"The gypsies assumed you were my husband. So I let them—and you— believe it."

She pressed her hands to her cheeks. She didn't know how she was going to face him again.

"Come and sit down, lass." His voice was dark and rumbling, and the sound of it caused impossible yearnings in her heart.

She took a deep breath and turned to him. He'd pulled the blanket over his lap, but his chest was still bare. As was one leg.

He crossed his arms over his chest. "You're sure we're no' wed?"

"Of course I'm sure."

Unable to stay calmly seated, she stood. "I know it was wrong to say so, but you were hurt, and it was cold and raining. And that man frightened me."

"Aye. I can see how it was." He grabbed her shoulders.

"You're still the most beautiful lass I've ever known," he said softly, drawing her close to him, "and my wanting you hasna changed."

Other **AVON ROMANCES**

Temptation
of the
WARRIOR

MARGO MAGUIRE

AVON

An Imprint of HarperCollinsPublishers

This is a work of fiction. Names, characters, places and incidents are products of the author's imagination or are used fictitiously and are not to be construed as real. Any resemblance to actual events, locales, organizations, or persons, living or dead, is entirely coincidental.

AVON BOOKS
An Imprint of HarperCollins*Publishers*
10 East 53rd Street
New York, New York 10022-5299

First Avon Books paperback printing: April 2008

Avon Trademark Reg. U.S. Pat. Off. and in Other Countries, Marca Registrada, Hecho en U.S.A.
HarperCollins® is a registered trademark of HarperCollins Publishers.

Printed in the U.S.A.

10 9 8 7 6 5 4 3 2 1

This book is dedicated to my husband and three kids,
always helpful, supportive, and caring.
I love you guys!

Temptation
of the
WARRIOR

Chapter 1

The Isle of Coruain, 981

"**M**errick, I doona know how long we can protect Coruain with you and Brogan gone," said Ana, falling into step beside her long-legged cousin, who was newly invested as high chieftain of all the Druzai people. "Allow me to go in your stead while you remain here to guard the isle. I can search for the stone while—"

"You have taken no warrior's training, Ana, and my quest in the Tuath lands will likely be dangerous." His father never would have sent a woman on such an errand, nor would he.

They hastened from the Chamber of Elders as Merrick peeled off the official blue Robe of the Chamber and tossed it to a nearby servant. There was no time to waste. Even now, Eilinora, the ancient enemy of the Druzai, was gathering her powers and uniting her allies to attack. The witch had escaped her prison and murdered his father, Kieran, taking the high chieftain's scepter of power. Every Druzai knew there would be no stopping Eilinora without the ancient *brìgha*-stones, hidden centuries ago in the realm of the Tuath, the nonmagical people of the earth.

No one, not even Ana, knew how the wicked sorceress and her Odhar followers had escaped the numinous bonds that had held them quiescent for nearly a millennium. Merrick and his brother suspected 'twas through the help of some powerful sorcerer, a force unknown to the Druzai. Somehow, Eilinora and her Odhar had found Coruain, then managed to hide themselves from Kieran's dragheen guardians and the Druzai warriors. They'd invaded Coruain House . . .

Merrick stifled a growl of grief and frustration. His father's death at Eilinora's hands weighed heavily upon him. So did his newfound responsibilities.

"Can you *see* Eilinora?" he asked Ana.

Ana gave a quick shake of her head. "She has shielded herself from me, Merrick."

"So we can assume she has gone to Tuath to find the *brìgha*-stones herself."

"Or she has sent the Odhar to search, while she remains nearby to mount another assault on Coruain," said Ana, the sound of worry thick in her voice. "Merrick, the oracle's prediction at your birth . . ."

"Has naught to do with what I must—"

"But such sights are never to be ignored!"

There was no time to speak of the events foretold nearly thirty years before. They would come to pass no matter what he did. "Is my ship ready?"

Taken aback by her cousin's abrupt manner, Ana nodded. "Aye, it awaits you at the dock."

Merrick headed toward the sea, conjuring a leather satchel as he walked. He filled it with the items he would need when he arrived in the Tuath land called England, then cast a spell that would seal it against the waters of the Coruain Sea and the trauma of the time portal.

"I hope to return in a day or two."

When he returned with the stone, the Druzai sorceress whose fate was tied with his own would emerge, as foretold by the oracle. Together they would battle the powers that would destroy the Druzai. There could be no doubt that he would succeed with the beautiful and powerful Sinann at his side.

"Your brother believed he would be gone only overnight," Ana countered anxiously, "yet 'tis nearly a full day since he left and—"

"Aye. There's no telling what Brogan found."

"Nor what you will find, Merrick. But you must hasten. If Eilinora returns wielding your father's scepter before we have the blood stones and are prepared to deal with her . . ."

She did not need to finish the thought. Merrick knew that she and the elders would exert all their energies to protect the isles. He hoped it would be enough until he and his brother returned.

"What more you can tell me about my quest?" Merrick asked, anxious to leave, to find the stone and return.

"I can barely see the stone, Merrick," said Ana, closing her eyes and rubbing her knuckles across her forehead as if it hurt to think. She was the truest oracle Merrick had ever known, but she'd been hard-pressed to locate the *brìgha*-stones, the only weapons the Druzai could use to vanquish Eilinora and her mentor.

"Search for Keating," Ana said suddenly, looking up at him.

"Keating? What does it look like, cousin? Where will I find it?"

Ana shook her head. "I know not, Merrick. 'Tis something . . ." She frowned at the vagueness of her vision. "'Tis so unclear. You must follow the northern road to . . . to a place called Carlisle. There you will find Keating."

Merrick did not know this road, but he had spent time in England under many different guises, and once had visited England's northern coast. He knew he could find his way. He only hoped Ana's instructions to his brother had not been so ambiguous. Brogan did not know England as Merrick did, and he had such disdain for the Tuath that Merrick thought 'twas possible he had erred in sending Brogan to find the other stone. Should he have sent Ana or one of the elders?

He touched the copper bracer on his wrist, the Druzai mark of the high chieftain, bestowed upon him only an hour ago. 'Twas too late to rethink his decision. He had to believe Brogan would find the stone and return quickly.

Ana went with Merrick to the ship, accompanying him all the way to the Astar Columns, the ancient time portals that had been hidden far beneath the Coruain Sea. A quick displacement would not suffice here. Merrick and Brogan actually had to pass through the magical columns to travel nearly a thousand years into the future.

He paused, listening to the shrieking calls of the mighty *wealrachs* as they soared high in the skies above them, then turned to gaze one last time upon his beloved home, at the high cliffs and rich earth of the isle. He felt the weight of his responsibilities and knew this challenge would define his tenure as high chieftain. If he failed, 'twould be a first for the distinguished Mac Lochlainn line.

The passage through the columns was the most difficult part of his journey, and he'd always had magic to see him through it before. This time, there was a danger of Eilinora or the Odhar finding him if he brought magic with him. He removed his cloak and the rest of his clothes, collected his satchel, and walked to the prow of the boat. He knew his spells would see him safely to the columns and propel him through them. Everything after that was uncertain.

"If only there were some other way, Merrick."

"I can think of naught, Ana. Even if I were to displace, 'twould only move me a few minutes back or forward."

She nodded. "Please take care, cousin. Doona draw Eilinora's Odhar hunters to you through your magic. You should be all right if you can avoid them."

"Aye. I'll have no reason to conjure. Once I locate Keating, I am sure the stone will become exposed to me."

"Then Godspeed, cousin. Take care."

Bresland School, Kirtwarren, Northumbria, early March 1826

It was freezing in the tiny room Jenny Keating shared with the newest teacher, Harriet Lambton. She broke the ice in the basin and braced herself for washing with the frigid water underneath. She and Harriet might manage to stay warm through the night if only the school allowed the use of coal past February's darkest, coldest days. But Reverend Usher's rules were strictly enforced.

The children were freezing, too, a fact Jenny knew from experience. She'd come to Bresland School when she was newly orphaned at age ten. Though her father had left enough money to support Jenny, her guardians had wanted nothing to do with her. Her aunt and uncle had sent her off to Bresland on the day of her parents' funeral, and Jenny doubted they'd given her a moment's thought in the eleven years since.

She hurried through her frigid ablutions and spoke to Harriet, but the other young woman, her head and shoulders huddled under her blankets, made no reply. "You'll lose your post for certain this time," Jenny warned, but Harriet remained quiet. Reverend Usher expected the teachers to be punctual, arriving in the dining hall ahead of the girls. He'd already spoken harshly to Miss Lambton. Twice that Jenny knew of, maybe even more.

Jenny had no time to spend trying to coax her up and out of bed. She barely knew the other young woman, and what she'd seen so far had not been impressive. Harriet was lazy, never doing more than what was absolutely required of her. Her language bordered on crude and her academic skills were minimal, but Reverend Usher had employed any number of odd teachers and servants over the years. No one of any distinction wanted employment here, and Jenny herself intended to leave soon. A new position awaited her at an estate called Darbury. She had only to give her notice to the headmaster and leave. The thought of it brought an unfamiliar twinge of peace to Jenny's breast, and she smiled.

With no further thought to Harriet and her troubles, Jenny quickly pulled on her clothes— the required black woolen frock with white cuffs and collar. It was worn and had been mended in so many places, Jenny was embarrassed to turn up at Darbury wearing it. She thought perhaps she might spend a few of her precious shillings to buy a replacement in Carlisle when she headed north.

Carefully rolling her curly, pale yellow hair, Jenny pinned it tightly at her nape before putting on her tattered white lace cap. She'd learned many lessons on her first day at Bresland, one of which was that her unruly locks were offensive to God and to Reverend Usher. More than once, the headmaster had given her a vicious thrashing because of them, calling her a vain and shameless little sinner and holding her up to the derision of all the other girls at school.

Wrapping herself in a dark shawl, Jenny descended the austere staircase. As was her habit, she felt for the old silver locket that she kept with her at all times, either concealed in a pocket of her gown or on a long chain around her neck. It was easy to hide, for it was only slightly larger than a robin's egg, and shaped just the same. It was not beautiful, and the latch had been jammed shut ever since Jenny could recall. But it was her only remembrance of her mother.

And now it was gone.

An unfamiliar panic overcame her as she stopped on the steps to search her person for the pendant. It had been the only memento she'd managed to hide from her aunt and uncle when they'd sold all her parents' belongings and sent her away.

Harriet!

The girl who shared her room was the only one who might have seen the locket and understood its value. After all Harriet's grumbling about being cast off to make her own way at Bresland School, Jenny would not put it past her to take the locket and sell it to a jeweler, probably in Carlisle, where she had some family. It would certainly fetch several pounds—enough to keep Harriet housed and fed until she found a position that suited her better than Bresland had done.

But Jenny needed it herself in case her own plans did not work out. If there was one thing she'd learned since coming to this bleak and hateful place, it was that she could rely only upon herself. She could not expect a rescue, or even a smidgen of help, from anyone else.

Very little had gone well for her since she'd come to this loathsome school. The headmaster had taken an immediate dislike to her, and the other girls had learned to stay away for the sake of self-preservation. None of them wanted to share in Jenny's punishments, none but her fearless friend, Norah Martin.

Jenny tamped down the stab of grief that always came with thoughts of Norah. She quickly headed back up the stairs in search of her locket.

"Jane Keating!"

She stopped dead in her tracks at the sound of Reverend Usher's cold, steely voice. Bracing herself, she turned to face the headmaster, the man who'd been her nemesis for eleven long, cheerless years.

He was a tall, angular man who never failed to belittle every rounded edge, every frivolous curl, and every pink cheek he discovered in the pupils at Bresland. He berated the girls, warning all his charges that their silly vanity gave offense to God.

Jenny did not understand why he was harshest with her. Even Norah Martin had said so, but

Norah was long dead, the victim of a chill she'd taken while locked inside the privy one cold winter's night as a punishment. She'd been deathly pale when Reverend Usher had finally let her out, and the fever that killed her had taken hold that very night. The headmaster had called Norah's death the Lord's own punishment for prying where she was not wanted.

Jenny had no doubt it was because Norah had witnessed one of her own humiliating punishments—a bare-bottomed thrashing—and had threatened to tell old Dr. Crandall about it when next he visited.

But Norah had been dead before Dr. Crandall had even been called. Swallowed by grief, Jenny had only vague recollections of that night, of whispers in the dark. But she remembered the teachers being shocked to learn of Norah's demise. While the headmaster had remained deadly quiet, the teachers had blamed one another for neglecting to call Dr. Crandall.

Reverend Usher's shameful punishments had continued unimpeded after Norah's death, and with each one, Jenny's anger and despair had unleashed a strange, uncontrollable force that caused inexplicable, shattering events. Frightened by these incidents, she spoke of them to no one, for she knew they were abnormal. She was abnormal.

Even so, she had not deserved even half the punishments meted out to her in the past eleven years. She certainly had not deserved to be struck so hard she'd lost the hearing in one ear.

Standing halfway down the stairway, she looked at Reverend Usher, meeting his gaze eye to eye, despising him with every ounce of her being. His close-cropped hair was white, and encircled his shiny, bald pate. His nose was narrow and slightly hooked at the end. Combined with his long, peaked brows, his features gave him the vague appearance of an owl. A malicious, flesh-tearing predator.

Jenny tipped up her chin, refusing to be cowed by him. He hadn't punished her physically since her sixteenth year, but he watched her incessantly with an unholy gleam that made her skin crawl. She reminded herself she would soon leave Bresland, and never have to deal with the hateful man again. "Yes, sir?"

"You are late."

She bit back the retort that warred against her closed lips, and forced herself to control her temper, to prevent one of those unexplained incidents—a shattered glass, or a bent tin cup. Sometimes she even cracked a plate, with her unbridled emotions.

"Go down to the dining hall."

"No, sir." She swallowed and somehow managed to refrain from wringing her hands. She kept them at her sides, feigning a calmness she did not feel. "I have something important to attend to. Something that cannot wait."

"Do you defy me, Miss Keating?" He came up the steps to face her, to intimidate her.

Jenny forced herself not to cower, and to put out of her head the memories of her degrading treatment in this institution. She was no longer a child. For the first time in her life, Jenny had options. She did not have to stay at Bresland.

She spoke firmly. "I do not mean to be insolent, Reverend Usher. But, as I said—"

"Headstrong, intemperate girl. You have not improved in your years at Bresland, have you?" He took hold of her arm. "Now, Miss Keating. In my office."

Jenny held her head high and jerked her arm away from the headmaster, repulsed by his touch. Yet she allowed herself to be led to the stark little office at the end of the hall, promising herself she would not submit to any penalty the man decided to mete out.

On the contrary, now was the time to inform the headmaster that she would soon be leaving. She had her letter from Darbury tucked into her Bible, confirming her governess position. It was the only offer she'd received after advertising for two years, and she was determined to take it, even though it was her last resort.

Reverend Usher opened the door and gave Jenny a push into the room. She quickly leashed her temper and stood rooted in place as he crossed the room, watching as he removed his coat. He unbuttoned his cuffs, and when he pushed up his sleeves, Jenny began to tremble.

He stood before her, with that eerie light that came into his eyes whenever he inflicted his punishments, and she realized he intended to strike her as he'd done when she was a child. She blushed with shame, unable to force away the memory of the terrible beatings she'd suffered, bent over his knee with her skirts over her head, aware that the only other girls who ever suffered the same outrageous treatment were the ones as fair as she was, with light eyes.

"Come here."

"No, sir. I will not."

She clasped her hands behind her back, surprised at the degree of satisfaction she felt. At age twenty-one, her life was her own now, and she gave no one the right to touch her. Especially not Reverend Usher.

"Satan still dwells in you, girl! You are s—"

"Meanness is not discipline, Reverend Usher." Jenny spoke quietly but firmly, her courage bolstered by the letter from Darbury, securely hidden away. "If Satan dwells anywhere on this earth, 'tis within the hearts of those who abuse little children."

"You dare—!"

She turned away defiantly and moved to the door, suddenly afraid he would rush over and stop her before she could put a safe distance between them. But he stood still. Jenny took a deep breath and looked back at him. "I'd intended to give you a week's notice that I am leaving Bresland, but your actions force me to leave immediately."

His knuckles turned white as he clenched his fists at his sides. *"What?"*

She felt light-headed with such unaccustomed boldness. Never before had she possessed the nerve to speak up to the headmaster. "Y-you heard correctly, sir. I am leaving Bresland and taking a position as f-far away from here as I can possibly go." No matter what the situation at Darbury, it would certainly be better than this.

"You will get no references from—"

"I do not need any," Jenny retorted bravely. "The position is already mine, and I will leave for it just as soon as I pack my things." And if she found the situation at Darbury unacceptable, she would leave there, too. She was done with serving everyone's whim but her own.

"You will regret this, young woman," Usher said, his voice shaking with anger. "No one leaves Bresland without my consent."

"I cannot think why you'd want me to stay. You've despised me since the day I arrived."

Two bright spots of red appeared on his sharp cheekbones, and his eyes darkened with hatred. He circled around to his desk and opened a drawer. "The sin in you is the blackest kind . . . tempting and taunting even the most steadfast of men."

Suddenly fearful that he might attempt to strike her with the wooden ruler he kept in his desk, Jenny gave Usher no further attention, but quickly took her leave, letting the door slam shut behind her. In spite of her careful control of her temper, she heard a row of books fly from his bookcase and crash to the floor. She hoped the old headmaster would assume it was due to the closing door. But Jenny knew differently.

She was responsible, even though she had not touched the books. She didn't understand how these things happened, nor could she control the strange accidents that occurred when her emotions were high. When she was far from Bresland, she intended to try to understand how these strange events happened, try to control the hot prickling in her chest when some freak event was about to occur. But now was not the time. She had to confront Harriet and get the locket, then take her leave of Bresland before Reverend Usher found some way to detain her.

It took only another minute to get up the stairs and into her room. Harriet had not moved a muscle in the time she'd been gone, and Jenny called to her again. She felt emboldened after her confrontation with the headmaster and did not bother mincing words. "Harriet, I am missing one of my belongings. A locket."

Still, Harriet did not move. Jenny crossed to the girl's bed and placed a hand upon her shoulder, but quickly realized she was not touching flesh and bone. Ripping back the blankets, she found that Harriet had only propped up her bolster and some old rags to make it appear as though she were lying there, sleeping. She was gone.

Angry and frustrated, Jenny made a quick search of the room, though she didn't expect to find her locket. Obviously, Harriet had taken it and absconded. How long she'd been gone was anyone's guess.

Jenny jammed her few belongings into the

sturdy traveling bag she'd brought with her eleven years before, and hurried down the stairs, ignoring the startled looks of the overworked maid and footman she met on the landing. But she could not ignore the headmaster, who stood in the entryway, his hands fidgeting in his coat pockets. His expression was one of a man still in control, one who thought he still had the power to turn her over his knee.

"Miss Keating," he said, "you are mis—"

He was interrupted by the exuberant entrance of Clara Tremayne. Jenny was grateful, for once, for the other teacher's appearance. "Miss Keating!" cried the young woman who would soon announce her betrothal.

To Jenny's fiancé.

The young woman came ahead of Mr. Ellis, the handsome young doctor who had courted Jenny all winter long. She eyed Jenny's traveling bag, then gave her a superior smile. "So Reverend Usher has finally dismissed yo—"

"On the contrary, Miss Tremayne," Jenny retorted, ignoring the other woman's scarcely concealed smirk. "I've just resigned my position here. Eleven years at Bresland has been quite enough for me."

She could not bring herself to look at Mr. Ellis, not after he'd jilted her so cruelly. He'd believed every horrible thing Reverend Usher had said about her, not once opening his mouth to defend her. Walking past them, Jenny decided she was glad to be quit of him, too. He had agreed with

Reverend Usher's disciplinary methods, even suggesting that Jenny had somehow deserved the beating that had caused her partial deafness. She was far better off without such a husband.

Without looking back, Jenny hefted her traveling bag over her shoulder. She ignored the sensation of Usher's hateful gaze boring into her back, and headed directly for the road to Carlisle, where Harriet had certainly gone. The woman had mentioned a brother there—a rum distiller, as Jenny recalled—so it would be the logical place for her to go.

And since Carlisle was directly on Jenny's path to Darbury, the estate where she would begin her new life, it made sense for her to go in that direction. She started walking and hoped to catch the next northbound mail coach.

There was nothing to keep her at Bresland.

Northumbria, late winter, 1826

Merrick Mac Lochlainn shook his head to clear it, then rose weakly to his feet to take his bearings.

England was cold, and he was soaking wet from his passage through the Astar Columns deep in the waters of the Coruain Sea. The spells he'd cast to travel through time had dissipated well before he reached the shore. 'Twas the only way to prevent Eilinora and her Odhar from finding any trace of him once he reached the correct time and place. But moving through time without the full protection of his magic was fraught with danger, not the least of which was his arrival at his destination feeling ill and weak.

Shivering and disoriented, Merrick collapsed to his knees and doubled over with pain in his belly. His muscles cramped and his head swam as he lowered himself to the cold ground. Remembering that he could not use his healing powers to restore himself, he realized he had to get some warm clothes on, before he froze to death and ended his quest before it had even begun.

With trembling hands, he reached for his satchel and struggled to pull out the suit of clothes he'd conjured before leaving Coruain. But two purple-black, long-fingered hands grabbed the satchel and tried to run with it. "Hold, sìthean!"

In spite of his weakened state, Merrick tripped the big-eared little beast, and watched him fall to the wet ground. He knew from past visits to the Tuath lands that sìtheans were not visible to the plain people here. Though the wicked little sprites had been commanded to leave the Tuath lands with the Druzai eons before, a number of them had defied the elders and remained here to plague the unsuspecting Tuath who could not see them. Missing possessions, unexplained clumsiness, strange accidents . . . the Tuath never knew 'twas a sìthean pest who caused them.

"Who ye be?" it shrieked, aghast at being caught, being *seen*.

"Aye, I can see you, little *deamhan*." Merrick

detained the leathery black sprite with a foot across its neck. "I'm no' some poor Tuath you can torment."

"You canna be—Druzai?" it squealed, narrowing its bulging eyes at him. "Ye be a magical one?"

"*Tathaich an bàrdach, sìthean!*" Merrick commanded. "Begone!"

The creature cried out again, shoved the satchel aside, and pried itself out from beneath Merrick's foot. It ran away through the rain, leaving a shivering Merrick to dress himself and hope he would not need to deal with any more sìthean interference while he searched for the *brìgha*-stone.

Somehow, Merrick managed to pull on his Tuath clothes and drag his heavy woolen cloak over his shoulders. He had to move along quickly in spite of his dizziness, in spite of the knives piercing through his abdomen and the grief that weighed so heavily on his heart. The truth of the Druzai tragedy struck him once more. His father was dead, his powerful scepter gone. Stolen.

If only Merrick had learned of Eilinora's attack right after it happened, he might have been able to displace himself in time to protect Kieran and prevent his death. Yet Merrick's father had been dead for many hours before he had discovered his body, making displacement useless. Nor could he make use of the Astar Columns and return in time to thwart Eilinora's attack. No one, not even Druzai, could achieve dual existence in such a manner. 'Twas impossible.

Merrick threw the satchel over his shoulder and trudged inland, staggering like a drunken Tuath. He needed to find a place where he could sleep a short while, to cast off the effects of moving across a thousand years' time. An inn would be best, but even a quiet barn would do. If nothing else, a sheltered corner in the woods would have to suffice. Unfortunately, there was no grand *wealrach* in any of the Tuath lands to carry him to his destination.

Merrick headed eastward, toward the road, his head pounding, every muscle in his body aching. He'd trained extensively with Brogan's men and was as capable as any Druzai warrior. But without magic, the Astar Columns took their toll. It was only a short time before his heart was pounding in his chest and his legs were wobbling as he walked. He had no choice but to find a place where he would be sheltered from the rain to lie down and recover his strength.

Coming out of the woods, he stumbled into a road and saw a pretty young woman in a black cloak being accosted by several ruffians. As weak as he was, Merrick could not ignore her plight when she screamed in terror.

Jenny had been walking more than an hour, and was far from Bresland School. She was far from everything, it seemed. The road was desolate, and when it began to rain, she despaired of ever meeting with the northbound mail coach.

She pulled up the hood of her heavy woolen

cloak and plodded on, only to stop abruptly when four men came out of the trees beside the road to confront her.

"Aye, what've we here?" drawled the tallest of them.

"A sweet bit o' skirt, Bob!"

"And carryin' some blunt, I'll wager," said a stocky one with thick, red side-whiskers.

Jenny said nothing, but held her bag tightly to her body and tried to edge around the four hooligans.

They did not let her pass, but closed in on her on all sides. "Leave me be!" she said defiantly, though her knees were knocking and her heart quaking.

"What's she got in 'er bag, Dickie?"

She pulled her arm away from the groping scoundrel and heard her sleeve tear at the shoulder. "'Tis none of your concern, you . . . you ruffian!"

Dickie laughed, showing rotten teeth, then wiped his nose against his sleeve.

The man in front shoved her, knocking her off balance. "Bet she ain't got much but what's under her skirts."

"No!" Jenny dropped her bag and tried to run, but one of the men caught her and knocked her to the wet ground. She screamed, slapping and kicking him away, but it was no use. The men were undeterred, even when a stout branch of a tree cracked and fell, barely missing them.

She screamed.

"Be still, dolly," said Bob, tearing her cloak from her shoulders. One of the others dumped her belongings from her traveling case, but Jenny's panic worsened when Bob pulled a pistol from his pocket and pointed it directly at her heart. She let out an unfamiliar plaintive sound, certain she was doomed.

Another voice called out sharply from the edge of the road, shouting unfamiliar words. *"Fosradh an ragair!"* he said in a commanding tone. "Stop!"

Her assailants turned to the intruder and Jenny managed to scramble to her feet. She hardly noticed her dress becoming soaked as the men converged upon the newcomer, a tall, striking man with black hair long enough to brush his shoulders. He looked pale and ill, but he dropped his greatcoat and satchel and came to her defense, throwing punches and shoving one ruffian into another. He was either the bravest man alive to take on four such scoundrels as these . . .

Or he was a fool.

The urge to whisk the blackguards into the air and toss them high onto the branches of the nearby trees came naturally to Merrick. So did the thought of displacement to arrive at this spot several minutes before the attack to prevent it. But he had the presence of mind to avoid such a mistake. He could not risk using magic, not when the Odhar might be searching this very locale for the blood stone. After all, Ana was not the only seer in the world. Surely the Odhar had someone with seeing abilities who also sought the stones.

In his weakened state, he had difficulty holding his own against the villains. But at least he could provide an adequate distraction while the young woman made her escape.

Only she did not. From the corner of his eye, Merrick saw her pick up a broken branch from the road and swing it at one of the men who'd attacked her. The scoundrel grunted with pain and fell to the ground in a disheveled heap.

Catching her eye, Merrick grinned in appreciation at her indomitable Tuath spirit and ducked another blow from one of her three remaining attackers. She was beauty and strength, an admirable combination. If she'd been Druzai, Merrick might well have wished she were the one foretold as his *céile* mate, the wife who would help him avert the crisis with Eilinora. As it was, everyone believed 'twould be Sinann whom he would wed.

Sinann was beautiful and talented, and any Druzai sorcerer would be proud to take her for his mate. Her blood would strengthen the Mac Lochlainn line, making their children capable leaders for yet another thousand years.

"Ye'll be sorry!" said one of the assailants, swinging his meaty fist, but Merrick made a quick turn and coldcocked him. 'Twas a simple maneuver taught him by his brother—a swift, fierce punch to the nose that incapacitated an attacker before he had a chance to realize what was coming.

Now there were two, and Merrick could see that the woman was trying to position herself to deliver another blow with her cudgel. But the taller of the two highwaymen turned suddenly away from him and grabbed her. She screamed when he knocked away the wooden club, but remained undefeated, even so. She kicked the scoundrel in the leg and he pushed away from her, yelping in pain.

Merrick made a quick move to dispatch the fellow who was still throwing punches, but a shot rang out and he felt a stinging blow to his head. Taken by surprise, he fell heavily to the ground.

He saw a bright flash of light before losing consciousness.

Chapter 2

"**G**oddamn it, Bob, you've killed 'im! Put that gun away afore any of us gets hurt."

Jenny barely heard the muttered curses of the highwaymen as they frantically gathered up their wounded. She rushed to the side of the handsome young hero who'd come to her rescue and dropped to her knees. He was unconscious, but still alive. The bullet had grazed him just above his ear, and his head was bleeding profusely.

He'd hit his head hard when he'd fallen, too, and Jenny knew such an injury by itself could be fatal. Her throat burned and she blinked back tears, aware that she should be running away as fast and as far as her legs could carry her.

But she could not leave her rescuer here to bleed to death in the rain, not the man who'd grinned so audaciously at her, in spite of their dire circumstances. Tossing a quick glance back at the villains who were busy rummaging through her traveling bag, she tore a strip of cloth from her petticoat and pressed it to the man's wound, wishing she could

somehow make an entire tree fall on the highwaymen, and not just a branch.

The highwaymen would be back for her as soon
as they saw she carried nothing of value, but she
could think of no way to combat them, no way to
get herself and the young man to safety. Even if
she abandoned the poor fellow and ran, it was just
a matter of time before they caught her.

"Wake up!" she cried softly, patting his cheek
in an effort to revive him.

If only he would get up, they might be able to
run into the woods and find a place to hide. But
he remained unconscious. He was much too large
for her to pull out of the road, and she doubted
she'd be able to support his weight even if he managed to get up. It was hopeless.

Jenny heard footsteps behind her, and her heart
pounded even harder than before. "Oh please,"
she whispered urgently as she gave him another
gentle shake. "Get up and help me!"

"Naught but *books* in yer case, dolly!" Bob said
angrily.

"I'm a teacher!" she cried. "I haven't anything of
value." Just the Bible and her favorite, an old edition of Malory's tale of King Arthur.

"Well, ye're just going to have to—"

Several horsemen came into view at the curve
of the road. The black-haired newcomers wore
vivid colors, and even their horses were draped
similarly. At the sight of them, the highwaymen
started to back away.

Bob put his gun in his pocket and fled alongside the others while some of the dark ones chased them down the road. Four of them—Gypsies—stayed with her. Jenny was afraid she might melt on the spot at their blatant, rude appraisal, but she managed to hold her head up and face the four men who dismounted and approached her.

"You, English," said the eldest, the obvious leader, his words spoken with a foreign lilt. His eyes were light brown, nearly the same color as the swarthy hue of his skin. His hair was black and curly, but for a few strands of gray at his temples, and a thick mustache covered his upper lip. He wore boots that he'd left unlaced, a garish coat, and baggy trousers, and he had a bright pink kerchief knotted at his throat. He looked as though he'd been thrown together with scraps from a ragbag.

Jenny had heard tales of these people. They wandered the countryside at will, stealing pretty English children from their beds, practicing dark magic, and who knew what else. The leader's companions unnerved her. One with a gold front tooth gazed at her intently, raking his black eyes over her sodden form, lingering at her mouth, then her bosom. When his gaze wandered downward, Jenny had the uncomfortable feeling that he could see through her clothes.

"Your man—he is bad hurt," said the leader.

She swallowed and glanced up the road. "Yes. Those men, they—"

"Narkri. Banditas." The man sneered and looked down the road where her attackers had fled. He looked at her, then at her traveling bag with its contents strewn about, apparently weighing the situation. "Come. We take you to camp."

An elaborately painted wagon drew up behind the horsemen. A man was driving, but a woman sat beside him, also dressed in vivid colors, and wearing gold bangles at her ears and wrists. Here on the isolated road, in the pouring rain, these Gypsies offered the unconscious man his only chance at survival. It was slim, but it was a chance nonetheless.

The leader spoke in his own strange language to his men, who dropped the reins of their horses and came to her. Carefully lifting the hurt man, they carried him to the back of the wagon and moved him inside. One of them picked up his leather satchel and her sodden traveling bag and tossed the whole unwieldy bundle into the wagon.

The leader pointed to himself and spoke in halting English. "I am Guibran Bardo. King of Rom."

Jenny swallowed her surprise. "K-king?"

"Of Rom. *Jip-see* as you say."

Jenny swallowed tightly. "Thank you for helping me. Er . . . *us*. I am Jenny Keating."

"And your husband?"

"M-my . . . ?" she stammered, then suddenly realized Mr. Bardo thought the wounded man was her husband. It was just as well for them to believe she was a married lady, especially while that black-eyed Gypsy rascal was near, watching her as he picked at his gold tooth. She could pretend to belong to her rescuer for a few hours, just until the weather cleared and she could go on her way.

"He is . . . er . . ." She swallowed nervously. "M-Matthew. Matthew Keating."

The Gypsy king took Jenny's hand and helped her climb into the wagon, where she slipped into place beside "Matthew." She hoped he would not mind that she'd claimed him as her spouse.

His head hurt abominably and his stomach felt as though one wrong move would make him heave its contents.

Worse, he couldn't figure out where he was. The smell of wood smoke was strong, but he seemed to be in a small, dimly lit room. The drumming of rain pummeled what sounded like a metal roof of the primitive chamber, and again he tried to understand what place this might be. There were two flickering candles amid the clutter on a tiny table a few feet away, and he could see pictures of strangers hanging on the walls. The windows were covered with colorful curtains, and a potbellied stove at one end warmed the room, the source of the smoke that hovered near the ceiling.

"You're awake."

A woman's voice startled him. Squinting his eyes, he turned and made out the delicate features of a disheveled young blond woman with a dark red gash at the crest of her cheek. Her black dress was torn and her hair a riot of sodden curls that drifted over her shoulders. He felt the sharp pull of attraction to her comely face and womanly form, but practical matters prevailed. "Where am I?"

She wrung her hands and stepped away. "They shot you."

"They? Who?" He didn't remember being shot. He thought back and realized he couldn't recall much. He couldn't recall . . . *anything*.

Surely this bewilderment would pass. Once the headache receded, his thoughts would clear. The nausea would disappear.

"The Gypsies came just in time," said the woman, adding to his confusion. Her speech was foreign to him, yet . . . he somehow knew it. "I think the highwaymen would have killed us both."

"We were attacked on the road, then?"

She nodded. "Don't you remember? No, I suppose not. First the gunshot, then you fell and cracked your head on the macadam. You only just stopped bleeding."

He felt the side of his head, but there was a soft cotton cloth wrapped 'round it.

The pretty woman started to speak again, but two swarthy men came into the room, drawing her attention. She was clearly even more nervous with the newcomers than she was with him alone.

"Ah, he is awake, your husband," said the older of the two men.

"Y-yes."

Husband?

"You have books," said the man with the mustache, while the younger man with a gold tooth watched every move the woman made with his intense black eyes.

Merrick felt a proprietary surge at the frank lust in the young Gypsy's eyes. The fellow had no business eyeing his wife—*his wife?*—so lasciviously.

She glanced toward a travel case on the floor. "Yes, I have a few."

"I need learn. Me," said the man. "And nephew. You teach?"

The woman looked uncertain, glancing from the case, then back to the men. "To read?"

"Yes. To read, Tekari Kaulo and me," he replied, pointing to the younger man. "You do for safe passage to . . . where you go?"

"I'm . . . well, *we* are going to Carlisle."

Merrick had trouble following the conversation as he tried to remember the events that had brought him to this place.

To remember his wife.

Surely he could never forget such a woman. He must have kissed those full, pink lips and caressed her soft, feminine curves many times. He must have seen her beautiful gray eyes go dark with pleasure when he—

"You teach, we take you to Carlisle," said the Gypsy. "Week's journey."

"To Carlisle?" said his wife with a hint of indignation. "But 'tis only sixty miles." She protested with spirit, but she was clearly uneasy, possibly even frightened. A good husband would get up from his bed and give her the support she needed. He would protect her.

He pushed himself up and garnered naught but a quick glance from the two dark men before they dismissed him and turned their attention back to his wife. *Mo oirg*, did he appear so pitiful?

"We go the Rom way," said the Gypsy leader.

Merrick's wife—*what was her name?* He wracked his brain to remember, but was momentarily distracted by the elegant movement of her throat as she swallowed. She bit down on her lower lip in a manner so sensual, he felt blood rushing to his groin. No doubt she'd always had this effect on him, but why could he not remember?

He could, almost.

The thoughts were there, just on the edge of his consciousness. 'Twas like a word on the tip of his tongue, one that teased at him, one he could not quite retrieve.

A gust of wind sent the rain hammering against the windows. His wife shivered and gave in to the man's request. "Yes. I will teach you, but only until we reach Carlisle."

"Good. We begin tomorrow, Mrs. Keating."

Keating. Finally, he heard something that sounded familiar, but still he could not remember his given name. Before he could give it further thought, a violent wave of nausea overtook him, and he turned to retch in the bowl he found beside his bed.

*   *   *

"I'm sorry," said the man. His very pronounced brogue led Jenny to believe he must be a Scotsman. "I'm a good deal of trouble for you just now."

He was not the only one at a disadvantage. Neither the rain nor the attack on the road had benefited Jenny's appearance. She turned her back to him and tried to arrange her hair into some semblance of order before facing him again.

And there was the matter of their "marriage." She had to apologize for taking such liberties with the truth. But that could wait until he felt better.

Bolstering her nerve, Jenny moistened a cloth with warm water from a deep bowl that had been provided, then returned to him and wiped his face when he lay back. He still looked pale—too pale—but at least he was awake and talking. His condition was far better now than it had been during the long ride to the Gypsy camp.

"Just try to rest," she said. "There's nothing we can do tonight."

Helping him to rinse his mouth and clean his teeth, Jenny was struck by her wifely pose beside him. Any onlooker would assume they actually were husband and wife. Yet he was a wealthy man, and she had only a few shillings to her name. The quality and cut of his clothes demonstrated their differences plainly enough, but Jenny had also looked in his satchel for some indication of his identity. She'd found none, but his other clothes and the gold sovereigns in his possession proved that he was a man of means. A nobleman . . . perhaps even a Scottish aristocrat. A man like her viscount uncle who would have little use for her once he regained his strength.

"We're going to stay here while you teach those men?" he asked.

"I don't have any choice," Jenny replied, glancing around the inside of the shabby, cluttered caravan. It had to be a dramatic contrast to the kind of environment he was accustomed to. There was only the one bed and a small table, a few boxes, a cloudy mirror, and several grimy pictures on the walls. Two small windows were covered by multicolored blankets that had been tacked down on all sides. The caravan was dry, reasonably warm, and safe. At least she did not think the Gypsies would attempt to accost her, as long as they needed her to teach them. An added protection was their belief that this man was her husband.

In truth, he appeared the kind of man who would have women falling at his feet in adoration. His black lashes were long and thick, his eyes a dark, warm blue, and his strong jaw slightly cleft. He'd fought for her like a bold and capable warrior of old, a chivalrous knight come to her rescue from Camelot itself. Even as ill as "Matthew" was, Jenny had never seen a comelier male. She did not doubt that he had a real wife somewhere, waiting, worried over his delayed return.

And as soon as he could move without becoming ill, she was going to get out of there. She knew better than to think she could rely on him for help. As usual, she was on her own.

"We'll stay until you're able to travel." Jenny moved away from the bed and took a seat on one of the boxes. "I don't want to run up against another band of highwaymen—"

"What happened to us?" he asked. He seemed genuinely puzzled.

"A group of men attacked . . . us . . . on the road. Don't you remember?"

"I canna remember anything. My brain feels hazy . . ." He touched his forehead pensively. "I doona think I know even my own name."

Jenny frowned. "Truly? You don't know your name?"

Closing his eyes again, he clenched his jaw, clearly struggling to remember, to understand what had happened to him. Then he looked sheepishly at her. "No. 'Tis no use. I canna . . . Nor do I know yours."

She took a deep breath and considered what to say. It might be another day or two before he was well enough for her to leave him, and Tekari Kaulo was clearly much too interested in her. This could not come out well, no matter what she said.

She could only hope the Gypsies followed a code of honor with regard to another man's wife and would leave her alone until she made her exit.

"M-Matthew," she blurted. "You're Matthew Keating. And I'm Jane. Well, I'm Jenny to my . . . my closest . . ." She cleared her throat as he repeated her name quietly to himself, then reached across the narrow space and took her hand in his.

His eyes bored through her as though he would devour her, given the chance. "How long have we been married?"

His hand was warm and firm, and nearly twice the size of her own. She closed her eyes and savored his touch, surprised by the unusual sense of security—and the heat—she'd never felt with Frederick Ellis. This man had risked his life to help her, and Jenny had no doubt he'd saved her from a terrible fate. She would have preferred to be honest with him, but this was anything but a normal, natural situation. She needed this husband only for a day or two, and by then his confusion would surely have resolved.

Once she told him the truth, they would split up and she would leave for Carlisle on her own, at a much faster pace than the Gypsy travelers would go. It was only a matter of getting back to the road and waiting again for the mail coach. She would start out much earlier next time so she wouldn't miss it.

"Not long," she said in reply to his question. "Er . . . only a few . . . days."

"Ah. So that accounts for your bonny blushes," he said. "Come here, lass."

Jenny's breath caught in her throat, and she wavered. She'd never shared such intimate quarters with a man before, not even with Mr. Ellis, who had been a most proper suitor until he'd discarded her for Clara Tremayne.

Matthew gave her hand a gentle tug. "Jenny."

She came to her senses and realized she could not do it. She had to tell him of her deception. "I need to—"

"Lie down beside me," he said, his voice troubled. He drew her into the intensity of his gaze. He was hurt and confused, and she was making it worse.

She pressed her fingertips to her forehead. "I need to think."

"Later, sweetheart. I want to hold you."

Such an endearment was completely foreign to her, but utterly compelling. Jenny found herself moving to the bed and easing onto the mattress next to him, allowing him to pull her into the circle of his arms. He drew her close, aligning their bodies tightly together. They lay face-to-face, his eyes searching hers, as though he might find the answers to all his questions there.

"I canna believe I am always this weak, Jenny." He lightly touched his lips to hers, sending wondrous prickles of awareness through her. "Can you trust that I'll take care of you?"

She could not speak, not when his strong hand was stroking the length of her back and his lips nipping tiny kisses along her jaw. She let out a shuddering breath and slid her arms around him, savoring his heat and the sense of being enveloped and sheltered by his powerful body.

She put Bresland and all its unpleasantness from her mind and allowed herself these few moments of abandon.

"No, you are not always so weak." She knew it because he'd come valiantly to her rescue, a brave knight without armor. And now he paid the price for his courage.

Jenny had always slept alone, shivering on a narrow pallet in one of Bresland's dormitories, then in the cold, stark bedroom assigned her when she'd become a teacher. She had never felt heat like this, not even on the warmest summer night. It was a heat that made her heart flutter and her mouth go dry. It made her yearn for something she'd never had any hope of attaining.

Matthew shifted, moving his leg between hers, sliding his strong thigh between hers, just above her knees. Jenny swallowed and allowed him to press against her, presumably as intimately as a husband would do with his wife.

"Jenny." He whispered so quietly that she hardly heard him before he kissed her, cupping the back of her head with his hand. He opened his mouth over hers, and she responded in kind, swallowing back her shock when his tongue swept into her mouth.

His leg moved higher, and hot sensations gathered at the juncture of her thighs.

She broke the kiss. "Matthew!"

He spoke as he touched her face with his fingertips, gently sliding his fingers over her scraped cheekbone, whispering so quietly, she was barely able to hear his strange words with her one good ear. *"A mo tàrmachadh, iocshlaint an ciùrr anns an aghaidh."*

Jenny could not understand his strange language, but she felt an odd, shivering chill at his touch that should have repulsed her, but was strangely alluring. Her cheek felt odd, the skin cold and tight, and then the sensation stopped as suddenly as it had begun.

"You . . . I-I . . ." She did not know if she could make herself do what was right, not while her heart pounded and her body demanded that she pursue the heady sensations he aroused in her.

"You are so beautiful." He gazed at her as though she were the most alluring female he'd ever seen. It gave her a quiet thrill, even though she knew it could not possibly be true. Reverend Usher had told her often enough that she was a vile, sinful creature who offended even the most generous of God's angels. Mr. Ellis had believed it, too. She'd given him her heart and all her affections, yet he'd jilted her with the cruelest of words. Words that were very likely true.

Jenny stopped Matthew's hand by taking it and stilling it in hers. "We m-must not . . . You are injured. We need to take care."

Gingerly, he rolled onto his back. "Aye. My head is splitting."

And Jenny's was reeling. If this was what husbands and wives did when they lay together . . . She took a deep breath and looked over at Matthew, at the thick eyelashes that lay in dark crescents over his cheeks, at the fullness of the lips that had kissed her senseless. She felt an unfamiliar liquid heat pooling between her thighs.

She had to contain herself, for none of this was real. In the morning, he would surely remember who he was, and what had happened to them. Jenny hoped he would understand her reasons for claiming him as her husband, but more than that, she hoped he would feel well enough so that she could leave the Gypsy encampment.

She had to find Harriet and get on with the safe, unfettered life she was meant to lead.

Matthew looked up at the stained and patched ceiling above him and muttered a few words in his own familiar tongue. Through some deep instinct, he'd known he could heal the scrape on Jenny's face, even though he hadn't managed to do much for his own wound.

"Jenny, am I . . ."

Her pensive expression quelled his words. He would not increase her worry with questions about the obvious. His memory was sure to return soon, and he would know more about his healing abilities. He did not need to ask if he was a healer, for he felt the power within him. Yet he could not restore his own memory. 'Twas puzzling.

He reached down to the edge of his tunic to pull it off, but it was too tight. His movements made his head ache, but he felt overwarm and nauseated. He wanted to feel the air on his skin.

"What are you doing?" she asked.

"The sherte is too restrictive," he replied. "Help me pull it off, lass."

She leaned over him and started unfastening a row of buttons that lined the center of the sherte, and Matthew realized his clothing was altogether unfamiliar. He could not quite understand. It was a question he could not refrain from asking. "Do I always dress this way?"

Jenny paused. "What do you mean?"

"This white tunic. Buttons," he said, his head pounding relentlessly. "Ach. I don't know what I mean."

He caught her gaze and noted her hair cascading in loose curls about her heart-shaped face. Her brow furrowed with questions, and her bright eyes seemed troubled.

Matthew cupped her chin, marveling at her uncommon beauty. He wanted her still, in spite of the knives spearing through his head. Again, he tried to remember the words to heal his own injury, but was only able to repeat the most basic of incantations. It was going to take weeks to heal his head if he continued in this fashion, but he seemed to be at a loss to do anything more.

She helped him out of his tunic, leaving him wearing another soft layer of cloth, a second sherte without sleeves, revealing a wide metal band that encircled his forearm, just above his wrist. The bracer seemed familiar, but Matthew could not remember who had given it to him, or why he wore it.

He pulled off the thin sherte and touched the bracer. "Where did I get this?"

Jenny did not respond. 'Twas as if her ears stopped working the moment he bared his chest. He felt his nipples pucker at her perusal, and when she bit her lower lip and turned her attention to the metal band 'round his wrist, he was charmed. And aroused.

"Jenny?"

"'Tis a family heirloom," was her hurried reply. "From your father."

He felt the tug of some dark emotion deep within him and he knew he could not avoid asking even more questions. "Where is my father now?"

"I, er . . . don't know, Matthew. Sc-Scotland, I suppose. You and I are on our own."

He knitted his brows together. "Have we quarreled, my father and I?"

"No," she replied quietly. "Not at all."

He closed his eyes, too weary even to try to remember his family. It was enough that Jenny was with him now, and he wanted her naked and lying beside him where she belonged. Releasing the fastening of his trews, he pushed them off and turned to her, but she was as shy as a new bride, blushing and quickly turning from his nakedness.

Yet he knew she was not unaffected. "Undress and lie with me, Jenny."

Abruptly, she left the bed and took on a pensive demeanor. "Matthew . . ."

"Come, bonny Jenny. I might be ill, but you are the medicine I need."

She whispered something under her breath, then blew out the candles, one by one. In the dark, he could hear the rustle of clothes as she removed her gown and slid in beside him.

Chapter 3

A weak and watery stream of daylight filtered through the multicolored-blanket curtains. The fire in the stove had burned low, but the cold did not penetrate the warm bed Jenny shared with her "husband."

She awoke to the exquisite sensation of Matthew's mouth on her nipple through her chemise and his hand between her legs. She heard herself moan with pleasure as she moved with him, arching her back to give him better access to her breast. Her body flared with arousal, moving against his hand as he shifted their positions.

He touched her intimately, creating a firestorm of sensation unlike anything she'd ever experienced. She knew she should make him stop, knew that his kisses and caresses were the result of a mistaken intimacy between them. But when her muscles tightened all at once and burst with the most intense feelings she'd ever known, she could barely think, let alone speak. Her womb tensed and stretched, and her entire body shuddered with pleasure.

Matthew took her mouth in a deep, possessive kiss as he moved over her, sliding his body between her legs. He was naked against her; the imposing male shaft she'd glimpsed earlier was hard and poised to enter her.

Yet she could not allow it! He was little more than a stranger who believed she was his wife. For all she knew, she was breaking the law by posing as such, and he would surely be angry with her once his memory returned and he realized she was not truly his wife.

"Sweet Jenny—" A loud banging at the door interrupted them, and Matthew pulled away abruptly. "What the devil—"

"It must be Guibran Bardo or one of the others." Jenny did not know whether to feel reprieved or deprived.

Matthew rolled away and lowered one thickly muscled arm over his eyes. He lay naked and exposed, the lines of his powerful muscles clearly defined, as was the thick shaft of his aroused manhood.

Jenny's breath caught in her throat at the sight of him, and her face heated as much from embarrassment as from sensual curiosity. She felt an insane yearning to touch him, to caress that male part of him as she kissed him, and return the same kind of pleasure he'd given her.

"Hey you! Missus!" called the man outside. Jenny shot to her feet and quickly threw the blanket to cover Matthew's naked form. Hastily wrapping herself in her cloak, she opened the door.

Bardo tossed her an annoyed look, then handed her a plate filled with a concoction of cooked potatoes, onions, and some kind of spiced meat. "You eat. Then teach."

"I'll need to wash and dress, too." She hardly recognized her own voice.

The Gypsy tipped his head in the direction of the mattress. "Your man. He is better?"

Jenny bit her lip. "Yes, somewhat."

"Good. You come. Soon."

Jenny closed the door and turned to Matthew, still shaky, unsure what to say. Her body hummed with the heat of his touch, and she wanted more. "Do you . . . remember anything?"

"No." His jaw clenched beneath the arm that covered his eyes, and Jenny was struck once again with the power that had lain hidden beneath his clothes. Her heart squeezed tightly in her chest at the thought of continuing their sensual encounter.

Yet she knew such a pursuit was not only wrong, it was foolish. Their liaison had no future, and Jenny had learned not to yearn for things she could not have. She had to leave the Gypsy camp and get away from Matthew before her body had a chance to betray her again. The weather had cleared sufficiently, and she needed to get back onto Harriet's trail before the woman got too far ahead.

Matthew was a big, strong man. He could deal with the Gypsies without her. She did not owe him . . .

Yes, she did. He'd risked his life for her. And what if his memory never returned? Would he always believe he had a wife who'd abandoned him?

It was all too much to think of. Matthew was ill enough that he still needed her, so she had no choice but to play the part she'd fallen into, and follow Bardo's command. At least they were inching their way toward Carlisle, and she would manage somehow to keep her distance from Matthew until he regained his memory.

"How do you feel?" she asked him.

He lowered his arm and looked directly at her, his blue eyes dark with intimacy. "Well enough to pleasure you in our bed. Come here, Jenny."

His words went directly to the muscles of her legs, making them feel shaky and weak, causing her nipples to tingle under the heavy cloak. As appealing as it would be to return to the bed they'd shared, Jenny knew better than to start believing in her own fiction.

"Mr. Bardo is waiting for me," she said.

"I doona want you to meet him alone," said Matthew.

"Nothing will happen." She had to get dressed, but Jenny doubted that Matthew would turn his back. Not after . . . not when he believed she was his.

She should never have shared his bed, never have allowed him to touch her as he'd done. If she told him now that they were not husband and wife . . . he would rightly conclude that she was a shameless wanton, a hussy with no sense of propriety.

It was such a muddle!

Turning away, she let her cloak drop to the floor and stood before him in her thin chemise. Her black gown was torn at the shoulder, but she pulled it over the long chemise anyway, hurrying as she heard Matthew start to climb out of the bed. She would not be able to resist him if he were to caress her bare skin again. He came up behind her and cupped her clothed shoulders with his big hands while she hurried to fasten the buttons of her bodice.

"We owe our survival to Bardo and the others," she said. "And I agreed to teach him."

"I'm coming with you." He pressed a kiss to the back of her neck and turned her to face him.

Jenny blushed hotly at the sight of his formidable nude form, her fingers burning to touch him, to caress him and allow him to finish what he'd begun. She curbed her fascination with the mat of dark hair that covered his nipples and belly, and trailed down to the hard, erect length of him. She took a deep, shuddering breath, aware that she needed to put some distance between them. "You're still unsteady on your feet. Are you dizzy?"

He nodded and winced at the movement, reaching up to touch the bandage on his head. "Aye."

"And your head still hurts."

He did not reply, and Jenny could see that his infirmity chafed at him. He was clearly unaccustomed to weakness of any kind.

A week ago, Jenny would have denied having a brazen bone in her body. Yet with every drop of her blood, she wanted to stay here with him. To take care of him and nurse him while he lay unclothed in the narrow bed they'd shared.

She was an idiot.

There wasn't a man in England to be trusted with her heart. Her uncle had dumped her at Bresland like no more than a charred and useless bit of coal. Reverend Usher had made it clear that she deserved nothing but disdain, and Mr. Ellis had betrayed her when she'd needed him most.

She knew better than to rely on the loyalty, the respect, and the affections of any man. As an educated woman, she could make her own way in the world without suffering the brutish wiles of the male sex.

She pulled on her cloak, as much a barrier to his touch as to the cold outside. "Go back to bed, then. I'll be all right."

"Jenny—"

"Honestly, Matthew." She cleared her throat, refusing to play into the fiction she'd concocted any more than was absolutely necessary. Perhaps when she returned she would confess her lie. "Bardo won't hurt me, not when he wants something from me."

"Aye. You're probably right." He retreated unsteadily to the bed and lay down.

Jenny pulled the blanket over him again, tucking him in snugly. Then she brushed a lock of his hair back from his forehead, past the band of cloth that encircled it. "Sleep awhile longer. I'll be back soon and bring you something more suitable to eat."

She added wood to the fire, then left him alone to go and face Guibran Bardo and his nephew on her own.

Jenny had not returned by the time Matthew awoke.

His head ached and the dizziness persisted, but at least the nausea had subsided. He eased himself out of the bed and looked at his surroundings. Somehow, he felt certain he was unaccustomed to such shabby circumstances, but his memory was still locked inside a dark hole that he just couldn't penetrate. It was frustrating and maddening, all at once.

He unwrapped the cloth bandage from his head and looked at his reflection in a dingy glass that hung on one of the walls. The bullet had torn a line of skin across his temple, just above his ear, but he seemed to have plenty of hair to cover the graze.

He glanced at the door, missing Jenny.

The strength of the sentiment surprised him, and he had the distinct feeling that he'd never experienced it with any other woman. No doubt that was why he'd married her.

He noticed the bracer on his wrist and slipped it off, studying it carefully, as though it could restore his memory. The reddish metal cylinder seemed familiar, but he could not recall how he'd gotten it, or who had given it to him. The markings on its surface seemed to be a kind of writing, and on closer inspection, he realized he understood the meaning of the symbols.

Let wisdom and kindness prevail.

The words seemed apt and fitting, but their significance was lost on him.

Sliding the band back onto his wrist, he found his trews hanging neatly over a chair and pulled them on, puzzling again at how strange they felt, how rough and tight against his skin. His entire experience since awakening inside the Gypsy wagon was weird, he reminded himself, certain that such a loss of memory could not possibly be a common event.

His confusion was even more disconcerting than the persistent headache and dizziness. Matthew had a feeling he was not often at a loss, and he had a niggling sense of some urgent business at hand. He knew not what it was, and no matter how he strained to remember, he could not.

A pot of water sat warming on top of the stove, and Matthew washed with it. He left the bandage off and cleaned his bloody scalp and hair with some soap he found in a dish on the table, awkwardly rinsing and pouring the water into a second pan. As he dried his head, he noticed a leather satchel on the floor near the bed. Draping the towel over his shoulders, he sat down and hefted it onto his lap.

'Twas a man's pack—undoubtedly his own. He reached inside and pulled out a clean sherte and another pair of trews, along with a handful of gold coins. Reaching in again, he found even more gold.

The sheer number of coins was astonishing.

Why would he be carrying so much money? Surely 'twas dangerous . . . which meant he must have a good reason for it. But try as he might, he could not think of any. He would have to ask Jenny. In the meantime, he needed to find a place to hide it. He did not trust Bardo or the other Gypsies in the least. Certainly not enough to leave Jenny alone with them any longer.

He wrapped the coins inside a square of cloth he found on the table, then shoved the whole package under the mattress, flattening it as much as possible. The hiding place was inadequate, but would have to do for now. He pulled on the clean sherte and slipped his greatcoat over it, then opened the door and went outside.

There were twelve or fifteen painted caravans parked in two rows, creating a wide aisle between them. Three large pit fires burned at intervals in the passageway, serving the cooking needs of the entire camp. An old Gypsy woman in ragged clothes crouched on her haunches beside one of the fires, smoking a pipe. A number of younger women worked beside their own "houses," the wagons on wheels like the one Matthew had just left. The dwellings were made of metal and wood, with an odd kind of aesthetic that gave unity to the camp.

Women cooked over the open fires, nursed their infants, and mended clothes while many of the men sat on overturned buckets and barrels, sipping hot drinks from delicate teacups.

Some eyed Matthew suspiciously, and some with interest as he moved through the camp, looking for Jenny and her two students. He forced himself to ignore the pounding in his head as he passed barking dogs and children who wore mismatched shoes and flapping coats while they played at kicking a ball at the far end of camp. When the children saw him, they stopped their game and fell into step behind him, a motley bunch following him as he searched for Jenny.

Matthew found his wife sitting on the steps of the last caravan. Bardo and Kaulo flanked her, and Matthew was struck once again by her beauty. The hood of her cloak had dropped to her shoulders, and her hair curled like a soft, golden halo 'round her head. Her cheeks were pink in the cool air, and her mouth, so soft and kissable, was a deep rosy color, just like her nipples would be, once he finally saw them without her chemise. Soon.

He was smitten with his wife, just as it should be.

He wanted to take her and get away from this ragtag troupe. Surely he had enough gold to provide her a decent home and better clothes. He had noticed how her frayed black gown was torn at the collar and shoulder, and it troubled him. Was he so miserly with his money that he provided only the most basic of clothes for her? And ugly ones at that?

If only he felt stronger, he would take her away from this camp and go on to . . . He had difficulty remembering where she'd said they were going, though he recalled her saying 'twas some sixty miles away.

Then he remembered it. Carlisle. He had plenty of money to buy clothing for her, and once they got to town, he intended to see that she had pretty tunics that suited her better. He could easily picture her in colorful, loose-flowing silk tunics and trews, but the image disappeared too quickly as he came closer to the rough wooden stairs where she sat teaching the two Gypsy men.

"This reading not so simple," said Bardo, and Matthew watched as the elder knifed his fingers through his hair in frustration.

The young one with the gold tooth moved closer to Jenny, and she shifted her shoulders to avoid contact with him. "This is the first step," she said. "You must learn the characters and then we will proceed from there." Matthew saw that her hands had gone red with cold and he wanted to take them between his own to warm them.

"No," said Kaulo. "Small English child do this. You show us wrong."

Matthew felt his ire rise, but before he could challenge the Gypsy, Jenny bristled with exasperation and spoke indignantly. "I most certainly am not teaching you incorrectly. Memorizing the letters is essential. You cannot proceed before you know them."

He grinned at his wife's indignation.

"She's right," he said, drawing a surprised glance from the two men on the step, although Jenny did not appear to hear him. He said no more as a sudden pain sliced through his head. He swayed on his feet as bright flashes of light pierced his eyes.

Jenny stood abruptly, concerned at Matthew's pallor. She hurried to his side and took hold of his arm. "Matthew, you're ill. Come, we must get you back—"

"Hey, missus! Not finished!" called Bardo.

"We're done for now," said Jenny to the man. She turned and started back in the direction of their caravan, through the crowd of children who'd followed Matthew.

"You should be in bed," she admonished, her voice sounding harsher than she intended. What was she to do about him? She could not go on allowing him to believe she was his wife, and she needed to get to Carlisle, sooner rather than later. "You're as pale as a ghost. And where's your bandage?"

"Jenny, I must lie down."

She swallowed, dismayed by her snappish tone. She felt confused and dishonest, and after the morning's intimacies in bed, completely wicked. Matthew almost certainly had a wife somewhere.

Scotland, by the sound of him. And he'd been on his way home to her when he'd stopped to help Jenny. "I'm sorry, Matthew. We'll soon be there."

He tried to walk without her support, but she felt him stagger. Jenny worried that if he faltered any more, she wouldn't be able to hold him up.

"Here we are," she said gratefully, as they started up the few steps.

"Doona worry, *moileen*," he said. "I willna fall."

"I sincerely hope not." *Moileen?* She supposed it was a Scottish endearment, one he used with his wife, and knew she had to tell him the truth. But when Kaulo appeared at Matthew's opposite side and watched them climb the few steps to their caravan, Jenny was grateful for the presence of a husband, even if he was infirm.

And not really hers.

"The lesson is done, Mr. Kaulo. We'll—"

"You teach more. I wait for you here."

"Then you've got a long wait ahead, lad," said Matthew, wincing as he spoke. He pushed open the door and went inside, taking a seat on the edge of the bed, his posture that of a man unaccustomed to illness. Jenny closed the door, then crouched before him. She skimmed her hands across the top of his head, her thumbs gently pressing his forehead as she lightly massaged his scalp. She could not tell him the truth now, not when he was so miserable.

It would be all too easy to forget the realities of her life for a while. It was about a fortnight before she was to report for her position at Darbury, but she still had to find Harriet and recover her locket. She had no time to waste with Gypsies and lost Scotsmen.

"Let me help you with your coat," she said, her tone businesslike and distant. She pushed the coat off his shoulders, and when she leaned close to take it from him, he slipped his freed arms around her waist and pressed his face against her breast.

"Matthew . . ."

"One kiss, *moileen*. Then I need to lie down." He placed one hand on her chin and brought her face close to his. The kiss was gentle and soft, hardly more than a touch. It left Jenny breathless, with her heart pounding for more.

She rejected such a desire for what it was, the pathetic yearning of a spinster who had elicited friendly affections from no one since Norah's death. Matthew was entirely reliant upon her at the moment, which could be the only reason he'd developed such an attachment to her. Once he regained his faculties, he would surely recognize the flaws that kept her apart. Jenny backed away, giving him room to move, putting some space between them.

"What about Kaulo?" Matthew asked.

His light kiss had dispelled every thought of the Gypsy. Jenny bit her lip and tried to figure a way to extricate herself from the mess in which she found herself. "Once you're settled here, I'll go out and work with him some more. The less time we spend here, the better."

"Stay close," Matthew replied, easing himself down to the mattress. He unbuttoned his shirt . "I doona like the way he looks at you."

His face blanched with pain as he lay down. Jenny pulled off his shoes and covered him with a blanket, worried about his head, certain he should have felt better today. If only his memory would return, she wouldn't have to explain her lies to him. He˙ would understand her reasons for the deception, yet he seemed so puzzled and vulnerable now, she could not think of leaving him yet.

"Turn over, Matthew," she said.

He complied without question, and Jenny sat on the edge of the bed beside him. She put her fingers on his head again and resumed the massage she'd started a few moments before. Her strokes became firmer, and he sighed as his shoulders began to relax. She rubbed the back of his head and neck, then pushed the blanket down to his waist to knead his shoulders. They were broad, and her fingers tingled at the feel of his thick muscles. He was masculine and hard, even while half asleep, and Jenny felt a stirring in her blood when she touched him . . . and a desire to feel his touch.

He made a low sound of pleasure. It would be so easy to slide the shirt off his shoulders and down his arms, then rub his bare skin.

Dismayed by the direction of her thoughts, Jenny quickly finished tending him and left him to drift off to sleep. She took a shaky breath and knew she had to get away from here—from him—and her romantic musings.

She knew better.

She'd escaped one bad situation, only to land in another. She knew what she had to do, and it did not include the man on the bed. Better to get away from him soon, rather than develop any deeper connection to him, one that would shatter as her few other connections had done.

A good position awaited her at Darbury, and that was the only certainty in her life. That, and finding the woman who had stolen her pendant.

Harriet had once mentioned that her brother was a rum dubber in Carlisle, and had seemed embarrassed to have let it slip that he was in the distillery business. A too-liberal use of liquor was deplorable, of course, but surely there was no shame in honest employment at a distillery, even though the wages might be inadequate to support his sister.

Having spent more than half her life at Bresland, Jenny knew little of big cities. She'd heard some accounts of dissatisfaction and difficulties among the weavers of Carlisle, but she did not think that would interfere with finding the distilleries in the city. At each one, she would inquire after a Mr. Lambton, and would soon find Harriet through him. And her locket.

Jenny had never been without it, not since the day her parents had drowned in a boating accident. She did not doubt her uncle Arthur would have taken it had he known of it, and her aunt would have done nothing to prevent him from confiscating it. Aunt Helen would have had no say in the matter, being only the wife. It did not matter that Jenny was the daughter of Helen's sister, and Arthur was no blood relative. A husband's will was always law.

It occurred to Jenny that marriage with Mr. Ellis would have been the same. He'd have assumed control of every aspect of their married life, as he would soon do with Miss Tremayne.

She shuddered at the thought of giving such power to a man. From her experience so far, few were kind or trustworthy. It was far better to keep her own counsel and rely upon her own abilities to survive than to trust a man to cherish her. She looked at Matthew, who slept peacefully with low and regular breathing. Jenny had no reason to believe he would be any different from every other man she knew . . . yet she did not like to think he might be just as uncaring as the others.

She intended to distance herself before she found out the hard way.

The caravan was small and close. Jenny's traveling bag lay forgotten on the floor under the table with her spare dress and underthings inside, a sodden mess. The highwaymen had dumped her two precious books on the ground, but since the Gypsy men had carried them separately, they were nearly dry.

Jenny draped her clothes over the two chairs near the table, stopping when quiet voices outside caught her attention. Opening the door, she saw a pretty young Gypsy woman standing on the step in front of Tekari Kaulo, holding a bundle of colorful cloth.

Smiling, she handed Jenny a needle and a spool of dark thread. "Guibran Bardo send," she said, pushing the sewing things into Jenny's hand and pointing to the torn sleeve and collar of her dress. "For you." She handed Jenny the bundle of cloth. "You mend. Wear these."

It was a skirt and blouse.

"Thank you," Jenny said. "You are very kind."

"I wait still," Kaulo said, his manner impatient and suggestive at the same time. Jenny had never encountered this kind of behavior before. During their courtship, Mr. Ellis had maintained a distant, formal manner, never allowing his eyes to wander brazenly over her body as Kaulo did. Reverend Usher looked at all the pupils and teachers with disdain, and the men of Kirtwarren averted their eyes whenever the students of Bresland came into the village, as if they did not want to acknowledge that the austere school existed outside Kirtwarren's borders.

But Matthew . . . Jenny suddenly remembered that expression of sheer delight in his eyes when she'd come to his aid and bashed the highwayman with the branch. As though she was not just a mere woman, but an equal in the fight for their lives.

Dismissing her foolish fancy, Jenny put the clothes and sewing tools on the table, then stepped outside and closed the door.

"You come now," said Kaulo.

Jenny ignored the young man's rude manner and spoke to the woman, who wore a colorful head scarf knotted at her throat. "What is your name?"

The pretty Gypsy looked askance at Jenny's slight of Kaulo. "Rupa," she said, pointing to her chest.

Kaulo tried to push Rupa aside, but Jenny bristled, placing her hand on the woman's arm as she glared at the young man. This was the kind of attitude she'd escaped on leaving Bresland, and she would not tolerate it from this grimy man who was in need of her help.

She spoke to Rupa. "If I could ask another favor, Rupa . . . I need some food for my husband. Something not too spicy. Some broth, perhaps, or eggs?"

Kaulo muttered under his breath and gave Jenny the same kind of harsh look Reverend Usher had used to intimidate her. She refused to feel threatened anymore, and ignored him, though she wished she had the nerve to meet his gaze with an obstinate one of her own.

He turned to leave, and Jenny let out the breath she'd been holding.

Rupa giggled and nodded at Jenny. "I will find eggs. Bread, too. I come back."

Jenny returned to the caravan where Matthew still slept soundly. Undressing quickly, in case he should awaken, she took off her torn gown and put on the multicolored Gypsy clothes. The skirt was made of four long panels of deep green, blue, gray, and red that swirled over the tops of her ankles, leaving her petticoat showing.

She decided to be reckless and removed the undergarment.

The Gypsy blouse was even less conventional. Made of the same colors as the skirt, but in a floral pattern, its sleeves were short and the neckline was gathered low, leaving a good deal of her chest and upper back bare. It exposed an indecent amount of her plain cotton chemise.

Jenny removed her corset, then rearranged the chemise, pushing her straps down just enough that the blouse covered them. She looked in the mirror, stunned by the change in her appearance.

She hardly recognized the smudged-faced wanton who gazed back at her with clear gray eyes. Her hair was a wild mess, haphazardly pinned to the nape of her neck. She turned her head slightly for better light, and saw that the scrape on her cheek was gone.

Or had she imagined seeing it the night before? Perhaps it had been Matthew's blood on her face, and she'd only imagined that it had felt sore.

She looked down at the colorful Gypsy clothes she wore and felt altogether different in the lively costume—young and pretty, and free. For the first time in years, she felt she could be anything or anyone she wanted to be.

She pulled the pins from her hair and let the mass of curls fall loose, allowing it to cascade down her back. Using her fingers to comb through the tangles, she turned her head this way and that, surprised at the dramatic change in her appearance.

A noise startled her, and she turned to see Matthew sitting up. A wave of embarrassment came over her to be caught in such a state, posing in front of a mirror as she'd done wearing her mother's finery in the years before Bresland.

"You are so beautiful."

He rose from the bed, and with one step, was standing before her. He cupped her chin in the palm of his hand and bent to kiss her. Jenny quickly moved away and picked up the gown that needed mending.

As much as Matthew wanted Jenny, he knew he was not capable, not when that excruciating pain could return at the least opportune moment. Besides, her reticence was clear.

'Twas not that she was unapproachable or entirely unwilling. He knew she was tempted, but he guessed she was unnerved by his memory loss. Likely she did not care to make love to a husband who did not actually know her.

"I may no' remember you, lass," he said, pulling her into his arms. "But you are no stranger to me."

"But I am, Matthew. You don't know me at all."

His finger skated across the bare skin of her back, and his cock rose with arousal. How he wanted her.

"I willna ask you do aught that strikes you wrong, Jenny." He pressed a kiss to her temple, then to her cheek as he lowered his hands to her hips, pulling her against him. He wanted her to know how she affected him, and that his memory loss meant naught. "But neither will I refrain from touching you as a husband ought."

"Matthew—"

"Time to answer the door, *moileen*." He released her, pleased to know she'd been so affected by his touch, she had not even heard the knock at the door.

Matthew returned to the bed as she opened their small home to a woman carrying two plates. Jenny exchanged a few words with her, then closed the door and returned to him, setting one of the plates beside him on the mattress.

"That was Rupa."

Jenny uncovered the food, and Matthew realized how hungry he was. He leaned his back against the wall and took the plate on his lap. Jenny set the other one on the table and avoided looking at him. By the way she chewed her lower lip, he could see that she was discomfited, mayhap even puzzled.

Aye, he was puzzled, too. He could not understand why she was so shy with him. If 'twas only because she felt she was a stranger to him, he could remedy it.

"You look verra fetching in your Gypsy attire," he said, and grinned at her blush. The upper portion of her chest had been left deliciously bare by the blouse, and the deep cleft between her breasts enticed him. Self-consciously, she placed one hand across her chest, as if she could hide her feminine bounty from him.

"Doona cover yourself from me, *moileen*. We are husband and wife, and you are beautiful."

"Matthew, you must not—"

"Come and sit by me. Are you no' hungry, lass?"

She sighed and did as he asked. "Yes. Starving."

Chapter 4

It was no use. With Matthew so completely convinced that she was his wife, Jenny worried that telling the truth now would do him some damage. She could only hope that with frequent naps he would awaken from one of them in his right senses, with his memory intact.

But she could not stay inside any longer, hovering so closely, watching him sleep.

Too restless to mend her Bresland dress, Jenny put on her cloak, gathered Rupa's plates, and went outside. The skies had cleared, and as she made her way across the muddy ground, she considered keeping on walking until she reached the road.

The watchful Gypsy eyes prevented her. They would know where she'd gone, and Bardo—or worse, Kaulo—would surely follow her. Besides, she could not abandon Matthew. Not yet.

She found the Gypsy leader near his caravan, sitting at a makeshift table, drinking black coffee from a chipped cup while he smoked a foul-smelling cigarette. Kaulo sat beside him, and they were poring over the chart of letters she'd left for them to study.

They raised their heads at a sudden commotion at the edge of camp. Visitors had arrived.

Bardo stood and looked toward the crowd that was gathering around two men in black uniforms. They looked like town constables, but they were not from Kirtwarren. Jenny was familiar with everyone in the village near Bresland, and knew that none of them had come to the aid of the girls at school. Yet they had to have known of the harsh conditions there.

"We want someone who speaks the Queen's English," said one of the men.

"You keep head down. Stay quiet," Bardo said to Jenny in a low tone. He pushed through the crowd and spoke to the intruders. "I Guibran Bardo. King of Gypsies."

The constable gave an audible huff of derision at the title. The Englishmen must have known that Bardo took the designation of king merely because he was the one who spoke enough English to represent his people. "We're looking for someone . . . a female runaway from a school hereabouts."

Jenny nearly gasped aloud in her concern for whichever student had decided to escape Reverend Usher's institution. As she had so recently discovered, the road was no place for a solitary traveler.

"We see nobody," said Bardo.

"'Tis a young woman with blond hair and eyes of gray. Goes by the name of Jane Keating."

"Or Jenny Keating," said the second constable.

"We keep to ourself, mister," said Bardo. "Don't know no runaway *gajo*."

Bardo turned his back to the constables and started to walk away in the opposite direction from where Jenny sat. She rolled up the chart of letters and moved quietly away, sinking more deeply into her hood and cloak.

The Englishmen followed Bardo, ignoring the children who started to pull at their coats, asking for money in pat phrases of perfect accented English.

"This particular girl has stolen something of value from the school," said the first constable. "I daresay there will be a reward for her recovery."

When the constables received no cooperation, they took the liberty of splitting up to wander through the camp. They used their batons to lift piles of rags, rugs, buckets . . . whatever debris they found lying about, as though Jenny might be hiding underneath. As unobtrusively as possible, she joined an old woman near a fire, crouching down beside her. The woman handed her the pipe she was smoking. Jenny took it between her teeth, but did not pull any of the acrid smoke into her mouth.

The children generally made pests of themselves. The old woman with the pipe began to scratch herself. So did Rupa, who sat on a thick tree stump near her own caravan. All the other Gypsies, who stood observing the proceedings, joined in, scratching their heads, their armpits and groins.

Their tactic worked. The constables were clearly unnerved by the prospect of taking home fleas or lice, and with the added nuisance of the begging children, the two men quickly took their leave. They admonished Bardo to bring the criminal teacher to Bresland if they ever came across her.

Jenny might have laughed aloud at such blatant aspersions on her character, but the implication of the constables' visit was grim. The headmaster had accused her of thievery. Hadn't he done enough to her over the years? Since she'd grown up, he'd left her alone physically, though his verbal insults had never stopped. She did not understand why her departure rankled so much. She'd have thought he'd be glad to see the last of her.

She tried to recall if she'd mentioned Darbury to anyone at Bresland. If someone had gone into her room and looked through her things, he might have found her letter from Darbury. But surely that was unlikely, so Usher would have no idea where to look for her. Once she went into Carlisle, no one would be able to find her.

With the constables' visit, Jenny felt a renewed urgency to get going. Moving at the Gypsies' slow pace was not going to serve her well. Yet if the authorities persisted in looking for her, she might be better off hidden here in plain sight.

"You shake your head, missus," said Bardo. "You steal from school?"

Jenny denied it passionately. "Of course not! The headmaster is a hateful, vindictive . . ." She clenched her teeth at the thought of all those dark and dismal years at Bresland. No child should have to bear such mistreatment, yet the pupils at Reverend Usher's school were forgotten innocents. It seemed that the headmaster answered to no one. Jenny firmly believed that he should be thrashed for his cruel practices, yet a beating would hardly teach him the error of his ways.

"The headmaster is angry that I left the school. I am certain he only wants me back in order to have the last word."

Bardo shrugged. "He is *gajo*, no?" As though that explained everything.

Kaulo brought the chart of letters to Jenny and handed it to her. "I have learn letters," he said, dismissing the constables' visit as inconsequential. "Now I read. Show me."

"My nephew has big hurry to know *gajo* ways," said Bardo, tossing an indulgent grin in Kaulo's direction. "We keep him happy. Have more lesson."

Jenny went along, even though she thought Tekari Kaulo should not be indulged quite so much.

Matthew knew he must be asleep, but he could not pull himself away from the all-too-real images and the urgent voices in his dream.

"You must make haste!" cried the beautiful, young, red-haired woman dressed in a flowing tunic of *àilean* green.

Matthew pulled her into his embrace and allowed her to weep against his chest. The dream room looked vaguely familiar, with walls paneled in rich, dark wood, and windows that spanned from floor to ceiling, looking out over tall, rugged cliffs. Huge, magnificent birds with sharp beaks swooped over the water in search of prey.

He did not want to leave the place, yet he knew he could not delay. He had to go quickly. Ana and the others needed . . .

His head pounded, and the pain blinded him. Whatever it was that they needed, he could not see it. He could not understand why Ana was weeping, only that he felt her unbearable sadness to the depths of his soul.

But he knew not why.

"Matthew."

He opened his eyes, and the images of sleep left him, replaced by the sight of his lovely Jenny in her colorful Gypsy clothes. She sat down beside him, her brow furrowed with worry. "You've been sleeping for hours. And not peacefully."

His mouth felt dry, but the rich aroma of something delicious brought him fully awake.

"Rupa gave me some soup and bread."

It seemed as though he'd just eaten, yet his stomach growled with hunger. He sat up carefully to avoid jarring his head. Surely it should feel better by now. If only he could remember the words that would heal it . . .

Jenny propped him up with a thick bolster, but he could hardly focus his eyes on her while he tried to remember the dream. It had seemed so real. Why had he been embracing the beautiful stranger who had not seemed like a stranger at all? He felt as if . . .

He closed his eyes and tried to recall the woman's features, what he'd felt for her, and why she'd been weeping. "Do I have a sister?"

Jenny seemed startled by the question, but Matthew assumed 'twas likely due to the abruptness of it. "No," she replied.

Then who was the red-haired woman? He had called her Ana. Was she even real?

Matthew decided she could not possibly be. The dream was just a result of his cracked head, no matter how real it had seemed. He was not going to mention it to Jenny. 'Twould only upset her, knowing he'd dreamed of another woman.

He ate the soup and tried not to think of the dream woman and her urgings to make haste. "Have your students learned their letters?"

Jenny nodded. "For the most part. Kaulo is quicker than Bardo."

"He's younger. Sharper eyes." Matthew reached over and smoothed a pretty yellow curl behind her ear. "But I doona care for the way he looks at you. Doesna the man realize you are mine?"

She looked away. "I pay him no mind. Soon we'll be leaving and never see him again."

Matthew narrowed his eyes and looked at her. "What's wrong? What's happened?"

"Nothing, Matthew." She stood abruptly and walked to the door of their caravan. "I'll just be glad when we can leave these people and go on our way."

Did she always wring her hands so nervously? Matthew didn't think so. She was keeping something from him. "Tell me again where we are going. I canna seem to remember."

"To Carlisle," she replied after a moment's hesitation.

"And what do we do there?"

"Nothing yet. We're . . . going to . . ." She came and sat beside him again. "Does it matter right now, Matthew?" She took his bowl and set it on the table. "Perhaps it would be best if you regained your memory first, before you have any new problems to worry about."

"Problems? Is something wrong?" It would certainly explain the urgency he'd been feeling ever since awakening here in this wagon.

"No! No, nothing is wrong. But, Matthew . . . I don't think we should talk about anything but this."

"This?"

"The here and now," Jenny explained. "Anything more is obviously too trying for you."

"Aye." He allowed himself to be swayed since he wanted to think only of Jenny and the soft skin of her throat, the fullness of her breasts, the curve of her hip. Had he ever been so enamored of any other woman?

He drew her down beside him, so that they were nearly lying together on the bed. "I'd rather think of naught but us. Come and lie with me, wife."

He kissed her gently, and felt his body change. Desire hardened him, made him pulse with need. He pressed a soft kiss to her ear and nuzzled her jaw. "I know why I married you, lass."

Her pale gray eyes went dark as she pulled back, gazing at him with bewilderment.

He laughed at her expression. "'Tis because you are so sweet. You worry over me and take good care of me, Jenny. I'd have been a fool to let you get away."

He wanted to know everything about her, but every time he tried to think things through, the pounding in his head worsened and his few fleeting memories disappeared. 'Twas best to do as Jenny had said, and dwell in the present, at least for now.

Pulling her close, he kissed her again and removed the pins from her hair, seducing her slowly. Matthew felt her reluctance, but he was certain 'twould take but little to convince her that their bed play would do no damage to his ailing head. In fact, he felt much better now. Her massage had worked wonders.

"Tell me how we met." He pressed his lips to her cheek, then her chin. "Was your hair curling down 'round your shoulders?" He moved his mouth to her neck, then lower while he slid his hands down to her hips. "Were you wearing a bright silken tunic that day, or your black gown with its prim, white lace collar?"

Her breathing changed, and he felt her body soften toward him. He pulled the ties on the Gypsy blouse and slid it off her shoulders, then ran his fingers across the bare expanse of her back. She moved slightly, allowing him to fit her body into the space between his legs. Matthew moved against her, enjoying her surrender. He rose to take her lips in a sensual kiss, spearing her mouth with his tongue, his cock hard and ready to do the same.

He slid her skirt up and ran his hand over the smooth length of her legs, then cupped her sweet bottom. She made an inarticulate sound of arousal, and he knew she yearned for another climax like the one he'd given her early that morning. But this time, he planned to be inside her when it happened. He pressed a kiss to her jaw, then moved down to her neck, and on to her breast. When he slipped the blouse and chemise from her shoulder, her breast came free, and he swirled his tongue 'round the nipple as she arched her back.

A loud explosion outside shocked them out of the moment. Jenny scrambled away from him, breathing hard, her eyes clouded with confusion and dismay. Aye, he felt it, too, especially when she stumbled to the door and grabbed her cloak. "Wait here!"

She moved so fast it made his head spin. For the moment, he remained where he was, puzzled and frustrated.

Jenny could not look back or she would be too tempted to stay with Matthew. Fastening her cloak on her way down the caravan steps, she ignored her wobbly knees and followed the sound of voices to the center of the camp, where all the Gypsies seemed to have gathered. She noticed several new caravans at the periphery of Bardo's camp, and that a number of strangers had gathered by the fire.

Rupa stood smiling near the edge of the crowd, holding a small, barefoot child on her hip. Jenny went to her, refusing to think about what had just occurred inside the caravan. She'd lost herself in Matthew's touch, in his sensual caresses.

Which was well and good for a wife. But she was *not* Matthew's wife. She did not even know his true name! At any time he could regain his memory, and then—

She closed her eyes and stood still for a moment, gathering her wits. That was exactly what she wanted, wasn't it? For Matthew to recover so that she could leave him to his own devices and go off to pursue Harriet? She tamped down her chagrin at the thought of leaving him. She was a practical woman and knew that a liaison with Matthew would come to no good.

She spoke to Rupa. "What is it? What's happening?"

The woman smiled broadly. "Tsinoria have come."

"Tsinoria?"

Rupa nodded. "Our *kompania* Lubunka. They . . ." She gestured toward the new caravans. "Tsinoria. We have much . . . er, fun and . . . foods—feasting—once brides chosen."

Rupa's explanation was far from adequate, but Jenny observed the embracing and cheek kissing of Bardo's clan with the newcomers, and concluded it must be a reunion of sorts. The Tsinoria must be another company—*kompania*—of Gypsies. Two young boys tossed something into the fire, causing another series of small explosions, startling Jenny.

She looked up and saw Tekari Kaulo staring at her from the other side of the fire, and recoiled at the expression in his eyes. She could not tell if it was disdain or pure lechery. Either way, he made her vastly uncomfortable, and she wished Matthew were close by.

Jenny pulled her cloak tightly around her and averted her eyes, troubled by her unfounded and unhelpful reliance on Matthew. There would soon come a time when he would regret the moment their paths had crossed. He would realize she'd lied to him and used him without consideration for his own situation.

"Many marriage soon," said Rupa.

"What do you mean?"

"Tsinoria and Lubunka," the woman replied, her words thickly accented. "Our *kompania*, their *kompania.* Soon old men choose good Tsinoria wifes for sons." She set her child down on his feet and allowed him to run with the older children. The barefoot toddler did not seem to mind the cold ground, yet Jenny's feet were chilled inside her shoes. She did not understand these people and how they survived their primitive hand-to-mouth existence. Few of them spoke English except for the phrases they needed to beg for money. None could read, and Jenny had noticed no livestock or stores of food anywhere. Yet Rupa had managed eggs and a thick soup.

She looked back at Rupa, who seemed happy and content in spite of her unstable style of life. "Fathers choose brides for their sons?"

"'Tis fathers' place to . . . to make match." Rupa nodded toward Tekari Kaulo. "My cousin soon take Tsinoria wife. He need . . ."

He needed a thrashing, but Jenny said nothing as she waited for Rupa to find the word she sought.

She hadn't realized that Kaulo was Rupa's relative, too. Now that she knew it, she saw the resemblance, but their personalities could not have been more disparate. Rupa's warmth and friendliness were directly opposite to Tekari's cold yet aggressive demeanor. Jenny dreaded the moment she would have to sit down with him for their next reading lesson.

"He need settlement. Family."

"Ah . . . settlement." Perhaps he would not be quite so abrasive once he had a wife, but Jenny did not believe that whatever drove Tekari Kaulo would be entirely remedied by an arranged marriage. There was always a burning impatience in his dark eyes, and his wiry body seemed perpetually poised for a fight, or perhaps for flight.

Jenny just hoped she was long gone when he exploded.

"Mr. Bardo is your uncle, too?"

Rupa nodded. "But I have father still. Tekari's— he die long ago. Fighting *gajo* with knife. He son now to Guibran Bardo."

The Gypsies built two more large fires between the rows of caravans, and Jenny went along with Rupa to her wagon rather than going back to the one where Matthew awaited her. She could not go back, not until he was asleep and she could enter without disturbing him.

Without having to deal with the wholly improper pull of attraction that raged between them. Jenny knew that her avoidance was cowardly, but there didn't seem to be any other way in the small camp, especially not with Tekari lurking nearby, his presence always threatening.

Other activities sprang up around the camp, giving it a festive air. All the women seemed to have tasks to perform, and many returned to their own caravans to prepare a welcoming meal for the newcomers. Rupa started to brew coffee at her own small fire. She pointed toward one of the far caravans where a group of men stood talking to one another as they poured liquor from a bottle into cups and drank jovially together.

"My husband. Name Pias Petrulengo. Very tall, but not so tall like your man."

Jenny doubted there were many as tall as Matthew. Or as strong. She'd seen the thick muscles of his arms and chest, and the powerful sinews of his legs. Yet he'd touched her so gently, as though he . . . cherished her. The same way her father had cared for her mother.

Jenny quickly squelched that painful memory. Thinking of happier times served no purpose but to make her feel miserable about all she had lost. She turned her attention to Pias, who stood drinking with his cronies, laughing and clapping one another on their backs. Small children ran circles around the adults, happily greeting the newcomers. The reunion was clearly a time of celebration.

"They talk of women. Pick brides."

"Now? They're choosing wives for their sons now?"

Rupa nodded. "Sure."

Jenny supposed it wasn't so very different from the way fathers in her own society chose spouses for their sons and daughters, though English girls were often able to accept or reject the proposed suitor. She wondered if the Gypsy girls had anything to say about the husbands chosen for them.

"They choose with ears not eyes," Rupa said.

"I don't understand," Jenny said, wondering if there was some ritual that involved blindfolding one of the parties.

"Pretty not always best," Rupa said. But Jenny was not so sure that Rupa's words were true. Mr. Ellis had chosen Clara Tremayne, whose dark beauty could not be concealed by Bresland's dowdy gowns and caps. Yet she was as harsh and unyielding with the children as Reverend Usher himself.

"Men . . . er, listen. Know who makes bad noise."

"They choose for temperament?"

Rupa furrowed her brow, clearly unfamiliar with the word.

"Temper," Jenny said. "Character."

"Ah yes. Husband want good temper."

Surely not all Gypsy women possessed easy temperaments. And what about the men? Jenny knew they could not all be fair and considerate husbands. "Who looks after the bride's interests?"

"You speak fast. What means this? Interests?"

Jenny covered Rupa's coffee tin and put it back on the shelf beside the caravan steps. "It doesn't matter," she said, but she wondered which unfortunate girl would become wife to Tekari Kaulo. The very thought of sharing her life with such a man made her shudder.

"You see. Tomorrow you see Gypsy way is good."

Jenny considered what kind of husband she might choose for herself if she did not know better. Not one like Mr. Ellis, who had listened to Reverend Usher's lies and decided she was not a biddable female, being much too opinionated for a woman. As though she should hold no opinions but his.

In the eyes of the law, a wife's property became her husband's, to do with whatever he pleased. Her children belonged to him. His word was law. Jenny knew that life on her own would be better than existing under some man's thumb.

Unless the husband were someone like Matthew. He could not have been more different from Mr. Ellis than Reverend Usher was from her own father.

Matthew had a commanding presence, a natural superiority that must have been bred into him. With Jenny having no noble background to raise her to Matthew's social standing, their attraction was entirely misplaced, and ill-advised.

No doubt Matthew would soon be missed and someone would come searching for him. Then all would turn out well for him, as he returned to his home and resumed the life he was meant to lead. With his clan and . . . very likely, a wife.

Jenny looked toward the caravan where Matthew rested and knew she could not go back, not when their attraction burned so fiercely between them.

"Look. Tsinoria begin," said Rupa.

One of the newcomers started out with an entourage of men toward Bardo's caravan, and when he was halfway there, started calling to its owner. Bardo gave an exaggerated appearance of being disinterested in what the visitor had to say, and everyone standing at the nearby caravans acted as though nothing unusual was going on.

But it was clear, even though Jenny could not understand the Rom language, that the visitor was trying to engage Bardo in marriage negotiations. With the way everyone in the camp participated in his own way, it was clearly a ritual they all enjoyed.

"What are they saying?" Jenny asked.

"Jivin Bovil tells Guibran Bardo his daughter very nice."

"I didn't realize Bardo had a daughter."

"Yes. Er . . . three daughters. One already go married."

"And Jivin has a marriageable son?"

Rupa nodded. "He want . . ." She struggled to find words to describe what was happening. "Show no hurry to Guibran."

"I think I understand," said Jenny. "Jivin cannot appear too anxious to engage Mr. Bardo's daughter."

"Guibran same. Much talk first. Bride price later."

"Bride price?"

Another nod. "Show value of bride."

Jenny had no dowry that she knew of. Her parents had lived comfortably, but any inheritance Jenny might have had had gone for her keep at Bresland. At least that's what her uncle had said when he'd shipped her off to school. She possessed nothing of any value to bring to a marriage. And there was that troublesome quirk that caused all kinds of havoc when she was upset or emotional. Could she hide such a thing from a husband?

"No childrens, you?" asked Rupa.

Jenny felt her face heat. "No. We, er . . . haven't been married very long."

Rupa laughed and touched Jenny's stomach. "Soon he fill you with babe. Then you be real wife."

Too embarrassed to reply, Jenny felt her heart skip when Matthew joined them and slid one arm around her waist, drawing her against his side. She would never be his real wife.

Forcing herself to ignore the heat of his body and the unearthly pull that drew her to him, she hoped he had not heard Rupa's words. He needed no encouragement.

Jenny sensed Tekari Kaulo watching them, and allowed herself to enjoy a few moments of security in Matthew's embrace. She introduced him to Rupa and told him Rupa was the one who'd brought them food and her clothes.

"I am verra glad to meet you, Rupa," Matthew said, earning a blushing giggle from the Gypsy woman, confirming Jenny's impression that Matthew held sway with the ladies with nothing more than a smile. In spite of her resolve to go her own way, her heart sank. Of course he had a wife. Or a fiancée at the very least.

"What was the explosion?"

"The children," Jenny answered. "They've been throwing something into the fire."

"Is *krábateysapa* . . . What English say?" Rupa tried to think of the word. "Burn powder."

"Gunpowder?" Jenny asked.

Rupa grinned. "Rom likes big noise. Come. We make tables for *kompania*. Much festive."

Matthew had come out of the caravan just in time to overhear Rupa tell Jenny he would soon give her a child. His loins tightened at the thought of it. Aye, he would give her his bairn, mayhap tonight. The headache and dizziness persisted, but they'd subsided sufficiently for him to make love to his wife, and he wanted to. Desperately.

Her worry that he did not know her was unfounded, and he was going to prove it to her. It did not matter that his memory was faulty. What he felt for her transcended mere memories of events they'd shared. He felt a connection to her that he knew—aye, he *knew*—he'd never felt with anyone else.

Clusters of men had gathered outside several caravans and were conversing cordially, all but Kaulo, who stood near one of the dark and deserted caravans, keeping his eye on Jenny. Matthew felt a surge of pure male possessiveness.

He'd come up behind Jenny, slid one arm 'round her waist, and pressed a kiss to her temple. She stiffened at first, but soon eased her body against his, making it clear to Kaulo, and every other Gypsy who could see them, that Jenny was his. No matter how infirm he might be, he would brook no male interference.

Matthew took Jenny's hand, and they accompanied Rupa to the center of camp. He admitted only to himself that he still felt a bit unsteady on his feet and dizzy when he turned his head too fast. But if Kaulo came close to Jenny, no amount of vertigo would keep him from laying the man flat.

There was a merry atmosphere among the Gypsy families, and Matthew noticed a second camp nearby. A few of the older boys began to light the lamps that hung on all the wagons, giving the grounds a magical, festive glow. The women set up tables and put out bowls of food and loaves of bread, while the men drank from flower-patterned cups and talked with the newcomers.

"Matthew, don't you think you should go back inside?" Jenny asked.

"Doona worry about me, *moileen*. I'm well enough."

In spite of her apparent desire to be rid of him, she clung to his hand tightly and glanced nervously about the periphery of the camp. "What is it?" he asked.

"So many people . . ."

"Then we should go," he said, drawing her close. He suspected she wasn't referring so much to the new group that had gathered, but to Kaulo. "Let's slip away, Jenny. The Gypsies are so occupied with their guests, they willna notice if we leave the camp and go on our way."

She dug in her heels. "No. 'Tis already dark and you are not well, yet."

"I am more resilient than you think, Jenny. Come," he said, turning back to their caravan. "We'll take a couple of the horses and ride to Carlisle."

She walked alongside him, but suddenly stopped. "No. I've seen how you cringe with pain every time you move your head. And you're still dizzy, aren't you?"

"No' enough to keep me here if you wish to go."

There was a loud cheer, and they were suddenly drawn back into the crowd by Rupa and the others, who laughed together and drank toasts. The Gypsy celebrations meant naught to him. He bent to speak into Jenny's ear. "Let's get away from here."

He took her away from the crowd and once again headed back to their own caravan, anxious to be alone with her. To show her that he remembered her well enough. He pushed open the door of the caravan and followed her inside.

Matthew didn't give her a chance to worry about his health or his memory. He took her in his arms and turned her, then lowered his head to hers. "'Tis been too long since I've tasted you, *moileen*."

He raised her hand to his lips and pressed a kiss to each of her knuckles. She sighed and started to pull away, but before she could form the words to try and send him to his sickbed, he touched her mouth with his own. He slipped his hands inside her cape and drew her hips tight against his erection.

Her nipples pebbled against his chest, and he felt her shiver. He deepened the kiss, moving to press her back against the wall of the caravan. She moaned quietly and tangled her tongue with his, skating her hands up his chest and 'round to the nape of his neck. Her touch sent flames of need darting through his veins and he rocked against her, wanting to be inside her.

But not yet.

Without breaking the kiss, he unfastened the ties at her neck and let her cloak drop to the floor. He wanted to touch and taste every inch of her, to explore her as though it were their first time. His heart hammered wildly in his chest as he loosened her blouse and lowered it to her waist. He brought his hands forward and cupped her breasts through the thin cloth of her chemise, then lowered her straps and bent his head to take one pebbling tip into his mouth.

Jenny made a desperate sound and held his head in place at her breast while he licked and sucked each sweet nipple in turn. She was so soft, yet she was possessed of a backbone of strength that drew him inexorably to her. Matthew tossed away his greatcoat and pulled his sherte free, ripping off buttons in his haste to feel her naked against him.

He lifted her into his arms and carried her two steps to the bed, laying her down gently. Her pale eyes glittered in the light of the candle he'd left, and they drifted closed when he took her mouth once again in a fervent kiss. She arched against him, tangling her legs with his.

She reached 'round to his buttocks, kneading his backside, pulling at the fabric of his trews. Her breathing was unsteady, as was his own, but he managed to unfasten his buttons, freeing his erect shaft to her touch. She moved slowly, but Matthew soon felt her fingers at the tip of his cock. Shyly, she began to explore him as he took her nipple into his mouth once again, sucking the honeyed tip as though it were the sweetest fruit.

Her tentative touch teased him and drove him mad. He jerked in her hand, then released her breast and shoved her skirts out of his way. Remembering how wildly responsive she'd been to his touch, he wanted to see her come apart with pleasure before he entered her. And again, after.

Using the pad of his thumb, he found the sensitive nub at her apex and rubbed lightly.

Her face became suffused with color as she bucked against his hand. He slid one finger inside her slick sheath and felt her shudder. "Oh dear heaven," she said on a breath. "Matthew . . ."

She tightened her hand 'round his cock. He growled with pleasure and placed his own hand over hers, showing her how to please him.

"You are so beautiful."

Her lips were swollen from his kisses, moist and pink. Her eyes were dark with passion, and the sound of her voice resonated deep within him. She was his life mate, the one woman who would satisfy him forever.

"Matthew . . . Oh, please . . ."

"*Moileen.* My sweet wife."

Her eyes changed suddenly, their focus becoming sharper. She let go of him and moved suddenly, drawing her hands up to his shoulders, caressing.

No, she was pushing, pushing him away and shaking her head. "Matthew . . ."

She shifted her position and started to move away from him.

"Aye. You take the top."

With one swift move, he was lying on his back with Jenny straddling him. He took her hands in his and placed them on his straining cock. "I need to be inside you, *moileen*. Now."

Her breasts, full and pink-tipped, swayed above him. She closed her eyes tightly, and her mouth quivered. "No," she whispered.

"Jenny . . ." 'Twas painful to wait any longer. He wanted her desperately.

"We can't, Matthew," she whispered. "I'm not your wife."

Chapter 5

The Isle of Coruain, 981

The wind on the cliffs whipped at Ana Mac Lochlainn with a fury that fairly matched her temper. She shoved her cloak behind her, and with fists clenched in worry and grief, resumed her pacing, her boots crushing the rich, soft moss of her island home.

"Eilinora and her Odhar will break through all our charms and protections, Ana," warned Cianán Mag Uidhir, leader of the Druzai elders. "'Tis no matter how—"

"Nay, they will not!" Not while Ana had breath in her lungs. She was as noble as her cousins, Merrick and Brogan, and wielded as much power as any Mac Lochlainn. The wicked Eilinora and her minions could—*would*—be held at bay with her own *lòchran* magic until her cousins brought the *brìgha*-stones home to Coruain. Even if the task drained Ana of all her energy and stole her life force, she would hold them, by God, until Merrick and Brogan returned.

Cianán clasped his hands behind his back and watched Ana pacing near the edge of the cliff, oblivious to the *wealrach* gliding over the waters before her, searching for prey, its wingspan greater than the height of two men. He turned to Ana. "You know the ancient tales of Eilinora as well as I, *mo curadh*. The witch will quickly learn to use the magic of Kieran's scepter and then we will be—"

"Brogan and Merrick will return with the blood stones before that happens," she snapped, resenting Cianán's intrusion. She needed to concentrate her full attention on her protective magic, as did he and the rest of the elders. Ana knew she would need all the help she could get.

Of course Ana knew the tales. The evil and capricious sorceress had instigated violent unrest between the Celtic clans eons before. Who she had been before taking the Druzai name Eilinora, for queen, was unknown. But she had cruelly used the Tuath Druids to foment petty jealousies that led to war. With her followers, Eilinora had caused many a bloody battle, resulting in the deaths of countless worthy Tuath warriors, as well as women and children.

The details of Eilinora's defeat had been lost in the mists of time, but 'twas said that the corrupt sorceress had been vanquished by one commanding Druzai who was her perfect antithesis. The two had met in battle, good against evil. And though the particulars of that contest were unknown, the result had been retold in Druzai lore for centuries. Eilinora and her minions had been imprisoned in some distant netherworld, a barren, *bòcan* forest. She and her vile Odhar were bound together in unbreakable numinous bonds, and destined to remain suspended in the colorless world forever.

Yet something had freed her. After a thousand years' imprisonment, some powerful force that Ana could not yet see had loosed the witch upon the world.

An ear-wrenching shriek forced Ana and Cianán to clap their hands over their ears. At the same time, a surge of dark magic spewed forth, suddenly piercing through Ana's protective *lòchran* field. She felt a crushing blow to her chest and some dark malevolence sucking at her mind. She sank to her knees, even as she launched what should have been a killing strike of her own.

"Cianán! Help me!" she cried.

But with the horrible roaring noise in her ears, Cianán's voice seemed very far away. A whorl of wind and debris rose up to swallow Ana, nearly pulling her to the very edge of the cliff. A harsh feminine voice pierced through the horrible howling in her ears. *"I will not relent, fledgling!"*

Ana resisted the torrent of pure evil that tore at the core of her power. Using every ounce of her will, she pushed herself up to her feet and caught sight of a female face, high above the magical shield, a filmy apparition that dissipated the moment Ana's eyes touched upon her. *Eilinora!*

"Nor will I, witch! Begone!" Ana raised both hands and drew upon every bright force, every decent power of nature that she could muster. Feeling Cianán's strength behind her, she repelled the witch's attempt to pull her thoughts from her brain.

"Do not fool yourself, *gurach*," the witch rasped in Ana's ear, her shrill voice making Ana wince in pain. "I will find your brothers. Their prize will soon be mine!"

"You doona even know who they are," Ana whispered as she launched an attack of her own and flung the apparition far from Coruain's shores.

She felt something cold upon her face. "Ana!"

"Aye." She opened one eye to see Cianán crouched over her.

"Let me help you."

Ana took hold of the elder's arm and pulled herself to her feet. She stumbled and would have fallen but for the elder's strong grasp. "'Twas Eilinora, was it not?"

Ana nodded. She felt weak and spent after her brief encounter with the witch. "You didna see her?"

He shook his head. "But I felt her evil assault. Did she learn where Merrick and Brogan have gone?"

"Nay. And she will learn naught from me."

"'Twas best that you kept their destination to yourselves. 'Twould no' do for the witch to tear that information from any of the elders."

"Aye," Ana whispered, feeling weak and drained. She and her cousins had decided not to tell anyone where they were going, on the chance that Eilinora might isolate one of the elders and coerce the information from him.

"You have not slept in the hours since your cousins left Coruain, Ana," said Cianán. "Have you eaten?"

"I am all right."

"No, you are no'. You are pale, and the light is gone from your eyes."

"I must keep watch."

Since Merrick's departure, she did naught but pace the cliffs outside the chieftain's dwelling, warding off the Odhar's attacks, shoring up the shields she and the elders had cast 'round the isles. The Odhar's surges of energy were more powerful than she'd anticipated, their attack more personal. And she'd just discovered that Eilinora was as formidable as the legends said. The witch had come close to penetrating Ana's mind and learning the details of her cousins' quest.

She knew 'twas only a matter of time before Eilinora's evil minions recovered from Ana's rebuff and mounted their next attack.

Cianán was correct—if the witch and her mentor learned to wield the chieftain's scepter, then Coruain would surely fall to Eilinora and the Odhar, who had nearly conquered the world without it. This time they would destroy the Druzai and enslave the Tuath.

"Your kin are the most powerful among us,

Ana," said Cianán. "Yet we can all see how this challenge exhausts you."

Fatigue was not the worst of it. Unable to see the outcome of this struggle, Ana worried that she would not have the power to withstand another attack. Brogan and Merrick needed to hurry.

Northumbria, late winter, 1826

Matthew's shocked expression was clear for Jenny to see, even in the flickering candlelight. He clenched his jaw and went perfectly still while she felt perilously close to tears.

"The Gypsies assumed y-you were my husband," she whispered shakily. "So I-I let them— and you—believe it."

She suddenly realized where her hands were, and yanked them away, awkwardly pulling up her blouse to cover herself as she climbed off him. "I was afraid you would die if I—"

He closed his eyes, and Jenny finally managed to right her chemise and blouse. She slipped away from the bed and grabbed the shawl that had been draped near the stove to dry. Wrapping it around her shoulders, she felt shaken and mortified by what had just transpired.

But she wanted him still.

She pressed her hands to her cheeks. They were hot, and Jenny knew they must be flushed. She didn't know how she was going to face "Matthew" again.

"Come and sit down, lass." His voice was dark and rumbling, and the sound of it caused impossible yearnings to stir in her heart once again.

"I-I—"

"I've covered myself, Jenny. Come and sit down."

She took a deep breath and turned to face him. He'd pulled the blanket over his lap, but his chest was still bare. As was one leg.

Jenny chewed on her lip and sat down beside the stove. She could not trust herself to go any closer, not when he looked at her like a fierce pirate, eyeing his valuable booty.

He crossed his arms over his chest. "You're sure we're no' wed?"

"Of course I'm sure," Jenny replied, her voice still shaky. She stood abruptly, feeling edgy and raw. "I know it was wrong to say so, but you were hurt, and it was freezing cold and raining. And that man, Tekari Kaulo, frightened me."

"Aye. I can see how it was."

Jenny began to pace in the small space. "I thought the highwaymen might come back—"

She turned and bumped into Matthew, who had come to his feet so quietly, she hadn't even heard him. He grabbed hold of her shoulders to keep her from crashing into him, and Jenny sent up a prayer of thanks that he'd wrapped something around his waist.

"You're still the most beautiful lass I've ever known," he said softly, drawing her close to him, "and my wanting you hasna changed."

Jenny swallowed the lump in her throat. He dipped his head and brushed her mouth with his. But her good sense prevailed before she could fall into his kiss.

"No! This is not . . ." She stepped back. "I'm not . . ."

"You are no' what, lass?"

"I am not your wife."

"Are you anyone else's wife?" he asked.

"No, of course not."

"Jenny, I felt your response to me."

"That doesn't mean I can sleep with you," she snapped.

"Sleep? I wasna thinking of—"

"I *know* what you were thinking of, Matthew!" She whirled away from him. How could he be so obtuse? Even without a memory, he had to know that their actions had been reprehensible. Immoral.

He pulled her against him, her back to his chest, and slid one arm about her waist. "Jenny, there is no one to gainsay us. Come back to bed and let me show you how good it can—"

"No. 'Tis impossible."

"You've said you are no' married."

"No, but *you* might be!"

Matthew's heart had not slowed since the moment Jenny had put her hands on his cock. He wanted her desperately, but even without a memory to guide him, he was quite certain he was not a man to beg. "I doona think I am wed."

"But you cannot be sure," she countered. "There might be a wife waiting for you at home in Scotland. With your children at her side."

He felt his brow crease as he tried to think, but all he got for his trouble was a sharp pain in his temple. He must have winced, for Jenny urged him to sit.

"I'm all right, lass," he said, his voice a harsh rasp.

But the dream of Ana, the red-haired woman, suddenly came to mind, and he sat right down. He wasn't all right, not at all.

"What is it? Do you remember—"

"I remember naught," he said sharply.

The woman in the dream could not be his mate, not when his bond with Jenny compelled him so. He'd not made a true physical connection with her, but what he'd felt was beyond a mere physical mating with a comely female. It had been a fiery passion unlike anything he could ever have known. He would surely have remembered such a bond, in spite of the damage to his head.

"Why did you no' leave me here with the Gypsies and go on your way, then?"

Wringing her hands together, she stepped away. "I couldn't leave you here, so ill you could barely move."

"We slept together last night."

"But nothing more."

"Until this morn."

"Matthew," she said sharply, "that was unintended. I didn't even realize—"

"Is Matthew my name?"

She gave him a look of utter dismay and answered in a quiet voice. "I don't know."

"I doona think it is."

"You remem—"

"No. But it doesna sound right. No' the way Keating does."

"Keating?" she asked. "My name is familiar to you?"

"Aye," he said, irked by his peculiar malady. "But I doona know why."

Matthew felt like a stranger to this place. He knew the language, but it was not his own. The people were entirely foreign to him, though mayhap it was because they were Gypsies. A sense of urgency tugged at the back of his mind, but he could not fathom the reason for it. Something to do with Ana . . .

He touched the bracer on his wrist and thought of the words etched there. *Let wisdom and kindness prevail*. The statement should help him to remember, but alas . . .

"Were we actually attacked by highwaymen?"

Jenny nodded. "*I* was. You came to help me."

Aye. He wouldn't have left this woman to face her attackers alone. "Was anyone with me when I came upon you and the highwaymen?" he asked.

"No."

"Of course, else my companions would have remained with me to help," he said, stating the obvious. "And you were alone as well?"

She nodded, and soft tendrils of her hair swirled 'round the delicate shells of her ears. She clung tightly to the shawl she'd wrapped 'round herself, clearly bent on discouraging his approach. "I was going to Carlisle, that much is true."

"Why?"

"I was going to . . ." She let her words drift as she eyed the side of his head. "Your wound. 'Tis nearly healed."

He shrugged. "Aye. Of course."

"I've never known anyone to heal so fast."

Matthew had an awareness that there were healers of all different abilities. He knew he was one of the best. He felt sure of it, but even his own formidable healing skills could not bring back the memory he had lost. 'Twas odd that there were certain things he knew about himself, yet his identity and purpose . . . his family connections . . . were deeply hidden.

"Why were you going to Carlisle?" he asked.

"'Tis a long, dull story."

"Humor me, lass. You might say something that will bring me a memory."

She sat down on the bed, then jumped to her feet again, as if the mattress burned her. With her cheeks flushed, she turned away from him. "I am—or I *was*—a teacher at a school a few miles away. I shared a room with another teacher, Harriet Lambton, who stole something of value from me and disappeared."

"Disappeared? Did you find her after her vanishment?"

She gave him a puzzled look, as though she did not understand him. "N-no, I think she must have gone to Carlisle. Miss Lambton once mentioned that her brother lives there, so I assume that's where she's gone."

He nodded. "It makes sense. What did the woman take from you?"

"A locket," Jenny said quietly. "'Tis a small silver pendant on a chain, all I have from my mother."

Denoting a deep sadness when she said the words, he went to her and pulled the edges of her shawl together. "We'll find her, Jenny. We can leave upon the morrow."

"Matthew, you can't come with me."

"Aye, I can."

"But what of your own journey? Clearly, you were going somewhere when you stopped to help me."

"Aye. I feel it . . . something tugging at my brain. Something I must do, but I canna think what . . ."

Another explosion of gunpowder startled Jenny. "There, you see?"

"No. See what?"

"You must try to determine what it is, what's tugging at you."

"Jenny, every time I try to force it, the thought escapes me and goes even deeper."

Something significant blazed between them. He wasn't about to let her go off to Carlisle without him. Besides, 'twas her name that had drawn him here. He was certain of it. Somehow, Jenny Keating was tangled up in whatever purpose escaped him.

* * *

Jenny put her hands on her hips. "Why do you suppose you're carrying so much gold?"

"I doona know."

"I do."

He tossed her a fierce, frowning look.

"You're a wealthy man, Matthew. I suspect you might be lord of some vast Scottish estate." He was certainly not English, not with his thick brogue and the Gaelic words that slid so smoothly from his tongue. Sometimes it seemed that he didn't understand the things she said, and there were times when his meaning escaped her, too. Vanishment, for instance. She'd never heard such a word.

"If I am such an important personage, then where is my entourage?"

He said the words in a scoffing manner, but Jenny could see that the question bothered him. He'd likely thought of it already.

He took her hand and guided her to a seat at the table. Then he sat on the bed across from her, their knees nearly touching. "Tell me all that you remember when you first saw me," he said.

She did not want to feel any sympathy for him. He belonged somewhere. Once he remembered his identity, he would return to that life, which included more gold than she could easily hold in both her hands. "I heard your voice first. You shouted to the highwaymen."

"What did I say?"

"I don't know. Something Gaelic, I think. Then you told them to stop."

He looked down at his clasped hands, at the bracer that encircled his wrist. "Naught unusual about that. 'Tis what any man would have said under the same circumstances."

Jenny nodded, although she doubted it. She could not imagine Mr. Ellis taking on four men in defense of an unknown woman. The young doctor hadn't even had the gumption to contradict Reverend Usher's criticisms.

"You saw no one near me?" Matthew asked. "Was this satchel the extent of my belongings?"

"Yes. There was nothing . . . Wait. You were pale and I thought you were ill."

"Before I was shot?"

"Yes. I had forgotten that. You looked as though you were in pain."

He looked at her intently. "So I might have been hurt before . . ." He rubbed his fingertips against his forehead, and Jenny kept silent to avoid interrupting any memories that might be emerging.

Jenny raised her brows and gazed at him expectantly, watching as every possible expression crossed his face. But for his fashionable suit of clothes, Matthew might have been a fierce Scottish warrior, come to the rescue of a helpless damsel.

He stood suddenly and moved to the stove, clasping his hands behind his back. She knew her honesty about their sham marriage had changed everything between them, which was as it should be.

He could not touch her the way he'd done only a few minutes before. Nor could they sleep together in the narrow bed. They could not even indulge in the small, affectionate gestures that seemed so natural for a man and his wife . . .

Because she was not his wife. She covered her trembling lips with her hand and fought tears.

She was no one. Her own aunt and uncle had wanted nothing to do with her, as though they'd somehow known of the aberrant force within her. She did not think Reverend Usher had connected her with the small accidents that had occurred with her anger, but he'd made certain she—and everyone else—understood all her other shortcomings.

She swallowed and looked up at him, bracing herself as he pondered all that she'd just told him, looking for the clue that might spark his memory.

"I think you're wrong," he said finally.

"I beg your pardon?"

"'Tis likely I'm running from something," he said finally.

"I don't understand."

"This urgency that I feel . . ."

"No doubt you are expected somewhere."

"Or I need to get away."

"From whom? Or what?"

"I think I must have stolen that gold."

Jenny could not help but laugh at the irony of Matthew believing he was a thief while Jenny was the one who'd been accused of it.

"'Tis no' amusing, lass."

"Yes, it is," she retorted. "Look at you. Your clothes, your shoes."

He glanced at the discarded items. "So?"

"They're of such a fine quality, Matthew. Very unlike the clothes worn by the highwaymen who attacked me. I cannot imagine any thief on the run wearing such expensive attire. And your satchel." She picked it up from the floor and slid her fingers over its butter-soft surface. "'Tis made of the finest leather I've ever seen."

She glanced at him then and caught him looking at her hand as it glided over the leather. Only a few moments ago, her hands had caressed him, had fondled the thick strength of his manhood, encased in silky softness. She heard his breath catch.

Jenny felt the same hunger, but she had no intention of giving in to it. She set the satchel on the floor and looked away from him. "The thief that's wanted is I, not you."

"What do you mean?"

She glanced at him over her shoulder. "Two constables came into camp looking for me this afternoon. They said I'd stolen something from Bresland."

"That's absurd."

She felt ridiculously touched by his confidence in her, and swallowed a sudden burning at the back of her throat. "Bardo and the rest of the *kompania* got them to go away."

"Will they return?"

"Perhaps. Bresland School is an important institution in Kirtwarren. The headmaster holds a great deal of sway in the district."

They heard another series of small explosions outside, followed by laughter and the lively strains of a fiddle and the rhythmic clapping of hands.

"Then we must stay hidden among the Gypsies for now," Matthew said. "As husband and wife."

"We can't."

"We canna change our story now, lass," Matthew said. "Besides, I doona like how Kaulo looks at you. I want him to understand you're mine."

It was merely a slip of the tongue. They both knew she was not his.

"I cannot stay here in this tiny room with you, Matthew."

He came to her then and touched her cheek, sending shivers of wishful thinking down to her toes. "You are so soft, so beautiful." He let his hand drop. "But I willna touch you unless you wish it."

Of course she wished it. She wanted to go back to that bed, pull the wrapper from Matthew's loins, and satisfy the burning need he'd kindled within her. But she knew better.

"Do you no' trust me, lass?"

"I trust you," she replied quietly. "'Tis myself I don't trust."

He took her hand. "Come to bed. Keep your Gypsy clothes on, but I plan to hold you through the night."

He blew out the candle, and Jenny followed him down to the bed, letting him draw her into his arms. True to his word, he made no advances, even though he'd discarded the cloth he wore and lay naked against her. She could hardly think when he pulled her close.

"Tell me about this place you came from. Bresland School."

Matthew felt her stiffen. "'Tis just a school."

"How did you come to be there?" he asked, fairly certain that the headmaster of "just a school" would not accuse an innocent teacher of thievery. And said teacher would not have found herself alone on a deserted road, vulnerable to attack.

"My history is quite dull, I assure you," she replied.

"Humor me. I canna recall my own, so let me hear yours."

She hesitated for a moment, then spoke quietly, her soft breath touching the base of his throat. "There's not much to tell. My parents were killed in a boating accident." She spoke steadily, but she took a deep, shuddering breath, and he skimmed his hand down her back.

"My mother's sister was my only relation. But she and her husband . . . They had no use for a scrawny, little orphan girl. They sent me to Bresland School, which is where I've been ever since."

"How old were you?"

"I'd just had my tenth birthday when my parents died."

Matthew's chest ached at the thought of Jenny as a wee, fair lass, her perfect eyes reddened with tears of grief and no one to comfort her. "Have you no brothers or sisters?"

He felt a slight shake of her head. "There was only my aunt Helen, and she . . . she let her husband send me away."

Matthew had difficulty grasping such a concept, leading him to believe his own family must be very different. 'Twas no wonder she had difficulty believing he might wish to help her.

"What of you? Who is your family?" Jenny asked, and he saw her question for what it was—a deliberate attempt to steer the conversation away from her own circumstances. She knew he had no knowledge of his own origins,. yet her question caused him a quick flash of a memory.

"I . . ." The thought was so fleeting, he could not grab hold of it. "You'll no' change the subject quite so easily, lass. Had you any friends at Bresland?"

She hesitated, and he knew she did not want to speak of this, either.

"I had Norah Martin," she finally said.

"But you left her to go in search of your locket?"

She shook her head. "No. Norah died at school. Years ago."

"Years?"

"She was about my age, maybe twelve, when she died."

Shock echoed through Matthew at the thought of such a thing. The death of a young child was unusual . . . was it not? "Was there no healer?"

"He was called too late."

'Twas unconscionable. "What happened?"

"Norah had been punished . . . and she took a chill afterward. When fever set in, she could not recover."

"Punished? How?"

"The headmaster locked her in the privy overnight. It was near Christmas, and cold . . ." In a strangely detached manner, Jenny described the appalling treatment of the child, and he knew that Norah was not the only one who'd suffered.

Matthew slid his hand under her skirt, moving up the smooth skin of her leg until he reached the raised welt on her buttock. He'd hardly noticed it during their lovemaking, but now he wondered. "Is this a scar?"

She pushed his hand away and lowered her skirts.

"Jenny, did the headmaster beat you?"

She nodded.

"And he broke the skin?" Matthew asked with more calm than he felt.

"Not every time."

He slid his hand over the area and touched it through her clothes.

"That happened my first day at Bresland," she said. "No one told me we weren't allowed more than half a slice of bread at breakfast."

"The headmaster struck you because you asked for more?"

"My . . . impertinence set the tone of our relationship for the rest of my years at the school."

Had Jenny not burrowed in closer, Matthew would have been tempted to go in search of the bastard right then. Instead, he gathered Jenny tightly to his chest. "'Tis no' natural for a grown man to lay hands on a wee lass, Jenny. Why did no one stop him?"

"I can assure you it was quite common at Bresland, at least with those of us who were fair-haired and small," she replied. "He never touched me after I . . . after I grew up."

The flickering fires outside cast colorful, muted light through the multicolored cloth over the windows. Reds and greens played over the features of Jenny's face and her light hair, like an artist putting paint on canvas.

Matthew heard Jenny swallow, and knew she was embarrassed. Anger seethed inside him, and he considered taking her back to Bresland with a champion at her side. *Then*, let the headmaster try to hurt her or any of the wee lasses still trapped at that miserable school.

He resumed his innocent caresses. "You became a teacher."

"I had nowhere else to go."

"Did you no' think of marriage?"

She hesitated. "Once. But it didn't . . . He decided I would not make a suitable wife."

Matthew's hand stilled. "Did you love the man?" His own throat thickened with dismay. He did not really want to hear of any other man she might have loved.

She hesitated, seeming to consider her reply before answering. "He became our school physician, and tended me when I was ill last autumn. When I recovered, he took an interest in me. He said he was ready to take a wife, and began to court me in earnest."

Matthew unclenched his jaw. "But then he decided you were unsuitable?"

She gave a slight shrug of her shoulders. "It doesn't matter what Mr. Ellis thought. I decided *he* was unsuited to *me*, too. I could never abide a husband who thought the headmaster's punishments were justified."

Matthew sat straight up. Was the man barmy? "He is a healer, yet he thinks 'tis acceptable to cause physical injury to a child?"

"I am lucky that he threw me over for Miss Tremayne," Jenny remarked offhandedly, though Matthew heard a note of regret in her voice.

"The man is a fool." And a betrayer. *Mo oirg*, had *everyone* forsaken her?

She would soon see that Matthew was not the kind of man to abandon her, no matter where he'd come from. It seemed impossible that he had

known her only a night and one day. She was as
much a part of him as his next breath.

"What will you do after you find your
pendant?"

"I'm to become a governess to a pair of brothers
north of Carlisle."

"Governess? I'm no' sure I comprehend the
word."

"A governess is a teacher. Don't they have such
women in Scotland?" Jenny asked.

Matthew shrugged, unable to recall if it were
so.

"We're an educated class without family or
connections. Wealthy families hire us . . . 'Tis very
likely you owe your early education to someone
like me."

"Believe me, lass. I doona think a knock on the
head could ever shake your memory from my
brain."

Jenny gave a bitter laugh, as though she did not
believe him.

"Someday I will learn all there is to know about
you, Jenny Keating."

"We should be trying to figure out who you
are," she said, "and where you come from. And
not waste time on my dull memories."

He gave a slight shake of his head. "The more I
try to remember anything, the worse it gets."

"What about that bracer on your wrist?" she
asked, sliding her fingers over the warm metal. "I
said your father gave it to you, but . . . you know I
lied. Can you recall anything about it?"

He'd tried, but his efforts to remember had come to naught. "No, I—" He saw a sudden flash of something. Dark blue robes. Deep chanting. "A ritual."

"A ceremony?"

"I doona know. Only that it feels . . . Aye, 'twas bestowed upon me, in a ceremony."

Jenny sat straight up in bed. "Then you remember!" she choked out.

"No." He pulled her back down to the bed. "'Tis gone."

"B-but you must recall something! Even a . . . a . . ." Her voice wavered, and Matthew realized she was on the verge of tears.

"You doona want me to remember, do you, lass?" he said quietly, smoothing her hair back from her forehead.

"Of course I want you to remember. It's just that . . ."

"Doona worry. I'll no' be leaving you to find your locket on your own."

"Don't be ridiculous," she huffed. "I'd planned on going after it by myself. You're just a distraction."

Chapter 6

They fell asleep in each other's arms, and when Jenny awoke, she knew Matthew had come no closer to remembering who he was. She was certain he'd dreamed, for he'd spoken in his sleep. In Gaelic. Perhaps one of his dreams would do more than give him a fleeting glimpse of his past—maybe they would even help him to piece those glimpses together.

He was not in the caravan when Jenny arose, and his absence bothered her more than it should. She'd lied the night before. He was more than a distraction, and she'd become much too attached to him. He'd been partly right in saying that she did not want him to remember, and the truth of his words forced her to face reality.

She washed her face and cleaned her teeth, brushed her hair and tied it back, then changed into her black Bresland gown. Unfamiliar sounds outside drew her to the door of the caravan. She pulled on her cloak and stepped out, and saw that the Gypsies were breaking camp. The men were hitching horses to the caravans while the women and children packed their belongings and put them inside, or put them in boxes or barrels and strapped them to outside storage areas.

Jenny stepped down and walked around to the front of the wagon.

"Brod fàir, moileen," said Matthew as he harnessed the second of two horses to their wagon. "Good morn to you." He wore a bright red shirt with no collar, and had a black kerchief knotted at his neck. His sleeves were pushed up to the elbows, and Jenny's breath skittered from her lungs as she watched him, the muscles and sinews of his forearms stretching and bunching as he moved.

He quickly skirted around the horses and came to her. Drawing her into his arms, he kissed her soundly, as though he still believed she was his wife.

"For Kaulo's benefit," he said quietly, releasing her before she had a chance to react. "We havena much time before they leave, so if you need to take a walk in the woods, you'd best get it done."

Jenny's blush delighted him, but she was the only aspect of his predicament to do so. His head wound was mostly healed, with the dizziness gone and the pain occurring only occasionally now. But the fleeting glimpses of his past were so fragmented, they were disorienting and not helpful at all.

While Jenny slept, he'd spent some time looking at the bracer 'round his forearm and tried to recall more details of the ritual when he'd received it. Naught had come to him.

He'd looked in the small mirror on the caravan wall, studying his face while he dispensed with his night's growth of whiskers, but again, he barely recognized himself. His satchel was unfamiliar, its contents meaning naught to him.

Jenny's notion that he was an important personage rang true somehow, but did not ease his mind. He had a great deal of money, and he was well dressed. Yet a man in a high position would hardly be traveling a backcountry road alone, especially carrying so much money. It made no sense.

Nor did Jenny's suggestion that he already had a mate. There was no one for him but Jenny, and he intended to keep her with him long enough that she realized and accepted it.

"You! *Gajo!*" Kaulo strode up to him. "This horse lame. You—"

"No. 'Tis no' lame." Matthew had seen to it earlier. There'd been a stone in its shoe, and Matthew had removed it and healed the sore spot. Naught was wrong with the mare now.

Kaulo went to the horse's left flank and lifted its fetlock to examine the hoof. He muttered something in his Gypsy language and went to the other leg. Frowning fiercely, he poked at the hoof, then dropped the leg to the ground as though he had no understanding of how easy it was to heal such a minor malady. Matthew decided to say naught about it.

Jenny returned, and Matthew slipped an arm 'round her waist. He pulled her close, keeping his eyes on Kaulo until the wiry Gypsy turned away and left, muttering under his breath.

"What was that about?" Jenny asked, extricating herself from his grasp.

"Naught but a slight misconception. Kaulo's."

Jenny had pulled her hair back and wore it loosely bound at her nape. Matthew reached for the tie that bound it, but Rupa approached, so he slid his fingers just under her blond tresses instead, and lightly rubbed Jenny's neck.

"You put up hood now," Rupa said, glancing behind her. "Again, *gajo* men come."

"The constables?" Jenny asked.

Rupa nodded. "And one old man. Guibran Bardo say pretend sleep. Your man drive wagon. No speak."

"Shouldn't I go inside?"

"No," said Rupa. With two fingers, she pointed to her eyes, then to Jenny. "Better he see no hiding woman."

Jenny covered her head, and Matthew helped her up to the seat in front. He climbed onto the bench after her and clucked his tongue, urging the horses to take their place behind the other caravans. It was a noisy departure, with the rolling of heavy wheels and the creaking of the wagons. Children and barking dogs ran alongside them, excited to be on the move again.

They had not gone far when Matthew saw three men on horseback, all dressed in black, though the old one wore a different sort of hat and his coat was much longer. They stopped every caravan and inspected the inhabitants of each. His own encounter with these men did not worry him, but he could feel Jenny's nervousness.

"'Tis the headmaster, come himself to see if I—"

"Jenny, doona worry."

He felt her tremble and slid his arm 'round her waist.

"They will see I am no Gypsy," she said quietly. "And Reverend Usher will—"

"No, they will see only what I wish them to see."

"Matthew, how is that—"

"Hush, lass. Doona make it more complicated than it needs to be."

He felt a strange, scratchy heat in his chest as he muttered a few quiet words in the language that felt most familiar to him, never taking his eyes from the old headmaster. He repeated the words once more for the two constables, and soon they were backing away from the train of caravans. All at once, they turned their horses and rode away.

"I don't believe it!" Jenny exclaimed, though she kept her voice down. "I wonder what Bardo said to them."

Matthew shrugged and continued on, though he kept an eye on the three men as they headed toward the road.

Of course he would do what he could to protect her. Matthew had no doubt the repelling words would never have come to him if he'd *tried* to remember them. Yet they'd slipped from his lips without effort, without thought. He looked at Jenny, who believed 'twas Bardo who had repelled the men. He decided to say naught to correct her, not until he understood it himself.

The Gypsies did not stop all day, but their rate of progress was slow enough for the children to keep up on foot. Unnerved by Reverend Usher's appearance in camp and his quick departure with the constables, Jenny jumped down and joined a group of women who walked beside the caravans.

They spoke their own language, but Rupa was among them, and she introduced Jenny to everyone. Their names were strange-sounding, and she had to repeat each one silently several times to remember it.

"Chavi will be bride tonight." Rupa put one hand on the shoulder of a young girl and nodded toward two others. "And Tshaya. And Dooriya."

The women all tittered behind their hands, but Jenny was shocked by the young ages of the brides. They could not have been older than twelve or thirteen. Rupa had mentioned that Tekari Kaulo would soon marry, but Jenny could not imagine sacrificing one of these girls to him. She shuddered at the thought of it. "And your cousin, Tekari . . . who will he wed?"

"Beti," Rupa replied, gesturing toward a slight, dark-haired girl riding on the back step of one of the Tsinoria caravans. Jenny judged her age at thirteen or fourteen years.

"Tonight?" she asked as Rupa's words suddenly dawned on her. "The weddings will happen tonight?"

"Sure. Good place. Village nearby. Mens go, um . . . They purchase feast," said Rupa.

Jenny thought perhaps it would be best to leave the group now. Matthew knew she was not his wife, and he was healthy enough to take care of himself. She was relieved that she'd finally been honest with him, at least about their marriage. She could never tell him—or anyone—of the abnormality inside her that sometimes caused bizarre, unexplainable incidents. She wondered if Reverend Usher was right . . . Did Satan dwell within her?

She did not feel evil, nor had she ever intentionally used the force to an evil purpose. But she needed to try to understand it, and discover whether she could control it. Experimenting was going to take complete privacy.

Jenny didn't think the Gypsies had progressed more than five or six miles when they stopped for the night. But she was tired when they arrived and set up camp, too worn out to think about finding a deserted place to test the force inside her. And she was much too tired to go off on her own to follow the road to Carlisle. While Jenny felt confused and at loose ends, Matthew unhitched the horses from their caravan and beckoned to her.

"You look weary, lass," he said, taking the reins of both horses into one hand to gently caress her face.

Jenny had a sudden, fierce desire to go into the wagon with him and lose herself in his arms, but she knew better. It did not help that Matthew looked as though he could carry her away and devour her, repeating the pleasures they'd begun the night before.

"Ach, lass. All I can think of is touching you . . . tasting your sweet mouth."

"Y-you must not, Matthew," she said, afraid he might have been reading her thoughts. He took her hand anyway, and they walked together toward the road.

A number of the men walked ahead of them, and one of the older boys came and took away one of Matthew's horses. "I'm going with Bardo and the others into the village," he said. "Promise me you'll still be here when I return."

She searched his eyes. "Have you been reading my mind?"

"Nay, 'tis no' one of my talents."

"What do you mean?" she asked, puzzled once again by his words.

"I doona know, lass. But I canna see what's in your mind."

"Then how did you know I'd been thinking of leaving the troupe?"

He kissed her lightly. "Because I know you, *moileen*. We might no' be man and wife, but you are part of me. I am part of you. When my memory returns, you'll see."

He mounted the chestnut mare and rode away, following Bardo and the other men as they rode into the village.

Jenny felt hollow as Matthew left. Their time together had been short, and illusory.

Some of the women began preparations for the wedding feast while others collected bridal finery from one another's wagons, and took all the colorful garments to Guibran Bardo's caravan.

"You come," said Rupa. "Help sew."

"Oh no," said Jenny, unaccustomed to such friendly overtures. The students and teachers at Bresland kept to themselves. "I should not—"

"Yes. Some fun. You see."

Jenny smiled at Rupa's warmth. "Soon, then," she said, taking her leave to go into the woods. It was her first opportunity to spend more than a quick moment alone.

She walked out of sight of the camp to a large, fallen log, and sat down to look up at the sky. Somehow, she'd caused a branch of a tree to fall when the highwaymen had attacked. She wondered if she could do it again.

Leaning back on her hands, Jenny turned her gaze to the tall trees that surrounded her, and concentrated, listening to the creaking of trunks as the trees swayed in the stillness of the forest. She only had to make it happen once, and then she would know. Just one branch.

Break! her mind called. *Crack and fall! Show me!*
"*Why do you wish us harm?*"

Jenny sat up straight. She heard the voice clearly,
but it was thin and reedy, like that of an ancient
man on his deathbed.

It had to be her imagination.

She focused her thoughts once again on the
branches of the trees, willing one of them to crack.
The same hollow voice called to her, "*Leave us be,
Ancient One!*"

Unnerved, Jenny got to her feet. She started back
to camp, stumbling as her gaze darted in every
direction, looking for whoever had followed her
out to the woods. She no longer thought it was her
imagination, but a real voice, perhaps one of the
Gypsies, out to frighten her.

It had not sounded like Kaulo, but whoever
had spoken might have disguised his voice. She
shivered with unease when she realized she'd
heard the voice with *both* her ears, even the deaf
one.

Moving quickly back to camp, she was anxious
to return to all that she knew was real and solid.
Some of the older children were tending the fires
and the pots that simmered over them. She asked
a young boy for Rupa's location, and he pointed to
Bardo's wagon, halfway down the line.

Jenny went to it, climbed the steps, and knocked
on the door. Bardo's wife opened it and gestured
her inside. It was just as small as the wagon she
and Matthew shared, and cluttered, but not with
castoffs. There was a large bed on one side of

the door, draped in dark red and gold silk. Gold tassels hung on similar red curtains against the windows, and two chairs stood neatly in place under a small table. There were two short cabinets near the stove, all of which filled the caravan with little room to spare.

There were so many people inside, Jenny started to excuse herself to leave. But Mrs. Bardo took her hand and pulled her inside, speaking rapidly in the Rom language. The three young brides had flopped onto the bed, their faces sullen and withdrawn.

Jenny caught Rupa's eye. "What's wrong?"

"They children. No want mens."

Knitting her brows together, Jenny looked at the three girls on the bed and thought of Beti, likely being fitted in one of the Tsinoria caravans for her own wedding finery. Jenny could easily understand if the girl did not wish to marry Kaulo, and wondered if the Tsinoria grooms were just as unpleasant. "Your girls . . . They do not wish to marry?"

"They no wish to grow . . . to grow up. Become womans."

Mrs. Bardo clapped her hands and spoke sharply to them. The women began to organize the clothing they'd gathered into three distinct ensembles. Since the garments had been pirated from the wardrobes of all the women in the company, they needed to be altered for the brides. Once they tried on all the frilly skirts and colorful blouses, the mothers decided who would wear what. Then Mrs. Bardo sent the brides and their mothers out, and spoke to Rupa, who nodded.

"Now we sew," Rupa said, taking Jenny's arm.

"Why me?"

Rupa touched the repaired shoulder of Jenny's gown. "You sewing very good." She smiled. "Besides, we like."

The caravan emptied, but for Rupa, Jenny, and one other woman, a dark-haired matron named Zurama Pooro.

"Where did the girls—the brides—go?" Jenny asked.

"For bath."

The logistics boggled Jenny's mind. "I did not see anyone carrying bathwater."

Rupa gave her a puzzled look.

Jenny rephrased her question. "Will there be baths for the brides in the other caravans?"

Rupa laughed and Zurama questioned her, presumably about what Jenny had said. They had a short interchange, and Zurama appeared aghast at what Rupa told her. She looked at Jenny as though she were mad.

"No," Rupa said. "Gypsy never have bath inside. Wash in river."

"In the river? 'Tis so cold!"

"Sure." She shrugged. "Water flow. Gypsy way."

Winter had mostly passed, but the thought of setting foot into one of Northumbria's frigid rivers at this time of year made Jenny shiver. It was one thing to wash face and hands with cold water. But to immerse herself? She did not possess that kind of fortitude.

"They be quick," said Rupa. "But no Gypsy stand in . . . what is word? *Marimé*. No tub. Dirty water."

It seemed to be a theme of Gypsy life . . . nothing should stand still. They moved every day unless there was a special occasion, and they preferred most activities outside.

"Do you sleep out of doors when the weather is fine?"

Rupa laughed. "Sure. Bad to stay in. Gypsy need air!"

Jenny sat on one of the chairs while Rupa handed separate bunches of clothes to her and Zurama, along with the needles and thread that were needed to alter the garments. Their informal friendliness was vastly different from what she'd known at Bresland. Everything was more relaxed here, and even though she was a stranger, a *gajo* to them, the women had made her feel welcome.

Matthew did not fare quite as well with the men. They stopped at a crossroads where a small village had sprung up. It looked as though it had been there for centuries, and its people seemed familiar with the Gypsies, welcoming their commerce. A few horse trades took place while some of the men wandered to the various shops, stopping at the butcher's and baker's, buying what was needed for the wedding celebration. Bardo beckoned to Matthew to join him in the tavern. He greeted the Gypsies who were already there, then turned to the barkeep and ordered drinks, paying with a few coins that he took from a kerchief in his pocket.

Matthew took a long pull of the drink that was set before him and gasped, choking as it burned his mouth and throat and everything else on the way down. The Gypsies laughed as Bardo thumped his back, all but Kaulo, who jeered. "You no manhood. Not drink whiskey."

"No' without warning," Matthew retorted, unfamiliar with the harsh drink. He lifted the glass and eyed it warily, calling to the barkeep. "Have you no decent ale, man?"

"Your woman," said Kaulo. "She is satisfied with half man?"

Matthew met Kaulo's gaze and smiled, but his expression infuriated the man, just as Matthew intended. The other Gypsies watched the two of them expectantly, while the barkeep placed a tall glass of dark ale on the bar. Matthew lifted it and drank half, all at once. He put his glass down on the bar and looked at Kaulo.

"You have your own bride waiting back at camp," he said. "Why are you so interested in mine?"

Matthew knew the wife chosen for Kaulo was hardly more than a child, and certainly not as comely as Jenny. He leaned his back against the bar and waited for Kaulo to answer. The Gypsy gulped down the rest of his vile drink, then slammed his glass on the table and narrowed his eyes.

Bardo put his hand on Kaulo's arm and spoke sharply to him, but Kaulo shrugged him off. He moved to stand directly in front of Matthew.

"Whatever you're thinking, lad," Matthew said as a strange heat prickled in his chest, "I wouldna try it."

"Tekari!" Bardo commanded.

Kaulo did not move away, and Matthew was not about to back down, either. This was about Jenny and his ability to protect her. Since they were not in a position to leave the Gypsies yet, he needed to make clear what would happen to any man who entertained unacceptable ideas about her.

He took a step forward so that he was toe to toe with the man. Kaulo was not as tall as Matthew, but he was muscular and strong, and Matthew had no doubt he would be a worthy adversary.

The Gypsy threw the first punch, but Matthew caught his wrist with accelerated speed. The men in the tavern went silent as they watched Matthew counter every blow without striking any of his own. 'Twas too easy, he thought, as he waited for Tekari to mount a serious attack. He didn't really know what he expected, only that Tekari Kaulo's overbearingly threatening posturing was entirely unfounded. The man had no extraordinary fighting abilities.

Kaulo worked up a sweat, cursing Matthew as he tried blow after blow, and Matthew overheard an undercurrent of quiet muttering among the

Gypsies. They seemed shocked to see Kaulo fail so miserably. Puzzled by their ignorance of his strategy, Matthew decided to end the encounter.

"If you're about finished, lad . . ." he said in a deprecating tone.

Two of the men pulled Kaulo away and took him outside. Unconcerned by the strange looks cast his way by the Gypsies, Matthew finished his ale and placed his glass solidly upon the bar. "Are we done here?"

"You shame my nephew," said Bardo.

"He shamed himself," Matthew retorted. "And he had best stay clear of my wife."

Bardo frowned. "Gypsy no like *gajo* woman."

"Tell that to your lad."

They heard women's voices outside, and a moment later, a group of dark-eyed, colorfully dressed Gypsy females came into the tavern. They were the same women who had seemed unable to communicate with him and Jenny. They spoke English to the *gajo* men they found inside, and collected pennies as their price for looking at the palms of their hands and telling their fortunes.

Matthew watched with fascination, acutely aware that they were going about it all wrong. Unless they were seers, 'twould take a glass ball to do any accurate auguring. Clearly, the Gypsy women were deceiving their patrons.

'Twas not his concern. One more night in the camp, and he would take Jenny away from the Gypsies to set out for Carlisle.

* * *

Jenny helped to dress the brides. The two Tsinoria and three Lubunka girls were quiet and subdued as they waited outside their parents' caravans. Beti seemed the most sullen, and Jenny could not fault her for it. The prospect of being tied to Kaulo was as unappealing to her as staying at Bresland would have been.

The women painted designs on the brides' hands with berry juice, then draped the girls with necklaces laden with gold coins. It was as though they wore their family fortunes around their necks, just as Jenny had always done.

Her silver pendant was the extent of her own fortune, and she needed to find it. If the position at Darbury did not work out, she would not hesitate to leave. And if that happened, she would need to live on the money her locket would bring until she found another position. Even if all was well at Darbury and she stayed, she still wanted the locket. It was her only connection to her parents, to her mother in particular.

How different her life would have been had her parents survived their accident. She'd have been schooled at home, would have attended country balls and soirees, and would have had some exposure to the society of young men. She might have known better how to deal with Matthew when he'd crossed her path.

She found herself glancing in the direction he'd ridden, watching for his return. Some of the men had already come back with large packages of meat and rice, crates of vegetables, and bottles of

alcohol. Until now, the meals she'd seen the Gypsy
women prepare had been moderate to skimpy. Yet
now they were busy preparing a banquet of huge
proportions.

None of them seemed to suffer from their
irregular meals and cold baths. They all seemed
healthy, the very young as well as the old women
smoking their pipes, and the grizzled men who sat
on wooden crates or overturned buckets outside
their caravans. The old men watched everything
that went on in the camp as they talked among
themselves, whittling wood or working on leather
tack for the horses.

Rupa and Zurama talked Jenny into changing
out of her black Bresland dress for the weddings.
She put on the colorful skirt and blouse Rupa had
given to her. Rupa took her hair out of its binding
and brushed it, letting it fall in loose curls down
her back. Zurama brought jewelry, draping rows
of colorful beads around her neck and wrists,
and helping her to attach heavy earrings to her
lobes.

She felt different, as though heaven might strike
her for being so primitive and sensual.

Once again, Jenny told herself the most prudent
thing would be to pack up and leave the camp
before Matthew returned, in spite of her promise
to stay. Glancing quickly to the woods, she shivered at the thought of being followed if she left.
Somehow, she knew it had not been Kaulo's voice
that she'd heard earlier. She touched her deaf ear
and rubbed it, testing her hearing as she'd done

hundreds of times after her injury had healed, not quite believing the ear no longer worked. It still did not.

Yet she had heard the voice with both ears.

She pulled her shawl tight around her shoulders and wished that Matthew would return and settle her ongoing argument with herself. Nothing was certain anymore. Perhaps she was wrong about him. His attractive appearance and obvious wealth did not necessarily mean he was already wed, did it?

"Your man return soon," said Rupa.

Jenny blushed, embarrassed by the transparency of her yearnings.

"That one, he make you smile with touch."

She blushed hotter.

"One day you have many children, many grandchildren, eh?"

Jenny felt as though her heart was in her throat. She swallowed and nodded, though she did not believe it. Rupa did not understand the ease with which the *gajo* abandoned each other.

The brides stayed hidden away while the younger children helped their mothers, gathering firewood, turning meat on the spit, carrying cooking water from the river. The savory smells of roasting meat, of leeks and garlic and spicy rice, permeated the Gypsy camp. The children of both clans, soon freed from their chores, ran together, laughing and playing, and stealing bites of food from their mothers' cooking pots. The women set up tables and gathered plates and flatware from every caravan for the outdoor feast. It seemed too cold for such outdoor activities, but the Gypsies were undeterred by the weather. They were impervious to the cold, some not even wearing coats.

It was nearly dark when Rupa said, "Mens coming." Jenny heard it then, the jingle of the horses' bridles, the muffled voices in the distance. Matthew came into sight, riding the chestnut mare that had pulled their wagon to the campsite. He used no saddle, riding in the Gypsy style, but seemed even more masterful than the most expert horsemen among them. His hair was long and loose, and when he caught sight of Jenny standing in the center of camp, he smiled and rode in her direction, dismounting before the horse had even come to a halt. He was magnificent.

Jenny did not want to think about his past or the obligations he surely had. She would just enjoy the moment tonight, before she did what she must. Now that Matthew's health had returned, she did not feel quite so guilty about her plan to leave in the morning.

The Isle of Coruain, 981

The sky over Coruain was nearly black, but for the flashes of the Odhar's magical *lòchran* energy, relentlessly seeking to penetrate the Druzai shields. Alongside Brogan's warriors, the elders managed to keep a powerful swathe of safety 'round the isles, but Ana feared it might not last. The elders were showing the strain of their sustained effort, and might actually fail. Ana could feel Eilinora's malevolent presence and sense her evil purpose, yet she somehow knew the witch herself would soon leave.

Not that the attack upon Coruain would cease. Eilinora's vicious Odhar would remain to bombard the isles with their evil attack while Eilinora went in search of Merrick and Brogan and the *brìgha*-stones.

A barrage of bright white lightning surged outside the protective shields, and Ana faltered. Each powerful *lòchran* blast was magnificent beyond anything she had ever seen before, and the elders struggled to hold off the attack. Ana could do naught to help them when a huge vortex of light and energy arrowed down from the sky above her. *Lòchran* pierced her shield and threw her off her feet, stabbing brutally through her skin and bones. Pain exploded all through her body, but she managed to hurtle an attack of her own, sending bolts of *lòchran* energy in the reverse direction. She rolled away, concealing herself, ignoring the tears in her skin and the pain of her shattered bones. She drew upon all her talents to close the shield above her.

Wicked laughter filled Ana's consciousness, and she knew 'twas Eilinora. She hated that the witch seemed able to reach into her mind, to fill her thoughts with the venomous muck that dwelled in Eilinora's own mind.

The dragheen guardians summoned help, and terrified servants came and carried Ana into Coruain House. As her body quaked in pain, the dragheen commander put out a silent call for Rónán the master healer, and every other Druzai of power who was not yet involved in their defense. Brogan's warriors and the elders were doing all they could, but Coruain needed more.

Soon, Ana knew, one of her peers would emerge from their midst to add her strength to their struggle. 'Twas assumed that Aenéas's daughter would be the one to wed Merrick and use her formidable powers to avert the disaster foretold nearly thirty years before. Merrick had shown his favor toward Sinann, yet the beautiful sorceress was conspicuously absent from the fray, which did not improve Ana's opinion of her.

She lay still as Rónán spoke the words that would heal the shattered bones in her legs, and wished Brogan and Merrick had not been compelled to leave Coruain. 'Twould have been so much better to battle it out with the Odhar legions, to destroy Eilinora once and for all, then deal with her mentor. But with the chieftain's scepter in the witch's possession, the balance of power had tilted in Eilinora's favor.

The Druzai might be able to win a few battles against the escaped sorceress, but possession of the *brìgha*-stones would even the odds. At least Ana hoped that was true. There was much about Eilinora and her mentor that she could not see. She could not imagine the extent of power wielded by Eilinora's mentor, but prayed the blood stones would defeat him.

Northumbria, late winter, 1826

Matthew quickly dismounted, gathered Jenny into his arms, and kissed her despite the crowd of Gypsies that had gathered 'round them. She did not notice their audience, melting into him as their mouths melded together. He stifled a groan and let her go, taking her hand and starting toward their caravan.

A crowd of cheerful Gypsies impeded their path. "Come," Rupa called. "Watch weddings now."

Matthew didn't see Tekari Kaulo anywhere, but the man's absence did not bother him. Likely Matthew had finally managed to make it clear that he would brook no interference with Jenny. He kept hold of her hand and drew her to the edge of camp. They watched a small group of Tsinoria men walk with deliberate casualness to the caravan belonging to the father of one of the prospective husbands. Many of those who were not part of the immediate negotiations pretended to go about their own business. Yet they listened carefully, as did the crowd that had gathered at the periphery.

The young man's father stepped out of his wagon and greeted the visitors as though nothing extraordinary was going on. They spoke together, and Matthew heard Rupa chuckle quietly, with delight.

"What is it?" Jenny asked.

"Tobar speak of fine weather."

"That's funny?"

"Weather is . . ." Rupa looked up at the sky and shrugged. "Nobody care."

Someone presented the bride's father with a bottle of liquor. He poured some of it into two cups, and then drank with the father of the groom.

"Where are the brides?" Jenny asked Rupa. "And the grooms?"

The question puzzled Rupa. With a creased brow, she replied, as though the answer were obvious, "Brides no come. Fathers make . . . er, pledge."

"I don't understand," Jenny said. "Don't the bride and groom make their vows to each other?"

"Papas make vows."

Matthew pulled Jenny's back against him and pressed a light kiss on the side of her head. The gesture was not calculated to prove his possession of this woman, for he was certain he'd demonstrated that very well in the tavern. 'Twas for the pure pleasure of holding her close. Of enjoying the sharp curiosity of her mind. Of smelling her warm, womanly scent, of feeling her soft curves against his body, something he intended to do every day for the rest of his life.

When he married her, there would be no proxies to make their pledge. He intended to commit to her, body and soul, and seal his vow with a kiss that left no doubt of his promise to her.

The first three "weddings" went well, though Jenny had never heard of such informal proceedings. There were no vows, no priest, no ritual. The bride and groom were not even present for the pledging. Yet the Gypsies considered them lawfully wed.

Jenny leaned into Matthew's chest and felt his arms at her waist, for the moment savoring his heat and strength.

Without warning, Tekari Kaulo rode into camp. He paid no attention to the proceedings, but walked directly to his uncle's caravan and went inside, letting the door slam behind him. He soon burst out again, holding a liquor bottle in one hand. Walking to a nearby table, he picked up a cup and poured himself a drink.

The mood of the crowd shifted slightly, but undeniably. The Gypsies had been quietly excited before, but with Kaulo's arrival, they'd become subdued, even embarrassed.

Rupa clucked her tongue. "So wrong."

That much was clear from the disapproving glances Kaulo garnered from both *kompanias* with his actions. He should probably have stayed out of sight like the other grooms until the marriages were complete.

"Can Beti refuse him now?" Jenny asked Rupa.

The woman shook her head. "Is done."

Matthew spoke. "Seems the lad is intent upon shaming not only himself, but everyone else tonight."

Bardo's wife was the first to recover, and she clapped her hands together to signify the start of the feast. Ignoring Kaulo, the men drank toasts to the health and prosperity of the new couples, and even Matthew took his turn. The Gypsy women put the food on the tables while taking sips of liquor from their own cups.

Inappropriately, Tekari Kaulo kept his eyes on *her* as the fathers drank to Beti, the pretty, dark-eyed, curly-haired Tsinoria girl who had married him. His gaze unnerved Jenny, but she felt Matthew tighten his arm around her. She shivered at the warmth of his breath on her temple.

"Doona worry, *moileen*. He knows you belong to me."

The brides were escorted out of their cara-vans by their fathers and taken to their new hus-bands. They took seats beside them and cast timid glances to the men whose families they would join, who would father their children. The girls looked flushed and nervous in their finery, espe-cially Beti. Kaulo turned his back on Jenny and the rest of the crowd, to take Beti's hand and pull her away from camp.

"No. No. Is very bad," said Rupa.

Several of the men took exception to Kaulo's treatment of Beti, and they turned to look nervously at Matthew, as though he might do something. Jenny did not understand the undercurrent.

She saw Matthew's lips move, but could not hear his words. He'd no sooner spoken than Kaulo turned jerkily back to the bridal tables and sat down with his new wife.

"What did you say, Matthew?"

Ignoring the question, he turned her in his arms and focused his attention solely on her. "Would that you were my bride tonight, Jenny Keating." He spoke directly into her good ear. "I would have you naked beneath me. I would taste every sweet inch of your—"

"Matthew, you mustn't say such things," she admonished, though shivers of heat skittered down her skin.

"No, stay close," he said when she would have moved away.

She was torn by her attraction to him and her common sense. Staying another night with him would be disastrous. She knew what would happen, but she yearned for it in spite of herself.

They joined Rupa's family at one of the tables.

"Why do the women pretend they doona understand us?" Matthew asked the Gypsy woman, surprising Jenny.

Judging by Rupa's expression, she was surprised, too. She laughed. "Most know only . . . to tell *gajo* fortune. No more."

Jenny looked to Matthew for an explanation.

"Some of the women came into the village this afternoon and started telling fortunes." He snorted. "'Twas entirely deceitful."

Rupa gave a knowing smile. "*Gajo* not understand."

"But *I* do. You can tell naught from looking at the lines inside a hand."

Rupa laughed at this and raised her cup. "To Matthew Keating. One *gajo* who understand."

As the Gypsies finished their feasting and smoked their pipes and cigarettes, some of them gathered near the largest fire and began to clap their hands in a quick, complex rhythm. It became even more complicated when they added the stamping of their feet and the joyous whoops of the men as they created a strange, compelling music. Two fiddles soon added to the mix, creating a sound and rhythm unlike any Jenny had ever heard before.

"Come! We dance!" Rupa pulled her away from Matthew to join with the other women who'd kicked off their shoes and were moving to the music. Rupa knelt and wrapped a string of tiny bells around Jenny's ankle, but she kept her shoes on.

Her skin felt exquisitely sensitive to the brush of her clothes and the primitive beat of the music. It called to mind the intimate touches and sensual exchanges she'd shared with Matthew. As her body heated, she threw off her shawl and moved her body sinuously. She caught his eye, his gaze hot and filled with the promise of dark pleasures to come.

Dancing for him alone, Jenny raised her arms over her head and heard the clink of the metal bangles Rupa had given her. She moved her hips fluidly, blatantly seducing the man who'd made his desire clear. She wanted to feel his mouth on her breasts, his hands on her body. She raised her skirts above her ankles and thought of his erect manhood, so huge and hot for her. She wanted the pleasure of holding it in her hands again. She wanted to hear his sighs of desire as she stroked him.

And she wanted to feel him inside her.

She put her future and his responsibilities out of her mind and danced mindlessly, throwing her head back as she moved with the music. With her body, she told Matthew that she was his, just as he'd been saying ever since he'd first awakened in the Gypsy caravan.

Jenny's hair dropped into wild, golden curls 'round her face and shoulders. Her skin seemed to glow as she danced, taunting Matthew with her soft curves and seductive movements. Matthew became aroused, just watching her move to the undulating Gypsy music. No other woman in camp could draw his attention from Jenny.

Nor did he pay any further attention to Kaulo, who had become completely absorbed in his own wife. The words that had pulled Kaulo back to camp had come into his head the same way the repelling words had come to him. Somehow he knew he could not do more—he could not make Kaulo a decent or loving husband. At least he'd kept the man from humiliating his pretty young wife.

Matthew still did not trust the Gypsy, but he was fairly sure Kaulo understood the consequences of infringing where he was not wanted. For now, he was compelled to stay at his wife's side and away from Jenny.

Oblivious to the music and laughter and drinking, Matthew approached Jenny. He took her hand and lifted her into his arms. He barely heard the hoots and suggestive male calls as he carried her to their caravan and took her inside.

Chapter 7

They did not escape the sound of the Gypsy music, and Matthew welcomed the primal beating of hands and feet. He felt primitive when he lowered Jenny to the floor and kissed her mouth, sweeping his tongue inside. She responded boldly, wrapping her hands 'round his waist and drawing his body flush against hers.

Groaning, he broke the kiss and pulled her blouse off her shoulders. She wore her thin shift underneath, and he nearly tore it in his haste to free her breasts, to lick and suck her pretty nipples.

"*Sibh ar mèinn*," he whispered, though he knew she did not understand. She would soon realize she belonged with him, even without the words.

She let her head drop back, and Matthew touched his tongue to the pulse point at the base of her sweet neck. He gathered her hair in one hand and pressed a kiss to the sensitive skin below her ear while she dropped her hands to his buttocks. Arousal shuddered through him.

"Ach, lass, I need you."

Kissing her deeply, he released the catch that held her skirt at her waist and let it drop to the floor, leaving her in naught but a pair of white drawers. At the same time, Jenny unfastened his sherte and pushed it off him.

Matthew took one of her hands and placed it on the front of his trews. She pressed her fingers against him, stroking him, caressing his hard length, torturing him with her touch.

He cupped her breasts, filling his hands with the plump globes as the tips hardened with his attention.

Intent upon slowing their momentum, he turned her 'round and pulled her back to his chest while he pressed his hard cock against the hollow between her buttocks and fondled her breasts from behind.

He pressed soft kisses to her cheek, then touched his lips to her ear and neck. Lowering one hand to her drawers, he released the tie that held them. When she was fully naked, he slid his fingers through the pale curls that shielded her womanly center.

He lifted one of her legs and eased her foot down to a nearby crate, her ankle bells jingling as she moved. "Open for me, *moileen*," he whispered.

She made a low sound when he touched the sensitive apex of flesh and slid a finger inside her. Shuddering against him, she tipped her head back onto his shoulder. He heard her breath catch with the pleasure he gave her.

"Aye, my sweet. Come for me."

'Twas enormously arousing to feel the tightening of her sheath 'round his finger, and his cock surged with need. But 'twas not enough. When her breathing slowed, Merrick turned her again. She fumbled with the fastenings of his trews, her touch driving him wild, even through the cloth. Impatient now, he pushed her hands away and made short work of divesting himself of the rest of his clothes. Jenny drew him down for her kiss as she took his cock in her hand. He jerked at her touch, beyond anxious to be inside her.

"I never knew a man was so . . ."

He did not wait to hear the rest, but laid her on the bed, opening her to his gaze, to his touch.

Slowly, he skimmed his fingers from the tiny bells at her ankle, all the way to her knee, then bent to press a kiss to the tender skin there. He inched his way up her body, using his mouth and hands to please her, to tease her before taking her to the brink of fulfillment once again.

He could not imagine anything more beautiful than Jenny. He heard her breath catch when he touched his tongue to the moist bud so responsive to his touch. Using his fingers, he opened her, licking and sucking the hard little center of her pleasure.

"Oh!" She raised herself up to her elbows and bit her lip, watching him. Her frank gaze delighted him. He pleasured her while she watched, and she went quickly to the edge of climax. But

Matthew wanted to be inside her when it happened this time. He wanted to experience *sòlas* with Jenny, wanted her to understand that they were *céile* mates.

With her whimper of need in his ears, he pressed a kiss to her stomach and moved up. He positioned himself at the threshold of her body as he licked each of her nipples in turn. She bent her knees on either side of him, and he slid inside.

"Ach, slowly, *moileen*."

But Jenny did not want it slow. She was frantic with need, impatient with the desire to feel him inside her, to make him part of her. He rose up over her, bracing his weight on his muscular arms, but she thrust her hips forward, pulling him into her. Fully embedded, he held his body still. Lowering his head, he touched his forehead to hers.

His breathing sounded harsh and labored, his voice a deep, rasping sound. "Are you all right, bonny Jenny?"

The burning discomfort quickly diminished. "I-is there more?"

"Aye, lass. There's more."

He moved, pulling partway out, and Jenny adjusted, moving so that the slide of his body against hers produced an exquisite tension in her nether regions. Her nipples tingled, and he was not even touching them.

"Oh my," she whispered when he slid back in, then out again. She wrapped her legs around his hips and watched his face take on a heated glow that had nothing to do with the fire in the stove.

She matched his rhythm and became mindless with the cadence of his movements. His body touched hers in all the right places, leading every one of her sensitive nerves toward the same culmination that had shuddered through her only a few minutes earlier.

She flew from her body, hand in hand with Matthew, as the shimmering aura of his body seemed to melt into hers. They remained separate, yet the shattering physical pleasure magnified and swirled through them again and again.

Jenny could not see where they were. There were no sounds or smells. She and Matthew were deeply joined in a world of pure sensation, and no other awareness was necessary. Such intensity should have been fatal, yet they survived.

It seemed to take a long time to drift back to their bodies. Matthew withdrew from her, but lay beside her, drawing her into his arms. He touched her face, gently smoothing her hair back from her forehead. He kissed her lightly.

"Have you any doubt now that you are mine?"

She felt confounded by what had just happened. Joining physically with him had somehow caused her—some part of her—to leave her body. "Where did we go, Matthew? Does this . . . connection—?"

"'Twas *sòlas*," he said, but his expression was one of puzzlement.

Jenny wondered if he was remembering sharing such solace with someone else. Wiping away a tear that slid down the side of her face, she knew she could not ask him.

While Jenny slept, Matthew made a sweeping motion with one hand and cleared the floor of the broken mirror. It did not surprise him that the mirror had fallen and smashed into a thousand pieces while he and Jenny had made love. But he wondered why the other pictures on the walls had not suffered the same fate with the energy they'd loosed in the caravan. It had been incredible.

Matthew had known how to please Jenny, leading him to believe he was no virgin. Even without a memory to guide him, he was certain his *bràth*—his essence—had never left his body to join with another's in *sòlas*. Only Jenny made him complete.

He added wood to the stove, and when he returned to bed, Jenny turned to him and situated herself into the hollows of his body, sighing with contentment. Matthew wrapped his arms 'round her and slept until morning. He awoke feeling better than he had since he'd been shot.

Leaving Jenny sleeping, he arose from their bed and pulled on his clothes. Outside, he saw that only one or two others were stirring. No doubt they would sleep late after the night's revels, so

Matthew headed out to the pasture where the horses had spent the night grazing freely.

They were fine animals, and Matthew was drawn to a snowy white gelding the Gypsies had acquired the day before at the *gajo* village. He had a sudden flash of memory—of mounting just such a horse, wearing naught but a pair of light-colored, loose trews. And he'd been barefoot. He struggled to recall more, but the vision left him as abruptly as it had come.

He closed his eyes and tried to empty his mind of every other thought, but the vision would not return. Nor was there any sense of where he'd been or who he was. Only that it was time to leave.

He intended to purchase this horse as well as another one from Bardo for the ride to Carlisle. Mayhap the white gelding's very proximity would shake loose a few more of his memories. No matter what was in his past, Matthew intended to go along with Jenny's quest to find her locket.

He touched the bracer on his arm, and though he could not understand the deep-seated sentiment he felt, he realized he would feel as lost without it as Jenny seemed to feel without her pendant. He was convinced she needed to try to recover it from the thief who'd stolen it, just as he knew that Jenny belonged with him.

He wanted her to decline the teacher position that awaited her, and stay with him. If those flashes of memory continued, he would soon be able to assure her that there was no other woman in his life. In the meantime, he believed the gold in his satchel was sufficient to support them indefinitely.

And he had talents no one else seemed to share, talents that might very well arouse suspicion if he used them. The Gypsies struggled in ways that seemed entirely unnecessary, yet they did not seem to have the wherewithal to make their tasks any easier. Kaulo had tried to strike him in the tavern the night before, but Matthew had easily prevented every blow. And the women pretended to read fortunes by looking at hands. 'Twas absurd. And he took it as a warning to keep his differences to himself.

After choosing the horses he wanted, he returned to camp, where a few more adults were up and about. He saw Rupa and her husband, who beckoned him to their wagon. They offered him a cup of dark, sweet coffee, which he drank while watching the children in a game of kicking a ball toward opposite goals.

"Your wife—she sleeps?"

"Aye," said Matthew, and Rupa nodded.

"Is good," she said with a glint in her eye, clearly aware of the way he and Jenny had spent their time after retiring to their caravan the night before.

Pias tapped Matthew's shoulder. He said something in the Gypsy language and pointed to the children.

"Aye. They are enjoying their game," Matthew said.

"My man—he say come and kick ball," said Rupa.

Matthew readily agreed, welcoming the exertion of running, a pastime he felt as though he'd often done.

The two men went to opposite sides of the field, each one vying for possession of the ball, but using no hands to do so. Pias was extremely proficient at moving the ball with his feet, and he passed the ball to his teammates more often than not, giving the young ones all the opportunities to score points.

Matthew's body was unfamiliar with the game, and he fumbled with the ball at first. The children were patient with him, demonstrating their technique, and laughing with him when he erred. He soon caught on and followed Pias's example, kicking the ball to his young teammates, enjoying himself immensely.

The cold woke Jenny. In the short time since she'd been with Matthew, she'd grown accustomed to sleeping beside his warm body. He must have added wood to the stove before leaving, and by the look of it, she reasoned he had not been gone very long. She heated some water and washed in the *gajo* manner, then donned her Bresland clothes.

She felt changed after last night.

Sliding her hands down the front of her gown, she closed her eyes and relived the moment when Matthew had entered her, when their bodies and souls had become one. She'd known so little about the relations between men and women . . . She had never imagined how much more vulnerable she would feel . . .

She'd been a fool to partake of such intimate activities with a man she hardly knew, a man who could very well give her the news that he remembered the wife he'd left behind.

Yet what if his instincts were correct and he had no wife waiting for him? Could she walk away from a man who seemed so different from Mr. Ellis, a man whose affections might actually be reliable and true?

Jenny's chest swelled painfully, and she covered her heart with one hand, wondering if she could risk it, knowing how shattered it would be if she chose wrong. How she would miss those sparkling blue eyes and that ready smile, and the warm caresses that made her feel so cherished.

She almost wished she had never met him, for then her path would be clear.

Bracing herself, Jenny set aside the elusive appeal of his embrace and decided what she must do. The Gypsy *kompania* had not traveled far enough from Kirtwarren to prevent Reverend Usher and the constables from coming back, but a long day's walk would do it. She had to go.

Bardo might object to her leaving without finishing their reading lessons, but when she reminded him of the trouble she might bring to camp, he would surely agree.

She packed her belongings in her traveling bag, then stepped out of the caravan, feeling torn. She could not leave without speaking to Matthew.

When she saw him in the midst of a game with the children, she went to Rupa's caravan and stood watching him play. He laughed as though he hadn't a care in the world, and she could easily understand that. With no past, Matthew truly had no worries, only the memory of what they'd shared the night before.

He cut a handsome swathe through the players, the corners of his bright eyes crinkling with laughter. He kicked the ball to one of the young girls, who then kicked it over the goal. Matthew cheered and lifted her into the air, delighting the child as well as her comrades.

Jenny felt her heart clench as her resolve wavered.

"He is good man, your husband," said Rupa.

Jenny could only nod in response. He was the hero who'd saved her from the highwaymen on the road; he'd seen to it that Kaulo kept his distance. He'd made love to her with a tenderness she would never have experienced with Frederick Ellis, or any other man. Yes, her Scotsman was a good man.

In a leisurely fashion, the Gypsies started to break camp, the women packing up while the men put out the campfires and carried the heaviest items into the caravans. Matthew and Pias Petrulengo quit their game reluctantly, even though the children pulled at their trouser legs and begged them to continue.

Matthew caught Jenny's gaze and smiled

broadly. He joined her at Rupa's caravan and slipped his arms around her. Unabashedly, he kissed her.

Jenny felt a blush heat her cheeks and found herself drawn into their kiss, reliving a fraction of what had passed between them in the night. When someone nearby cleared her throat, she came to her senses and pulled away.

Matthew took her hand and drew her out of the camp.

"Matthew, I—"

"Come, there's something I want to show you."

Jenny set aside her reservations for the moment, unable to resist his appeal. She walked alongside him toward the pasture, vaguely aware that his mere proximity was interfering with her ability to reason.

He stopped suddenly in the midst of a stand of trees, out of sight of the camp. "Come here, lass, and give me a proper kiss." He swung her around and pulled her into his arms, drawing her up to her toes and lowering his head to take possession of her lips.

Jenny could not resist the powerful attraction that arced between them. She slid her hands around his neck and held him tight, opening her mouth for his welcome incursion. He pulled her hips close, and she felt the hard ridge of his shaft. His arousal fueled her own, and as he deepened their kiss, Jenny felt driven to join with him, to make love as they'd done the night before.

He broke away from her suddenly and grabbed her hand, grinning wickedly as he led her into a clearing where the sun shone brightly in a cloud-dappled sky. He found a mossy patch of ground alongside a few large stones, and laid her down on her cloak. Coming down over her, he kissed her deeply. With one hand, he touched her breast through her woolen gown and opened the placket of his breeches with the other.

"Ach, how I want you, lass."

They did not undress, and Jenny trembled when she caught sight of Matthew's thick erection jutting from his trews. He raised her skirts and touched her intimately, pressing his fingers against her most sensitive flesh.

"Matthew!" She could hardly catch her breath.

"Aye, lass. You're ready for me."

Jenny was still trembling when 'twas over. Matthew righted her skirts, then buttoned his trews and gathered her into his arms. "Ah, my sweet Jenny." He pressed a kiss to her forehead, but she slipped out of his arms and stepped away.

"Matthew, we . . ." She bit her lip. "I cannot believe I just . . ."

She looked up at him, and he felt a tenderness that paralleled the *sòlas* they'd just experienced.

"I've chosen horses for us."

"Horses?"

"Aye, lass. You want to leave, do you no'?"

She turned away, crossing her arms against her

chest. Matthew thought he'd convinced her they were meant to be together, but it seemed she still had doubts.

He moved behind her and gently brushed a few bits of grass from her hair. "*Moileen*, my memory has started to return in small pieces. Soon I'll be able to assure you—without reservation—that there is no one else."

He slipped his arms 'round her waist, and when she leaned back against him, he knew she'd surrendered.

"I have plenty of gold, surely enough to purchase horses to carry us to Carlisle." Keeping his arm 'round her, he turned her and pointed out the white gelding.

"This one . . . And the mare." He showed her the gray palfrey he'd chosen for her. "I know what Bardo paid for these two. He'll take my gold for them."

"Matthew, I don't know how to ride."

Her words took him aback. He'd assumed . . .

'Twas strange how his lack of memory functioned. Why would he assume she could ride? Was everyone a proficient rider where he came from? A memory of the white horse came once again, and Matthew forced his brain to reach into the past and come up with a solid memory. Yet 'twas as patchy as the sky above them.

"Then we'll buy only the gelding," he said. "I prefer to hold you between my legs as we ride, anyway."

* * *

Jenny walked to the edge of the field, then turned to watch Matthew as he made himself known to his new horse. He ran his hands along its neck, its withers and flank, then his lips moved as he spoke quietly to the beast. Jenny felt spellbound as she watched him, entranced by the slow, deliberate movements of his body.

Ignoring the alarm bells ringing in her heart and soul, she left him with the horses and returned to camp to collect their belongings. Matthew seemed so sure, and he was so ardent with his attentions . . .

Jenny could not bring herself to abandon him. She could not help but risk her heart with him.

Matthew had had no doubt that he could convince Bardo to part with the white gelding, but Jenny wasn't sure how the man would react to losing his teacher. She decided to let Matthew handle that as well. Leaving the cover of the trees, she walked into camp, where all was quieter than usual.

Three saddled horses stood at the edge of camp, tethered to a nearby shrub. Reverend Usher had come back!

Controlling her panic, Jenny darted back behind the nearest caravan to avoid the constables, and pulled up her hood just in case they caught sight of her. None of them had seen her yet, but she could take no chances. She made her way to Rupa's caravan, well behind the area where Usher and the constables were walking. Poking her head around to the front of the caravan, she called quietly to her friend. "Rupa!"

The woman did not turn, but stood and casually retied her head scarf, then picked up a bucket and carried it to her door. When the caravan's door blocked her from the constables' view, she waved to Jenny to come inside.

Jenny moved quickly, scrambling up the steps as Rupa followed her into the caravan. She went to the window and pushed aside Rupa's bright yellow curtains, just far enough to see Reverend Usher talking with Bardo at the opposite end of camp. The two men in black uniforms had split away from the headmaster and were making their way toward the caravan she shared with Matthew.

"He is in the pasture! What if he comes back when they're—"

"Your man, he . . ." She tapped a finger to her forehead. "He know."

"But if they surprise him . . ."

"They look for woman, not man."

That was true, so Jenny allowed herself to relax a fraction. Still, all this meant that Reverend Usher had not given up. Perhaps it would be better to stay yet one more day with the Gypsies.

Matthew came into the camp and found himself face-to-face with the men Jenny had wanted to avoid. He wished he understood why the headmaster of Bresland School was so determined to take her back.

"What have we here? A blue-eyed Gypsy?" said one constable to the other.

Matthew was dressed as a Gypsy, and since he'd seen many a variation in eye color between the two *kompanias*, the comment did not worry him. He knew he could mutter a few words and make these two disappear, just as he'd done the day before, but he held back this time, shrugging as he'd seen the Gypsies do, as though he did not understand their language.

He wanted to avoid calling attention to Jenny, so he walked away from his caravan and went in search of Pias, with the hope of drawing the Englishmen away from her. But Pias was leaving with some of the other men, and heading toward the pasture. Matthew took a quick glance 'round and saw no sign of Jenny. Rupa gave him the slightest hint of a nod, and he felt immediately reassured. He caught up to the men who were on their way to get the horses, confident that Rupa would take care of Jenny.

When he returned to the camp, the *gajo* were gone, and Jenny was still out of sight.

Matthew went to his caravan and vaulted up the three steps to his door. He pushed it open, but Jenny was not inside. His first thought was that the constables had found her, but he quickly dismissed it. He understood the Gypsies well enough to know 'twas a matter of honor to prevent such a thing. He tied the horses to the wheel and went in search of Rupa, certain the woman would know where Jenny was hidden.

Her absence made him acutely aware of how empty his life would be without her. No matter what his past, Jenny was going to be his future.

She was descending the steps of Rupa's caravan when he approached, and her worried expression tugged at him. He took her into his arms and wished he could reassure her with facts. "Doona worry, *moileen*. I will take care of you," was all he could say, firmly wishing he would have an opportunity to throttle the despicable headmaster. Matthew was going to relish the moment when Usher realized his adversary was not a small girl child, but a warrior chieftain with . . .

Matthew cursed silently when the memory flitted away. If he was a warrior of some kind, then where were his weapons? And if he was chieftain . . . who were his people?

"I think we should stay with the Gypsies one more day, Matthew," said Jenny. "Just until we're a few more miles away from Kirtwarren."

"Aye, if it will make you feel better." He hoped Usher made another foray into camp. Matthew would blast him beyond the horizon with his . . .

"Matthew, are you all right?"

He swallowed. "Aye, sweet."

She looked 'round. "I'm afraid they might be keeping watch from a distance—"

"I can make a search of the area, lass," he said, discomfited by the incomplete bits and pieces of memory that came so quickly, then evaporated before he could make sense of them.

"Let's just stay another day, Matthew. By tomorrow, we'll be that much farther away, and they'll likely be out of their jurisdiction."

"Are you sure, *moileen*? Moghire could carry us far today, much farther than the Gypsies will travel in their wagons." He took her hand, and they started back toward their own caravan. All the others were packing to leave, but he and Jenny had naught to carry but her bag and his satchel.

"Mog-hara?"

He laughed at her English pronunciation of his horse's name. "Aye, Moghire. My comely white gelding."

"'Tis a strange but lovely name. Do you know where you got it?"

He shook his head. "Nay, lass. It just came to me. I know it connotes beauty and magic, all in one."

"You still cannot remember anything else?"

Could he tell her he was a warrior who would protect her with his life? Or that he could crush Reverend Usher with little more than a thought?

"I've had a few strange flashes of sights that might be memories, but naught of substance. The only thing I *know* is that you are mine, Jenny Keating. You belong with me."

She actually gave a shy smile at his words and did not hesitate to return his quick kiss.

"You! English!"

Bardo's approach separated them, and the Gypsy looked to Matthew, rather than speaking directly to Jenny as he'd done before. He showed none of the swagger and confidence she'd noted before, and he spoke to Matthew with deference.

His attitude toward Matthew was decidedly different, and Jenny wondered if something had happened in the village the day before.

"Good day for teach, eh? Your wife . . . she give lesson?"

Matthew kept her close, and Jenny felt more at ease than she'd felt in eleven years.

"I have no objection to letting her teach you, Bardo. But she stays here beside me while I drive."

Bardo nodded his agreement.

"And you keep your nephew away from her."

Matthew drove the caravan while Jenny sat on the wooden bench beside him, managing somehow to avoid looking back every few minutes for signs of Usher and the constables.

"Why is the headmaster so determined to have you back?" asked Matthew.

Jenny shook her head, puzzled by the question. "I cannot imagine, since he took a dislike to me when I first arrived. His opinion never changed."

"But he kept you at school beyond your time as a student."

"I wanted to leave, but I needed a position first."

"And Usher gave you one."

"Yes, when my advertisements came to naught."

"Good of him," Matthew said dryly.

"What do you mean?"

"Only that it seems quite convenient for his purpose."

"Of keeping me at Bresland?" Jenny asked.

Matthew nodded. "Aye, lass. He wanted you to stay. Can you think of no idea why?"

Something Norah had once said struck Jenny now.

"What is it?" Matthew asked.

"Probably nothing." She pushed away the distant memory of her poor, dead friend.

"Anything you remember, *moileen*, might be of importance. The man is passionate about getting you back. There must be some reason."

Yes, there was, but Jenny was too ashamed to speak of the pleasure the headmaster had derived from his cruelty to her, especially those horrid beatings when she was draped across his lap. They were perverse, and Jenny never wanted to think of them again, much less speak of them.

She shrugged, though she wondered if Norah had been right, and Reverend Usher could face censure if those thrashings became known.

With the row of Gypsy wagons moving so slowly, Matthew had one hand free. He guided the horses easily, managing to touch Jenny frequently. He whispered strange, fascinating words in her good ear, and she found herself looking forward to the moment when they would stop the wagons and retire to their own bed for the night.

She would not allow herself to dwell on what would happen once he remembered his identity and his past, but prayed that he was correct in his belief that he had no wife.

Bardo soon came to their caravan and climbed up with his letter charts to sit on her opposite side, putting her between the two men. "Where is Tekari Kaulo?" she asked, though she did not miss the annoying Gypsy. She just wondered if she would need to repeat this lesson later.

"He stay with Tsinoria bride. Come later."

"Where?

"At last camp."

Jenny shuddered at the thought of Beti being stranded with such a husband, far from her own family. "What of the others who were wed last night?"

"Same. Come now. You teach."

Jenny turned in her seat to hear him better, and they stayed at it most of the day. She was surprised at the man's stamina. He'd memorized the letters and learned their sounds during lessons the day before, so Jenny was able to teach him a few simple words. By the end of the day, Bardo was able to read simple sentences.

"Why do you want to read English?" she asked.

"Most times, Gypsy way best for us," he replied with a shrug. "But comes a time . . . *gajo* makes troubles. Gives papers with words. Someone need know."

"I see," Jenny replied, aware that the Gypsies would find themselves at a serious disadvantage if the Kirtwarren constables or any other English authority wanted to give them trouble. The Rom were ingenious people, and Jenny was sure they were able to avoid most confrontations. But their inability to speak and read English would be a detriment if they were presented with warrants or other legal documents.

"These basic reading lessons will not help you to understand official papers," she said.

"Oh, aye. Does help."

Whether her lessons were enough or not, Jenny intended to leave with Matthew in the morning. She'd learned enough about the Gypsies to understand that they were no different than any other people. Bardo would keep her only for as long as she was useful. The moment he no longer needed her, she had no doubt the Gypsy would leave her.

When they stopped for the night, Matthew lifted Jenny from the caravan, his eyes warm with the promise of pleasures to come. They had sat close together all day, barely exchanging a word, yet their connection had grown immeasurably.

Bardo jumped down behind her.

"How much farther is it to Carlisle?" Jenny asked him.

"Oh . . . maybe four days," Bardo replied.

"Do you mean to say we only went four or five miles today?" Jenny asked, unable to keep the frustration out of her voice. She'd hoped to make at least ten miles! How was it possible to travel so slowly?

Bardo gave his usual shrug and started walking toward his own caravan. He turned and pointed toward Jenny and Matthew. "You. Come to Bardo table. Eat with wife. With me."

It was nearly dusk, and had turned much colder. Jenny and Matthew settled their wagon, then joined Bardo and his wife for supper. The man's ten-year-old daughter, Patia, sat on her father's lap throughout the casual meal. She looked like a younger twin of her sister who'd been one of the previous day's brides. Jenny wondered how the older girl fared with her new husband.

And how Beti had survived the night with Tekari.

"I marry off two daughter. And nephew. Two, three year more," he said, patting his daughter on her head "my Patia take husband."

Jenny thought of her own tenth year with fondness. It was the year before her parents' death, the year before she'd been sent to Bresland. By then, she'd felt so young and so lost, she could imagine how the child brides felt, being given away to their husbands at such an early age. Yet Jenny's own lot had been neither easy nor simple.

The Gypsy marriage customs were not all that differed from the English. Jenny had seen that the Gypsies had a very different understanding of stealing, too. Taking a chicken or a few eggs from an English farmer who might not miss them was not considered thievery, though the farmer would surely think differently.

"Why old man come for you so much?" Bardo asked.

Jenny looked into the Gypsy leader's dark, piercing eyes. "The headmaster has accused me of stealing, but I—"

"You bring nothing," said Bardo, casting his glance toward her caravan, obviously thinking back on the possessions she and Matthew had brought with them. To Jenny's knowledge, the Gypsy had not looked inside Matthew's satchel. But then, Matthew was not the one accused of theft. "You know bad things from school? From . . . head man?"

"Bad things?" Jenny asked, noticing Matthew's interest in the question. "I'm not sure I understand you."

"*Gajo* care for two things." Bardo reached over to his wife's arm and slipped a gold bracelet from her wrist. He held it up for Jenny and Matthew to see. "What calls this?"

"Bracelet."

Bardo shook his head.

"Jewelry?"

"No. Different thing."

"Valuables," said Matthew

The Gypsy nodded. "Valu-buls. *Gajo* care for valu-buls and name. You take no valu-buls. Must be you take away bad story of *gajo* man. Hurt his name."

Jenny was aware of many terrible things about Bresland School and Reverend Usher. But she knew of no one to tell. The parents or guardians of the students certainly did not care, or else they might have visited. Their children would never have been sent there. Jenny could think of no authorities in Kirtwarren who would challenge the headmaster for his harsh treatment of the girls. Not even the village doctor had objected to his abuses.

But Norah . . . the memory of her last night came to Jenny suddenly, and she recalled Norah's confrontation with Reverend Usher . . . her childish, naïve threats . . .

He'd punished her, and then she'd died among a flurry of whimpers in the night.

Matthew saw the light go out in Jenny's eyes when she spoke of the school, and considered Bardo's theory. The Gypsy was right. If Jenny had not stolen anything of value, 'twas likely she knew something she should not.

Her past was nearly as mysterious as his own.

He took her back to their caravan, determined to dispel her melancholy. He added wood to the stove, then removed her cloak and drew her down to the bed.

"'Tis freezing in here."

"Aye. I plan to keep you warm."

Matthew pulled her close and felt her shivering. As their bed warmed with the heat of their bodies, he touched his mouth to hers in a long and sensuous kiss. He nipped her lips and sucked her tongue into his mouth while he skimmed his hands down her back.

She wore the black Bresland gown, and Matthew was anxious to divest her of it. He made quick work of the buttons that held her bodice together while Jenny did the same to his sherte. Soon he was bare-chested against her soft breasts. He released the hooks of her skirt and pushed it down to her feet.

Jenny draped the quilt over her shoulders and rose to straddle him. Matthew's breath caught at the sight of her naked breasts, swaying just inches from his mouth. He lifted his head to reach one, swirling his tongue 'round her succulent nipple. "Naught has ever tasted so sweet, Jenny lass."

She slid her fingers through the hair on his chest. His cock roared up when she flicked her fingertips over his nipples, then leaned down to suck one into her mouth. She opened the buttons of his trews and slid them down his legs, agonizingly slowly. He finally took charge and kicked them off, anxious to feel her mouth upon him again.

She skimmed her hands up his legs, stopping short of his cock, teasing him as her fingers retreated from the target he most wanted her to reach. She lowered her body onto his legs and skimmed her breasts against his thighs, then higher, soon brushing them against the tip of his willing cock.

"Jenny."

"You are not the only one who can tease," she whispered, pressing her face to his belly. "I will have my revenge for your torture this morning in the pasture."

She kissed his abdomen, then slid lower,

dropping kisses on every surface but the one that strained to feel her mouth. Matthew's heart seemed to stop when her breath warmed his cock. She encircled it with her fist, then touched her mouth to it.

"Pull me in, sweet Jenny," he rasped, and Jenny complied, sucking his hard cock deep inside her mouth. She swirled her tongue 'round it, and made a low sound of satisfaction as she did it. Matthew's body was on fire, every nerve burning for completion.

But Jenny had no mercy. She tortured him just the way he'd done to her earlier, nipping and sucking, licking the length of him as though he were a tasty morsel and she had all the time in the world to enjoy him. Matthew watched her pleasure him, and when she looked up and caught his gaze, she released him and smiled audaciously at him.

"Come here," he rasped.

With one quick move, he switched their positions, shifting her to her back. She slipped her legs 'round his waist and opened for him, as anxious as he was to complete their joining. Matthew wasted no more time, but plunged, stopping to relish the exquisite sense of being sheathed tightly inside her.

Jenny moved her hips and set their rhythm, slow at first, her eyes locked on his as she moved. Their pace increased until he felt her muscles tighten and the spasms of her climax begin. Only then did he let go, leaving his body to experience true *sòlas*.

And when 'twas done, they fell asleep, content and secure in each other's arms.

Matthew dreamed of the red-haired lady again. This time, she wept and begged him to hurry home. The clarity of the dream roused him from sleep, and he sat up abruptly in bed.

"What is it?" asked Jenny, suppressing a yawn.

"Naught," he replied, gently stroking her cheek. "I'll stoke the fire. Go back to sleep, lass." He pressed a kiss to her forehead and went to the stove, adding another wedge of wood to the glowing coals within.

The image of the red-haired woman disturbed him. He still could not bring up any memory of her, but he knew she must be someone of significance from his past, else he would not dream of her so repeatedly. Yet he'd never joined with her, never known *sòlas* with her. Of that he was certain. Only with Jenny . . .

She was as much a part of him as his next breath. He had to find a way to force his memory to return, for this uncertainty was frustrating and exasperating, all at once.

He returned to bed, and Jenny gravitated toward him. She curled her body into his as she slept, while Matthew wracked his brain until the pale light of dawn seeped through the colorful curtains on the windows.

And he had no more understanding of his history when dawn broke than he had when the sun had gone down the night before.

Matthew watched Jenny make small, feminine movements, stretching her legs, then turning over to press her backside into him. She sighed and then made a sound of pure satisfaction. He smiled, turned onto his side, and slid his hand 'round her waist. Sleeping with a woman felt as intimate as the act of making love with her.

He drew her hips against his erection, and she wiggled in place, inviting his touch. Matthew could not resist. He closed his eyes and savored the moment, then slipped inside her, rocking slowly and deeply as he touched the nub of feminine pleasure at her apex. He nuzzled her neck and whispered sweet words to her in the language he knew she did not understand, words that came naturally to him. "*Sibh ar mèinn.*"

They slept another hour or more, and when Jenny awoke again, she saw that it was cold and overcast, giving her a strong sense of foreboding. She dared not wish that going to Darbury would be unnecessary, or that she would never need her locket. But she had no assurance of a future with Matthew.

He must have swept up the mirror that had shattered the first time they'd made love, but he'd said nothing about it. Jenny managed to hide evidence of the cups she'd broken and the other damage she'd unwittingly caused on subsequent occasions. But it was only a matter of time before her weird quirk became known to him.

How she dreaded that moment.

Quietly, Jenny left the caravan and headed for the woods alone, unsure whether it would be worse if Matthew found out about her strange talent, or if he suddenly regained his memory. Either revelation would surely change everything between them.

Since Tekari Kaulo had not returned, and there'd been no signs of Reverend Usher or the constables, Jenny felt safe enough going into the woods alone. Gathering her cloak tightly about her, she made her way to the river's edge. She found a low ledge nearby, and sat down on it, taking a moment to gather her thoughts.

The last time she'd gone into the woods to force an unexplained occurrence—the breaking of a branch—she'd heard strange voices. This time, she was not going to allow anything to deter her. She concentrated on the rocky banks, mentally calling to the heaviest rocks, commanding them to fall into the water.

She closed her mind to everything but the rocks on the far bank, focusing her attention and all her energy on them alone. She pictured them moving, and saw an odd light that shimmered like long strands of silvery hair, emanating from the region of her chest and spreading to the rocks on the far bank.

One of the rocks fell, pulled into the water by the shimmering strands!

Jenny jumped to her feet, stunned. The luminous threads disappeared, but her skin tingled with heat at the center of her chest. Bright yellow sparks shimmered around her and dropped to the ground. She scrambled up and away from the river, unnerved by what she'd done, what she'd seen. She could not imagine how she'd acquired this strange ability, or why she had never been able to control it.

To her knowledge, it had come upon her suddenly, soon after her arrival at Bresland. She'd been shocked and infuriated by her first punishment, and the window of Usher's office had suddenly shattered. Jenny had been stunned by the realization that she was somehow responsible for the mess.

Luckily, the headmaster had assumed the breakage was caused by a stone being thrown by a passing carriage. He would surely have denounced her as a disciple of Satan had he realized she could cause such strange and unnatural events.

Jenny choked back a sob and looked down at her chest. When she pulled away the edges of her cloak, there was nothing to indicate that those strange, luminous strands had come from her chest. But they had! And the sparks that had fallen to the ground still remained as proof of her aberration.

She felt ill as she gazed at the rock she'd disturbed. Such things should not be possible. But now she knew, without any doubt, how peculiar she was.

Dazed, she returned to camp. Matthew was not inside their wagon, but she noticed some of the men already hitching the horses to their own caravans for travel. Matthew was not among them.

Still feeling bewildered and dismayed by her experience at the river, she walked through the center of camp and saw Matthew outside Bardo's caravan, haggling with the Gypsy leader. Jenny reached them just as a deal was made. Matthew dropped some coins into Bardo's hand, then the two men raised their cups of coffee and drank to their agreement.

"Ah, Jenny," Matthew said. "Here you are, lass." Bardo's wife wrapped bread and cheese into a square of cloth and handed it to Jenny, along with another large, wrapped parcel of food.

"Moghire is ours," Matthew said, taking the packages from her hands. "And here are provisions for a couple of days on the road. Enough to get us to Carlisle."

She looked at him blankly. "Mr. Bardo does not mind my leaving before our lessons are complete?"

"Nay, lass. I took care of that."

Jenny did not question him as they walked through camp, making their farewells to Rupa's family. They were halfway to their own wagon when Matthew suddenly stopped at the caravan of an old woman who was packing her belongings. He pointed out a glass ball that rested on a lead pedestal.

"You wish to know what future brings?" she asked, her words heavily accented and sounding rehearsed to Jenny's ear.

"I thought they did not know any English," Jenny said to Matthew.

"They doona," he replied as the woman waved her hands over the clear glass. "Only enough to swindle the *gajo* with their sham predictions."

"But I've heard tales of the Gypsies' mysterious powers," Jenny said. "Why do you say they are sham?"

"Because everyone knows this is no' the way to use a *ceirtlín*." Jenny had never heard of a *ceirtlín*, much less known how to use one. Perhaps she'd been sheltered from such items at Bresland.

Despite the old woman's protests, Matthew used two hands to lift the glass ball from its metal stand. He spread the fingers of one hand a few inches above the ball and muttered a few Gaelic words.

The ball darkened, then a fog of blue began to swirl inside it. The old woman gasped when she saw it change.

"Aye. *This* is how 'tis done," he said forcefully.

"Is this some kind of trick?" Jenny asked, struck by the vivid display.

"Nay, 'tis no . . ." His voice trailed off as a face took shape in the glass, that of a young woman with vivid red hair and bright green eyes. Her beautiful features contorted into an expression of worry, and her lips moved. They could not hear her words, but it was clear she was calling out to him. Quickly, Matthew returned the ball to its stand, relinquishing it as though it had burned his fingers.

"Who is she?" Jenny whispered.

"No one," he replied. "No one."

A lump formed in Jenny's throat, and her mouth went dry. She closed it and forced back the tears that were suddenly welling in her eyes.

She'd been right. He had a wife.

Chapter 8

A fierce wind suddenly whipped through the camp, lifting cloths from tables and laundry from clotheslines, and tossing small items through the center of it all. Jenny's heart felt as though it might burst. She turned abruptly and hurried back to her caravan without Matthew. Tears burned her eyes and her chin quivered, but she would not weep. Instinct had told her from the first that Matthew was not free. She should have trusted it.

She ran into the wagon and grabbed her bag, shoving her remaining belongings into it. How many days had she wasted here, she wondered, while Harriet lost herself in Carlisle? How long would it take Jenny to catch up?

How had he made that face appear in the glass ball?

"Jenny."

She brushed away her stupid tears and turned to face Matthew as she threw the strap of her bag over her shoulder.

"She is no' my wife."

Jenny felt an instant of relief, then cast it aside. "Your memory has returned, then?" she asked, somehow certain that it hadn't, not when his expression was one of a man grasping at straws.

When he did not answer, she slipped past him and left the small dwelling, the refuge they'd shared so intimately for the past few days. It was the last caravan in the line, so no one noticed that she left without her supposed husband.

Matthew could not blame Jenny for being upset at the vision of Ana in the *ceirtlín*.

Mo oirg, he was upset, too. He did not know who the woman was, yet now she plagued his waking hours as well as his dreams, warning him and urging him to hurry.

Regardless of who Ana was to him, he could not let Jenny go off on her own. With haste, he collected the coins he had hidden and tossed them into his satchel, then did the same with the provisions he'd purchased from Bardo's wife. A moment later, he started for the pasture where Moghire awaited, but found himself sidetracked by the arrival of a cold, misty rain, along with the newlyweds' caravans. He was in a hurry to catch up to Jenny, but something was wrong.

All the brides were distraught, and one bore the marks of a beating. Her eyes were red and swollen, and one was bruised. The couples dismounted from their caravans and started speaking rapidly to their elders. An argument broke out between one of the Tsinoria men and Guibran Bardo. Matthew looked for Tekari, but he was nowhere to be seen.

Taking a quick jog to Rupa's caravan, he found the woman watching the men's argument with a horrified expression on her face. Her husband, Pias, bore an expression of anger and disgust.

"What is it? What's happened?"

"Lubunka honor . . . hurt."

"How?"

"Tekari—" Rupa covered her mouth with her fist. "He leave Beti. He . . ." Her eyes filled with tears and she turned away. Pias put his arm 'round his wife to give comfort, even as he muttered words that sounded like curses on Tekari.

"Where is Kaulo now?" Matthew asked.

"Gone," Rupa replied. "So bad. He go away. No Gypsy man do."

Matthew did not like the idea of Kaulo unaccounted for, not while Jenny walked the deserted landscape alone. He hastened to the pasture and slipped the Gypsy bridle onto the white gelding, then mounted and headed northeast, the direction Jenny must have gone.

The weather worsened, with falling temperatures and increasing winds. He took to the path toward Carlisle, riding as fast as Moghire could carry him and considering, for the first time, the reaction of the old woman and the others who'd seen the face in the *ceirtlín*. 'Twas as if they'd never seen it used properly before.

Matthew decided they had not. Somehow, that woman had acquired a *ceirtlín*, but had no idea what it could actually do. Matthew wasn't sure how *he* knew how to use it, only that the words and actions had come naturally to him. Before he could give it any more thought, he saw a hooded figure ahead, walking through the drizzling rain with her cloak whipping 'round her legs in the wind.

He kicked his heels into Moghire's flanks and galloped to Jenny's side, dismounting as he arrived alongside her. She ignored him and kept walking. "Jenny, you are soaking. You will freeze this way."

"No, I won't Matth—" She stopped herself from using the name she'd given him, the experience with the *ceirtlín* forcing both of them to face the truth of their situation. Neither of them knew who he was.

"I intend to see you to Carlisle, *moileen*." After that, he would convince her to let him find the woman who'd stolen her locket. But he would be content if she allowed him the first step for now.

Her eyes were bleak when she looked up at him. "'Tis not a good idea. We've become too—"

He did not allow her to finish, but took her bag from her and lifted her onto a rock that would serve as a mounting block. "I'll mount first, then pull you up."

She did not resist as he situated her in front of him on Moghire's back. She was cold and trembling, and he pulled her close to warm and dry her. "The woman in the glass is no' my wife, *moi-leen*," he said close to her ear. "I would know it—would feel it—if she were."

They rode for hours, making more miles in one day than they'd made in all the time they'd traveled with the Gypsies. It seemed wholly impossible, yet Jenny felt the heat of Matthew's body warming her face and hands as well as her back. She felt his warm breath at her deaf ear, but she was too upset to tell him she could not hear the words he spoke. His denials did not matter. The vision of the red-haired woman and her pleading expression had been clear enough.

As dusk approached, there was no sign of a village or town where they might spend the night. Eventually they came upon a solitary stone farmhouse on the rain-swept landscape where they stopped and asked for shelter.

"Aye, 'tis a bruising storm," said the housewife who opened the door merely a crack. "Take yer horse to the barn. Ye'll find my husband out there."

She pulled Jenny inside, taking her bag and sending her to stand by the fire. "'Tis an awful night to be out and about. Where ye headed?"

"To Carlisle," Jenny replied, inhaling the scent of something hot and delicious in the cook pot that hung on a hook over the fire.

"Well, ye've a ways yet to go. But ye'll be warm enough and dry here. I'm Kitty Moffat. These be my bairns—Sally, Jamie, and Paul. And my youngest, Susan," she said, referring to the baby she carried on her hip.

Shivering, Jenny nodded to the woman and her shy but curious children. "I'm Jenny Keating. My . . . husband is Matthew."

"Ye can hang yer cloak there," Mrs. Moffat indicated a hook near the door. "We'll soon have our soup. There's plenty t' go 'round. 'Tis lovely to have a bit of company. We don't get much here."

The children were all rosy-cheeked, with curly brown hair. None was older than five or six years, and Jenny saw by the roundness of Mrs. Moffat's middle that she was with child again. Jenny touched her own belly under her cloak, and it struck her that she might be carrying Matthew's child.

"What is it, lass?" The woman asked. "Ye've gone all pale, like."

Jenny gave a quick shake of her head and forced a smile. She took off her cloak. "I'm just tired, I suppose. We've been riding all day. You have handsome children, Mrs. Moffat."

What a fool she'd been, risking pregnancy with Matthew, a man who had a beautiful, red-haired wife worrying and waiting for him. She turned to face the fire and rubbed some heat into her arms as she blinked away fresh tears. When she felt composed enough to turn back, Mrs. Moffat was organizing the children into their places at the dining table.

"Would ye take Suzie for me, Mrs. Keating?" Jenny had not a moment to reply before the child was thrust into her arms. The bairn could not be even a year old, for she had only two teeth, and could do nothing but bat her arms and smile happily.

Jenny felt numb as she watched Mrs. Moffat tie the next youngest child into a chair so that he would not fall out during the meal, then took bowls and spoons from a cupboard and placed them on the table. "Tom—my husband—thinks the sleeting rain is going to keep up all night," said the woman. "Here now. Take a seat."

Keeping the bairn on her lap, Jenny sat down at the table and gave the rest of the children a hesitant smile. They kept their eyes on her, certainly curious about the stranger who'd suddenly turned up in their house, but each one too polite or too shy to question her.

Mrs. Moffat drew up a wooden stool and an extra chair, and put them at the table. "We have plenty, Mrs. Keating, and ye're welcome t' sleep in here by the fire for the night. 'Tis sorry I am t' say that th' floor will have to do, but we've got a few rugs to soften it, and spare quilts t' keep you warm."

"You're very kind," said Jenny, grateful that she would not have to force her aching legs and hips onto Moghire's back for a few more hours. At least they'd stayed relatively dry for their ride this far, though she did not know how that had been possible. By the time they'd stopped at the farmhouse, the cold mizzle had turned to sleet, and was coming down in icy sheets.

"How far is it to Carlisle?" she asked.

"Twenty miles as the crow flies," the woman replied. "But in this horrible weather—"

The door blew open and the two men came in with the wind. Everyone shuddered at the cold blast as Mr. Moffat pushed the door closed and latched it tight against the weather. Mrs. Moffat took her husband's coat, and then Matthew's, hanging them both by the door.

"Ye'll be Mr. Keating, then. I'm Kitty Moffat, and ye're welcome here. Tom, come and say hello to Mrs. Keating."

The farmer gave Jenny a friendly nod and went to the fireplace, lifting the pot off the hook while Matthew took the Gypsy bread and cheese from his pack and laid it on the table. "We've something to share, too," he said.

The sight of Jenny holding the pretty, dark-haired bairn took Matthew's breath away. He knew the recovery of his memory was the only thing that would convince her that the woman in the glass ball meant naught to him. And once that happened, he would take her home and fill his house with their children.

He'd had a few more inklings of memory while they rode, but not enough to solve the question of who he was. The persistent sense of urgency was stronger, as was the echo of a warning. About what, he still could not fathom. He only knew he lived for the day when Jenny would sit in Coruain House with his bairns in her arms.

"Coruain?" he muttered aloud.

"What's that, man?" asked Tom.

Matthew looked up. "Coruain House. I . . . just remembered it. Do you know of it?"

Moffat shook his head. "Canna say I've e'er heard of it. In Carlisle?"

Matthew sat down on the three-legged stool beside Jenny. "No. Mayhap." He sighed. "I'm no' sure." He felt the excitement of being on the verge of discovering something important about himself, but at the same time, disappointment, knowing the words told him little. Unless his memory returned, he would still have to search for someone who knew of him . . . or of Coruain House.

"Sounds Scots, or Gaelic," said Moffat. He opened the shutters and looked out at his land being battered by the freezing rain, then turned to his wife. "I doona know what this storm portends for the rest of our spring."

"Likely a harsh one," the woman remarked with a visible shudder. She ladled a thick potage into each of the bowls, then bade her husband to come and sit down. She took her own seat and bowed her head, speaking a short prayer of thanks.

"I'll take Suzie now if ye'll be so good as to slice yer lovely bread," she said, reaching over to take the bairn from Jenny.

The Moffats were friendly and gregarious by nature, and lately deprived of company, so Matthew had no difficulty steering the conversation from himself and Jenny, and concentrated on farm matters and the weather. It was fully dark by the time they finished the meal and Tom went to the mantel for his pipe. He sat in one of the worn but comfortable chairs near the hearth and took the smallest bairn on his lap while his wife cleared the cups and bowls with Jenny's help.

The older three children climbed all over their father, playing a game they called "tickle the bear." Tom roared while the children squealed and ran away, giggling. Then they sneaked back and tried to tickle him while one of them distracted him. They got the best of him until his wife came and took the bairn, then each of them was eventually caught by the bear, and tickled mercilessly.

Matthew watched them, distracted, as he tried to make sense of Coruain House. He could not picture any such place in his mind, nor did it call any other memories to him. Coruain was just a word, as the red-haired woman was just a face. He thought of her, looked into her grass-green eyes, and felt naught but a vague familiarity. Likely because he saw her so often these days.

Naught was real to him but Jenny. But until he knew his own history and could swear he was free to take her as his mate, he was sure she would have little to do with him.

She and Mrs. Moffat came along and sat by the fire, and Jenny took a book from her traveling bag.

"Ye'll ne'er guess, my wee ones! Mrs. Keating has promised to read to us!"

"'Tis good of ye, ma'am," said Mr. Moffat, insisting that Jenny take his chair.

"Ach, 'tis a fine auld book," the farmer's wife said when Jenny placed the book on her lap and opened it carefully, showing the illustrations to the children.

"'Tis a treasure to me—Sir Thomas Malory wrote it hundreds of years ago."

"The book is that auld, then?" asked the farmer's wife.

Jenny smiled. "No, but 'tis an old edition . . . printed many years ago."

The children settled themselves comfortably near Jenny and begged her to begin. Matthew could easily imagine her reading to their own children. He thought of the games he would play with them, mayhap in Coruain House—a place that must have some significance if it came into his mind, like all the other disconnected bursts of memory.

"''Twas New Year's Day in those ancient years,'" Jenny began, "'and all of England's barons rode unto the field, some to joust and some to tourney . . .'"

Her voice was magical, sliding inside Matthew and settling just below his heart, where he could feel it. He stretched out on the floor and listened, almost dozing, to the legend she read, a tale of an ancient kingdom and its knights.

"''How gat ye this sword? said Sir Ector to Arthur. Sir, I will tell you. When I came home for my brother's sword, I found nobody at home to deliver it to me; I thought my brother Sir Kay should not be swordless, and so I came hither eagerly and pulled it out of the stone without any pain.'"

Matthew's eyes shot open. Arthur? It sounded familiar, but . . . No, 'twas *Arthwyr* whom he remembered, quite clearly. The warrior Arthwyr was a man of short stature with a barrel chest and fair hair. Matthew rubbed a hand across his mouth and tried to remember more. Had he served with Arthwyr? Were they somehow related? There had been war . . .

Matthew recalled a vast number of mounted knights, all bearing swords and lances, wearing the green and gold colors of Arthwyr, the king.

The memory flitted away, leaving him even more confused than he'd been without any memory at all. Why did he remember knights in thick leather armor? Where on earth . . .

"'Then all the kings were passing glad of Merlin, and asked him, For what cause is that boy Arthur made your king? Sirs, said Merlin, I shall tell you the cause . . .'"

"Merlin?" The hair on the back of Matthew's neck stood on end.

Jenny nodded. "Merlin, yes," she said as though it were the most common name in Britannia, and continued to read until the farmer and his wife started to doze.

Three of the Moffat children had fallen asleep, and the fourth nearly so. Mrs. Moffat stopped Jenny and rose to her feet. "I'd best get these wee ones—and ourselves—off t' bed. Thank ye for the tale . . . Mayhap ye would finish it for the children in the morn."

"Of course," said Jenny, stifling her own yawn.

The family went to the back of the house, and Matthew could hear their faint voices as the couple put their children to bed. Jenny busied herself with arranging the thick rugs Mrs. Moffat had provided, and set the blankets on top of them.

"Jenny . . . That last part of the tale."

"When Merlin explains how Arthur pulled the sword?"

"Aye." The name resonated, even more than Arthwyr. He pressed a couple of fingers to his forehead and started to pace.

"Matthew?"

He looked up at her, puzzled and unable to explain why he felt as though he *knew* Merlin. "The tale you read . . .'tis strangely familiar."

"'Tis likely you've read, or at least heard the tale of King Arthur. Everyone knows it."

"Aye, I suppose so."

"But you remember nothing more?" She took a deep breath and appeared to brace herself, as though she feared his answer.

He shook his head and touched her cheek. "No, my sweet lass." And what he remembered about Merlin was unclear.

Jenny did not think it would be much longer before Matthew remembered everything. If he recalled the characters from Malory's tale of King Arthur, and the name of that place—Coruain House—then the rest was sure to follow.

Kitty Moffat's thick rugs made a comfortable bed, and when Matthew lay down beside Jenny and pulled her into his arms, she did not resist. He made no advances, but seemed lost in his own thoughts, as she was in hers.

The sound of the sleet lashing against the windows had Jenny considering their journey from the Gypsy camp. Surely the icy rain had been falling just as viciously then as it was now. Yet they'd somehow managed to stay relatively dry, and she wondered if she'd been responsible. She'd *willed* the rock to fall off the riverbank, and those silver fibers had carried out her desire. Jenny wondered if she might have used the same force unconsciously to make herself and Matthew impervious to the weather. She dozed off before coming to any conclusion.

Tom Moffat was up before dawn. Matthew left the house with him, offering to help with his chores. Jenny passed a pleasant enough morning with the rest of the family, entertaining the children with the end of *Le Morte d'Arthur*, while Mrs. Moffat started her own chores.

Jenny and Matthew were ready to take their leave well before noon. It was still cold, but at least the storm had played out overnight. Tom helped Jenny to mount the white gelding in front of Matthew, and they made their farewells.

Just before Matthew turned to ride away, he stopped and spoke to Tom. "There's a lone Gypsy who might come this way," he said. "Black hair and eyes, with a wiry build. He rides a bay mare. Beware of him. He's a bad character."

"Thank ye for the warning," said Tom, glancing toward his wife. "We'll take care."

"Kaulo left the *kompania*?" Jenny asked when they returned to the road.

"Aye. The newly married couples returned right after you left." He told her about the disturbance in camp and what Rupa had said.

Jenny shuddered, and Matthew pulled her tight against his chest. "Doona worry, lass. Kaulo willna hurt you."

"I know," she said, aware that he thought he had to protect her. But Matthew did not know she could probably make a rock fall on Kaulo's head, or do some other damage before she let him touch her.

Jenny tried to sort out the issues that faced her, and steeled herself to refrain from talking with Matthew. She was certain Matthew had recognized the redheaded woman in the glass ball, though she had no idea how that face had come to be in the glass.

The recognition in his eyes was what had spurred her to leave. She'd known better than to let her wishful thinking dictate her actions. She had to get to Carlisle and find her pendant before Harriet could sell it, then go on to Darbury as scheduled. No matter how ardent Matthew had been, Jenny could not let go of her fear that he would abandon her. And now she knew his insistence that he was unattached and unwed was unfounded. She'd seen his face when the other woman had appeared in the glass, and she was no stranger to him.

Jenny had been right all along.

Taking a shuddering breath, she faced the same future that had been in front of her the moment she'd left Bresland. It was the only one she knew with a certainty, before she'd become sidetracked by highwaymen and Gypsies . . . and Matthew.

At midday, they stopped in a grove of ancient oak trees, where they saw a grouping of rocks as tall as Matthew, arranged in a circle. Two of the stones lay on their sides, disturbing the symmetry of the scene. All of the rocks had patterns carved into them—circles inside circles, with straight lines and small holes beside them.

"What is it?" Jenny asked.

Matthew dismounted, then reached up for Jenny. "'Tis a *màrrach cearcall.*"

"I don't understand."

"Nor do I. I canna translate the words. I doona even know where they came from. Yet I know they signify an ancient power. I canna explain."

"The language," Jenny said. "Is it Gaelic?"

Matthew shrugged. "Mayhap. I doona . . ."

"Right. You don't remember."

Matthew had to force himself to sit still on one of the fallen rocks and eat some bread and cheese, but some strong force tore at the core of his body, making him feel as though he were being burned from the inside out. He stood abruptly and walked away from the stones, away from Jenny.

Bits and pieces of memory assailed him, none of them making any sense. His other language seemed much more natural to him, yet he was not uncomfortable with English. He knew about Merlin and Arthwyr, but he somehow knew the story Jenny had read was not accurate. He could not understand how he knew about a king who'd lived more than a thousand years past.

The vision of himself in a dark blue ceremonial robe was equally puzzling, and Matthew knew he had an urgent task before him. He'd recognized the *màrrach cearcall*, yet had no understanding of where this knowledge had come from.

And there was the red-haired lady. Ana.

Matthew jabbed his fingers through his hair and forced his thoughts to the vision of her face, to her eyes and hair. He tried to sense her touch and her smell . . . but he could not. As far as he knew, she was a stranger to him. And he had to make Jenny believe him. Ana was most definitely not his *céile* mate.

They did not stop for long, but continued on their road, arriving at Carlisle's gate as heavy clouds began to gather, threatening another spate of icy rain.

The sight of the city was overwhelming. Jenny did not want to separate from Matthew and proceed alone, but she did not see that she had any choice. He'd seen that she'd arrived safely at Carlisle, but she could go no farther with him. "Stop here."

"Why?" he asked. "We're so close to the city gates—"

"This is . . . must be . . . where we part ways, Matthew," she said, struggling to keep the quiver from her voice. She turned to look at him, at his handsome features, memorizing the arch of his brow and the dimple that appeared in his cheek when he spoke or laughed. She would have touched him then, but she could not prolong her anguish. "If you'll h-help me down . . ."

"No. I willna let you go off alone. Where will you go? Where will you stay?"

"I don't know. I'll find a room somewhere until I can locate Miss Lambton. Then—"

"Jenny, let me help you."

"Matthew, you don't even know if you've been to Carlisle before. How can you possibly—"

He took her lips in a deep kiss, holding the back of her head and tipping his own so that he had full possession of her mouth. Jenny felt her heart give way, and she kissed him back, tasting him, feeling the heat of his lips and the texture of his tongue. She suddenly pushed away, her eyes filling with tears, her chest moving in short, pitiful breaths.

"Matthew, 'tis over—"

"No, *moileen*. 'Tis no'."

"Please let me go."

He looked past her toward the crumbling walls of the city, to the castle in the distance and the river ahead. It was nearly dark, and Jenny could barely see the cold, dark waters beyond the river-banks. But there was a bridge, and she intended to cross it, alone.

Matthew dismounted, then reached up and lifted her down from Moghire's back. He took the reins in hand, then started walking toward the bridge. "We'll go in together."

He was determined, and Jenny knew that arguing was pointless. Besides, she had not been away from Bresland and the small village of Kirtwarren since her parents' death, and Carlisle was more than a bit intimidating. As she walked into the city beside him, she wondered when she had become such a fearful little mouse.

"What do you suppose that is?" Matthew asked, indicating a large dark building, looming quietly in the shadows across the road. They could see faint light emanating from some of the windows.

When they came closer, Jenny read the sign above the door. "'Tis a workhouse."

She'd only heard of such places. Two years before, when she'd told Reverend Usher she wished to leave Bresland, he'd threatened that she would end up there, destitute and unable to find work without references.

"Workhouse? What kind of work?" Matthew asked, keeping his eyes on the place as they walked past.

Jenny shuddered at the thought of living in

such a place. "'Tis where the poor go when they cannot support themselves. They are given food and shelter in exchange for work."

They continued silently, and Jenny could see that Matthew was troubled by the building and her explanation of it. She thought perhaps he had personal experience of the workhouse, but quickly reminded herself that a man who carried as much money as Matthew would hardly be familiar with such hardships. Perhaps that was it—he was wholly *un*familiar with it.

"I doona understand," he said. "*This* is what's done to take care of those who canna provide for themselves?"

"Are there no such places in Scotland?" Jenny asked.

"Ach, no."

She noted his furrowed brow. "Can you remember what you do for the poor in Scotland, then?"

A muscle tightened in his jaw, and he gave a brief shake of his head. "No, lass. I have merely an impression of . . . of dealing with the unskilled among us."

"Unskilled?"

"I canna even tell you what I mean by that," he said, with frustration coloring his voice. "'Tis just that some are more able than others to care for themselves. And those who are most capable ought to do what they can for the rest."

Jenny nodded, deep in thought. She was fairly sure she'd heard of workhouses in Scotland, yet

Matthew did not know of them. She wondered if his brogue was not Scottish. Perhaps he was a Welshman or an American.

They followed the road into the city, and soon turned down Castle Street to head toward the center of town. The street was well lit with gaslights, and they saw increasing numbers of people hurrying about as they walked south, past the cathedral.

In the town center was a tall, narrow monument. Beyond it was the Guild Hall, all closed up, and a darkened tea shop. A chemist was just closing his store, and as he bent to lock his door, Matthew approached and asked him if he knew where they might find a room to let.

The man pulled up the collar of his coat and looked at Matthew, quickly taking his measure. Apparently satisfied with what he saw, he nodded toward a narrow lane back in the direction from where they'd come. "Respectable houses will let rooms to a man and his wife down that way." Then he pointed up another street. "And the Queen's Hotel is not far. But it's expensive."

It seemed much colder now, and as the rain threatened, the very air became icy and uncomfortable. Jenny's feet were freezing as she started toward the houses that had rooms to let. Matthew took her arm and joined her.

"Matthew . . ."

"Doona even think I'll leave you alone in the street, lass."

"But I—"

"Come on."

She allowed herself the luxury of his presence for just a short while longer, turning into a poorly lit lane with houses that had signs advertising rooms to let.

But that was all. He had to leave her soon, and pursue the life he'd left behind.

Before she could take another step, Matthew handed her Moghire's reins and approached the most promising of the houses. Jenny started to call to him, but stopped herself, unwilling to attract the attention of the neighbors who were already peering at her through gaps in their curtains. She shrank back into her hood and cloak as a woman opened her door and spoke to Matthew. He gestured toward Jenny and the woman nodded, then accepted payment, pointing to a narrow track between her own house and the next.

Matthew came back to Jenny and took Moghire's lead. "Go inside, *moileen*, and get warm."

"Matthew, we can't—"

"Can you no' trust me to take care of you, Jenny?"

She swallowed, not trusting him in the least, but trusting her own heart even less.

Matthew led Moghire to Mrs. Welby's shed at the back of the house, then brushed him down and fed him. He took his time, wanting Jenny to get settled in their room, allowing her to claim her space. Matthew had no intention of leaving her, no matter what she might think.

He took his satchel and Jenny's traveling bag, and returned to the front of the house. Two men were walking past, wearing similar dark jackets and the same kind of high hats worn by the constables who had come searching for Jenny in the Gypsy camp. They also carried thick wooden batons in their belts, as though they expected trouble.

Matthew gave them a nod as they continued walking toward the town center, then dismissed them from his mind as he climbed the steps to the house where he and Jenny would spend the night.

"Mr. Keating," said the stern landlady as she picked up a lamp and started for the stairs. "This way."

He followed Mrs. Welby up the steps to a door with a wooden number two nailed to it. "Here she is," she said without humor or friendliness. The woman never smiled, nor did she have a single word of welcome. But she'd been glad enough to take his money for the room and a few amenities.

"I do not abide any drinking in my house, Mr. Keating, nor any loud or lewd behavior. I'll thank you and your wife to keep to yourselves and respect the peace of the house."

"Aye, madam. You'll hardly know we're here," Matthew said, aware that the woman would toss them out if she knew he and Jenny were not married. She started to leave, but Matthew stopped her. "Is there a place nearby where we might buy a meal?"

"Yes, of course," she said sourly. "At the Queen's Hotel, a short walk from here, past the cross in the town center and down the street a short way. You'll see it. But mind you watch for pickpockets. The city is rife with 'em."

"Thank you, ma'am," Matthew said, even as she walked away muttering disparagingly about Scotsmen.

The room was sparsely furnished, with a bed no bigger than the one he and Jenny had shared in the Gypsy caravan, and a chair near the hearth. There was a low table beside the bed with an oil lamp on it, and it shed scant light into the room. Jenny did not turn away from the narrow little hearth when he entered, and Matthew refrained from reaching for her, even though he wanted nothing more than to hold her in his arms and assure her—assure himself—that all would be well. But now was not the time.

He shoved his hands into his pockets. "Are you hungry, lass?"

She faced him then. "Matthew, we cannot continue sharing a bed. I—"

"I'll no' be leaving you, Jenny."

He could not read the look in her eyes, and did not know whether 'twas relief or annoyance. It mattered naught. This was no place to leave Jenny unprotected. A city like Carlisle was no place for a young woman alone. He'd seen signs of danger lurking 'round enough corners to make him concerned for her safety as she went in search of the thief who'd stolen her locket.

"Come then and we'll go for . . ." He felt the familiar tingling sensation in the center of his chest. A vague sense of it had preceded a number of his actions, from eliminating the whiskers from his chin every morning, to preventing Kaulo from striking him that night in the tavern. But now it was stronger, hot and compelling.

"Matthew? Are you all right?"

Her reticence disappeared with her concern for him. She came to stand right in front of him, cupping his cheek with her hand. She dropped it self-consciously when he turned his attention to her.

"Aye. Just hungry, I think. Shall we go?"

But the sensation persisted, as well as the knowledge that he could control it, could actually *project* it out of his body.

Yet, like the healing, and the way he'd kept the rain off them the day before, no one else seemed to have these abilities, and prudence made Matthew refrain from using it to feed them now. He did not want to give Jenny further reason to be wary of him. Besides, there was some niggling warning in the back of his brain, a vague, half-formed memory that begged him to be cautious with this power.

They left their few possessions in the room,

then wrapped themselves in their cloaks and walked to the town center.

"What's that noise?" Jenny asked.

There was a crowd gathering in the streets somewhere nearby. Matthew and Jenny soon saw a large group of poorly dressed men and women, shouting and carrying torches and signs. They were moving quickly, rushing toward them, like a stormy sea. "Stay close, *moileen*." Matthew pushed her behind him and started to retreat toward the Welby house.

But another ragged group suddenly appeared behind them, and Matthew quickly realized they were surrounded by a loud, fast-moving crowd that was growing angrier with every step. He could hear them yelling the words, "Blood or bread!" repeatedly.

The sound of whistles suddenly screeched from somewhere farther up the street. There were frightened screams and more angry shouts from the crowd, and some of the people started to run away, creating chaos. Matthew caught wind of a few loud voices ordering the crowd to disperse.

Many of the women carried young children in their arms, the small urchins looking pale, thin, and unhealthy. Bottles, stones, and other projectiles flew through the air and crashed to the ground, and Matthew had no doubt that many would be hurt. He hoped 'twould not be any of the children.

"They're going back to the Guild Hall!" Jenny cried above the din of the crowd.

Mayhem ensued. Matthew drew her close and moved her 'round to his back. "Hold on to me, Jenny!"

She latched on to the back of his coat and held tightly while Matthew used his size and strength to push his way through the stampeding crowd, heading back toward Mrs. Welby's house. But the crowd pressed in on them on all sides, moving in opposite directions. "This way!"

Their only option was to head toward the buildings at the edge of the street. Matthew forced his way past the angry people who shoved and pushed to get to the other side of the town center. In a split second, he felt Jenny's grip torn from his jacket, and she was lost. He whipped 'round to grab for her, but she'd been swallowed into the mob. Her scream sounded loud in his ears.

"Jenny!" Matthew called as a wave of bodies pulled him into the flow. He was going to lose her!

He caught sight of her and started to grab for her with the force that emanated from his chest. Instead, he used brute force to toss people out of his way, and pressed through the path he created to get to Jenny.

The mob closed in all 'round her, and Matthew roared with frustration. Her head dropped completely out of sight, and Matthew knew she had fallen. Without thinking, he reached for her and raised her above the jostling, teeming herd. To any onlooker, 'twould appear that the crowd had lifted her to their shoulders, and were moving her across their bodies, toward him. Matthew plowed forward and caught her in his arms, then drew her out of the fray into the indentation of a nearby building.

The door did not open at first, so Matthew let his power surge once again. He muttered the words that unlocked it, and they fell together into a tobacconist's shop. Setting Jenny safely inside, he slammed the door shut behind him, muting the sounds of the mob outside. The light of their torches cast wild shadows on the cluttered shelves, but Matthew pulled Jenny into his arms, desperate to touch her, to hold her and know that she was unharmed.

"*Ainchis*, Jenny!"

She whimpered and clung tightly to him, and when she pressed her teary face into his chest, a much more primitive need roared through him.

He turned and pressed her back against the wall, taking her mouth in a possessive kiss that branded her as his own. No other man would ever touch her. He sucked her tongue into his mouth, tasting her, reveling in all that he felt for her.

Jenny slipped her hands 'round his neck and pulled him closer, as needy as he. She tilted her head and deepened the kiss, closing her eyes and melting into him.

He broke the kiss, and whispered the words that had never rung more true. *"Sibh ar mèinn, moileen."*

He pressed heated kisses to her ear, then to her neck, as he drew her skirts up above her knees. With every pore of his body, he wanted to be inside her, to become one with the only woman who would ever dwell in his heart.

She slid her leg 'round one of his, and he opened his trews, then lifted her, quickly finding the split in her drawers. With one swift move, he was inside.

Their climax overtook them all at once, and they soared to that place where his filmy essence blended with hers, creating a pleasure that shuddered through their *bràths* as well as their physical bodies. He felt her quake against him, and heard her sighs of satisfaction. And when it was over, he did not withdraw, but kept them joined as he looked into her eyes.

"I'm sorry, Jenny . . . I shouldna—"

She touched her fingers to his lips and closed her eyes, then touched his cheek as though she were committing every detail of his face to her memory. He bent down to touch his forehead to hers, then gently lowered her to the ground. She stepped away and righted her clothes while Matthew fastened his trews. In the dim light, he noticed that the shelves behind the counter were empty now. He looked over the counter and saw that the tobacconist's wares lay all over the floor.

"We should get away from here," Jenny said quietly, her voice distracting him from their surroundings. Rising up onto her toes, she looked out the window. "It's not so bad now."

He came up behind her and saw that she was right. There were some stragglers, but the mob had passed by. And here they were inside a locked shop, which was surely not permissible.

Stealing one more kiss, he took Jenny's hand and let them out of the shop, correcting the disarray behind him, for he was certain the shelves had been intact when they'd come inside. He had no explanation for what had happened to all the pouches and boxes, but could only imagine it had something to do with the intensity of their joining. A similar mishap had occurred every time he'd made love to Jenny in the Gypsy caravan . . .

They entered the street and saw that they were still unable to pass in the direction of the Queen's Hotel. They headed back toward Mrs. Welby's house, giving a wide berth to the straggling groups that remained in the street.

They were nearly at the Welby house when a mean-looking giant who was armed with a long stick grabbed Jenny. "Ye're one o' them from King's Street, ain't ye, now?"

"No! I'm a visitor—"

The man pulled Jenny off her feet, and Matthew reacted. Without touching him, Matthew shoved the giant off his feet. The man released Jenny as he flew across the brick pavement, crashing into a number of his cohorts.

"Come on!" Matthew shouted. He grabbed Jenny again, half lifting her off her feet, and ran all the way back to the Welby house. When they were safely inside, she turned to him with astonishment in her eyes. "What happened back there? What did you do to that man?"

Chapter 9

"**N**aught, Jenny. He just lost his footing and fell."

That was the most likely explanation, but she'd seen Matthew raise one hand and make an odd gesture, then suddenly her attacker was lying on the far side of the street. His explanation was the only reasonable one, but yet . . .

After all that had happened in the past hour, Jenny could not comprehend one more thing. She should never have allowed that fast, intense coupling inside the darkened shop, but their joining had felt impossibly right. She'd wanted him with more passion than she had experienced before.

She stood with her back against the wall in Mrs. Welby's entryway, with Matthew looming over her as he leaned on the arm he'd extended to the wall beside her head. He touched her gently with his other hand. "Are you all right, *moileen*?"

She should have felt embarrassed to look into his eyes after behaving like such a wanton, but he'd felt the same driving need. They'd been perfectly matched.

"Yes. I-I'm fine." Except for the red-haired woman in his past.

Mrs. Welby came into the entryway, carrying a lamp and looking worried. "Such a commotion out there."

Matthew pushed away from the wall, and Jenny's heart finally started to slow. "A huge, angry crowd gathered—"

"Oh aye," said Mrs. Welby. "The Irish and Scots weavers. Complaining about their wages. She bolted the door and went to peek through the shutters of the first-floor windows. "They'll need to call out the militia. Their leaders ought to be put into the House of Corrections this time."

"They looked verra poor," said Matthew. "What can we do?"

"Do? For those ruffians?"

"Aye. Their bairns looked half starved."

Jenny had noticed the same thing and felt pity for the small ones, but since she barely had enough to keep herself from starvation, she did not know what she could do. She felt a surge of warmth for Matthew and his concern for the children.

"They should go back where they came from, so our own good English weavers can get enough work to keep them," Mrs. Welby said as she retreated to her sitting room. They heard her locking the shutters of the rest of the windows.

Jenny and Matthew climbed the stairs and went to their own room, but she no longer had any appetite. The evening had been fraught with upheaval, and she did not know what to think or what she should do about Matthew.

He opened his pack and took out the food they'd brought from the Gypsy camp, bidding Jenny to sit in the chair by the fire. He laid the food on the table and sat down at her feet.

"I'm not hungry anymore, Matthew."

He ignored her and handed her a thick slice of bread and some cheese. "Try just a few bites, *moileen*."

Jenny had to resist the urge to sink down beside him and slip her fingers into his hair. She craved the flavor of his lips and the intimate slide of his hands on her shoulders and neck, around her waist and hips.

She wanted more than the quick coupling they'd experienced in the tobacconist's shop.

Perhaps the red-haired woman was not his wife, but merely someone Matthew had known before he'd been injured. Possibly a sister. Or the wife of a friend. Maybe she shouldn't have jumped to the worst possible conclusion.

Or maybe she was deluding herself.

Her troubled thoughts fled her mind when he took one of her shoes in hand and unbuttoned it. He removed it and rubbed her cold foot through her wet stocking.

"Take it off, Jenny," he said quietly.

"Matthew . . ."

"Or I will."

After a moment's hesitation, she reached under her skirt and rolled down both stockings, so that when he removed her other shoe, he was not impeded by her hose. He rubbed her feet with his big hands, returning the warmth and circulation to them, reducing her bones to putty at the same time.

Jenny closed her eyes and leaned back in her chair, her emotions painfully unsettled, but unable to resist his touch.

"You've bonny wee feet, *moileen*," he said quietly, his voice easing any misgivings she had.

After only a few minutes, her feet were warm and her body languid. Her mind grew complacent and irresponsible. Matthew's touch was all that mattered.

He skimmed a finger lightly up her leg, from her ankle to her knee. Then his hand circled behind it, searing the sensitive skin with his touch. Pushing her skirts aside, he pressed a light kiss to her thigh, then treated the other leg to the same sweet torture. Jenny's body hummed with arousal.

"So soft," he murmured, looking up at her, "like silk." He stood and took her by the hand, drawing her to her feet, leading her to the bed. Jenny could not deny him—or herself—the pleasure she knew would follow.

They undressed each other slowly, taking time to kiss and caress the skin they bared, while Jenny forced thoughts of tomorrow from her mind.

Standing naked together in the small room with only the dim light from the hearth, Matthew pressed a gentle kiss to her lips. "My bonny Jenny," he whispered, then laid her on the bed.

Jenny slid her fingers through his hair as he touched a kiss to her jaw, then another to her neck. He moved down and took one nipple into his mouth, swirling his tongue around it and making her quiver with a yearning that she felt through to her soul.

His breath feathered lightly over her belly, then the hollows between her hipbones. He slipped his hands under her hips and pulled her close as he pressed kisses to her soft skin. Easing one finger inside her, he flicked the sensitive nub with his tongue.

As Jenny came close to shattering, he drew his mouth slowly away and moved up, kissing the indentation of her navel, then her breast. She took a deep, shuddering breath and shifted position, so that she was beside him, facing him.

Inching her hand down the length of his body, she was gratified by his growl of arousal when she encircled his manhood and ran her thumb over the tip. He jerked as if in pain, but Jenny knew her touch pleased him. She kissed his broad chest, then ran her tongue over one taut brown nipple as her hands stroked him, exploring him, learning all she needed to know from his gasps and moans.

"Jenny . . . *mo oirg.*" His words were a mere gasp.

He rolled to his back, pulling her with him, then positioning her on top. Jenny's hair was a wild mass of light curls around her face, dropping over her shoulders. Matthew reached up to brush it behind her, then cupped her breasts in his hands as he slid inside her.

"Matthew," she moaned as she arched her back, giving him more, wanting more.

"Aye, lass. Move on me," he whispered. "Any way you want . . ."

Jenny found a rhythm, her movements pleasing them both.

"Ainchis!" he groaned, and though she did not understand the word, she knew he was consumed by the same fire that drove her.

The tempo increased and Matthew began to move, too, sliding in and out of her, finally slamming his body into hers as they met in a tumultuous climax, shuddering their release at once. They came together in the otherworldly fog, their inner selves transparent as they slid into one another, becoming one.

At length, they returned to their bodies. Jenny raised her head and looked into his eyes, wishing she could see into his mind and help him retrieve his lost memories. She would give anything to be certain the woman in the galss ball was not his wife.

The sound of glass shattering somewhere outside broke the mood of the moment, and Matthew stood and quickly extinguished the lamp beside the bed. Then he went to the window and looked down.

"Stay back, Jenny," he said when she started to rise from the bed. "They are moving this way again, and I doona trust that crowd. They are desperate."

The Isle of Coruain, 981

Ana's cousins had been gone nearly a week, and Eilinora's assault had not abated. Ana could barely move. Her bones were nearly healed, but the pressure in her chest was likely to kill her if it did not stop soon. She was weakening by the hour.

Several of the elders had gathered 'round the pallet on which she lay inside the great hall of Coruain House, adding their strength to her resistance against the Odhar. 'Twas only their combined assistance that kept Eilinora from succeeding in killing her, just as the she-*deamhan* had killed Kieran.

"No, witch, I doona give you access to my mind!" she whispered, her voice a harsh rasp that barely scraped past her dry throat.

"Then I will have your life, little gurach!"

Ana wasted no energy on a response to the words that only she could hear, but kept her full attention on bolstering the shielding swathe that encircled the isles.

"Shall I take one of your pathetic elders and destroy her?"

A terrible, hot wind burst through the ceiling, shattering wood and glass, and the elders scrambled to close the gap in the shield. Before it could be done, a horrible cry sounded in Ana's ears. The elders gasped, then called out in horror. With intense effort, Ana turned her head and saw the tortured form of Nessa, burning to cinders as they watched. The fire burned her horribly from within, and there was naught that any of them could do to prevent it.

Sickened by the terrible assault, Ana felt more vulnerable than she had since her cousins' departure. With supreme effort, she pushed up onto one elbow and shot a fatal blast of *lòchran* back through the shield, and though Eilinora escaped it, Ana saw two of her Odhar fall. Ana focused her energy on another attack, but saw the witch raise the Druzai rod of gold, the chieftain's scepter.

"Tighten it! Reinforce the shield now!" she cried as her own powers surged forth to protect them. "She wields . . . the chieftain's scepter . . ."

Cianán acted immediately, his horror and fear etched upon his face, and with good reason. Eilinora was using the scepter to burst through the shields that were their only protection without the blood stones.

"It gives her more power than we can withstand!"

Liam fell to the floor, clutching at his throat. Ana tried again to demolish Eilinora, taking the witch by surprise with the strength of her assault. "Begone, *deamhan*!"

Eilinora suddenly released Liam from the invisible claws that held him, and he crawled to his knees, struggling in pain, gasping for breath.

"How can she do this?" cried Cianán as the others helped the elder to his feet. "Not even the scepter should give her such power! Will she destroy all of us, one by one?"

"We can hold her until Brogan and Merrick return!" Ana whispered with vehemence. She fought the weakness brought by the strain of defending Coruain and the pain of her mending bones. "Be strong!"

Carlisle, March 1826

The mob moved away from the Welby house, but as much as Matthew wanted to remain in the bed with Jenny, he felt he needed to keep watch until the unruly mass of people dispersed. The house would not provide much protection if the crowd decided to break windows and press inside.

He crouched beside the bed and reached over to push a stray curl gently from Jenny's forehead. Doubt had replaced the passion in her eyes, and there was naught he could do to dispel it. At least not yet. She'd experienced the same joining of souls as he had, and would soon come to understand what it meant.

Matthew stood and pulled on his trews, then moved the chair over to the window where he could see beyond the curtain. Taking a seat, he propped his feet on the end of the bed.

"Do you think they'll come back?" Jenny asked. They could still hear the raucous voices shouting in the direction of the town center.

"'Tis doubtful. Those constable men will soon disperse them, I'm sure."

"And the militia. Mrs. Welby mentioned that."

She said it as though he should understand the word, but it meant little to him. Wherever he came from, they had no such thing as a militia. But the memory of fighting men, warriors, men who trained and fought to ensure peace and security, came to him. "Do you mean the *ulhabar*?"

"*Ulhabar*?"

Matthew heard her turn over to lie on her side, facing him in the dark. He would much rather climb in with her and curl his body 'round hers, keeping them both warm through the night, and ponder his vague inklings of *ulhabar*.

But the danger from the encroaching mob was very real. He wanted to be ready to take Jenny away in case the crowd got any uglier.

"Is it a Gaelic word?"

"I suppose," Matthew replied, although he was not so sure of it. The word "Gaelic" itself was not as familiar as it should be if it were his native tongue. 'Twas so puzzling. There were many aspects of this place that seemed wholly unfamiliar. And yet much that he knew.

"Jenny, can you tell the rest of Malory's tale without having to read it?" 'Twas a way to keep their connection, even though they were not touching. And mayhap something else would sound familiar.

"Of course. The tale has long been my favorite. I memorized it years ago, and only brought out the book last night so the Moffat children could see the illustrations."

She began to recite it, and Matthew listened to her voice as she described events he vaguely remembered. Yet he had an awareness that her recounting of the ancient king's history was not quite accurate.

"Arthwyr had a temper," he said suddenly.

"Arthwyr?"

Matthew shrugged in the near darkness. "'Twas how he was called. He didna care for anyone to cross him, either."

"According to Malory, he was a fair and just king who—"

"Aye, but sometimes his temper was unreasonable. Unfair."

"Perhaps," said Jenny. "Do you want to hear the rest?"

"Aye. I'll . . . Go ahead."

He felt more confused now than he'd been ever since his injury. He could not understand why he would feel so certain about this legendary king who'd been dead for centuries. He could picture the man in his mind, and could see his red-gold hair and thick, red brows. He clearly recalled Arthwyr's fiery temper and had tested his skill with a sword.

"Tell me more about Merlin."

She yawned, her voice soft and drowsy. "He was an old wizard with white hair and a long, grizzled beard."

Matthew felt his forehead tighten. "What was his role in Arthwyr's court?"

"Matthew, is the tale familiar?"

"Aye, lass."

His eyes had adjusted to the shadows of the room, and he could see that she'd propped her head on her hand. "Do you recall where you heard it?"

He did not think he'd heard it, but *lived* it. How else could he picture it so vividly? "No, I canna recall exactly. Only that . . ." Feeling surprisingly irritated, he knew that Malory had gotten it wrong. There'd been no affair between Gwyn and Lancelot. And Merlin was no wizened old man.

Matthew was Merlin.

He stood abruptly.

"What is it? Are they coming back?" Jenny asked, alarmed. She sat up in the bed.

"Ach no, *moileen*," he replied, realizing her alarm was about the dangerous crowd and not his ominous memory. "Lie back down."

"Then what—"

"Naught. You should try to sleep now."

"But you—"

"Just felt a cramp in my leg. I'll move 'round a bit and be all right."

She settled down to sleep, and Matthew tried to sort out what he knew of Merlin, of Arthwyr, and of the court at Camelot. 'Twas not much, but he felt certain he was Merlin himself. He surely could not tell that to Jenny, or she would question the sanity of a man who claimed to be a mythical character from a millennium ago. After the injury to his head, mayhap he should be questioning his own sanity.

Matthew raised one hand to his eyes and studied it in the faint light from the street. During their encounter with the crowd in the town center, he'd shoved that man away from Jenny without touching him. He was certain of it, even though he'd denied it to her. Such a thing was not commonly done, or he would have seen it happen. He'd felt that tingling heat in his chest, and without the slightest difficulty, had opened the locked tobacconist's shop. And later, he'd felt the same heat just before replacing all the shopkeeper's wares onto the shelves. Matthew did not understand why *he* had such power when no one else seemed to.

He returned to the window and turned his attention to the gaslight perched high upon a pole some distance down the street. With the conscious intent of extinguishing the light, he managed to pour that odd heat from his chest into his hand, and with one finger, flicked it at the light.

The flame disappeared.

It did not surprise him in the least, and he suspected there were many other feats he could accomplish, just by channeling the energy that glowed hotly in his chest. Yet some deep instinct warned him to be cautious.

He relit the flame in the lamp and sat down again, considering what he knew of himself. Gaelic or something similar to it was his natural language. He was a wealthy man, judging by his clothes and the amount of money he carried. He'd known how to use the Gypsy's *ceirtlín*, and caused the face of the red-haired woman to appear in the glass.

There was an unrelenting sense of urgency that Matthew had pushed to the back of his mind because he was unable to do anything about it. As he struggled to remember why he felt such a demanding pressure and what action he should take, he envisioned the face of the redhead again. This time, she looked pale and ill. The color had gone from her lips, and there were dark shadows beneath her eyes. She did not speak to him when he pictured her this time, nor did she even try. She was dying.

"Ana," he muttered quietly, aware that something was horribly wrong.

Matthew closed his eyes again and called forth everything he could remember about Ana. He felt certain she was a woman of influence, of power, possessing the respect and admiration of her people. She was a comely lass, her beauty second only to Jenny's. He felt no pull of attraction to her, yet there was a closeness between them. He knew her well. But she was not his mate, nor was she his sister . . . He clenched his fists . . . Not his sister . . . But they were as close as . . .

Mo oirg! She was his cousin!

And he was Merrick Mac Lochlainn. He had to get back to her and . . .

Ainchis! The *brìgha*-stones!

It all came back to him in a flood of memory. In a flash, he knew who he was and why he was there in the Tuath world. He flew out of his chair once again and started to pace, horrified by the precious time he'd wasted. He knew that his brother had gone in search of one *brìgha*-stone, and Merrick was responsible for finding the other. He just hoped he was not already too late.

Jenny made a soft sound of sleep, and Merrick dropped down into his chair once again, lowering his head into his hands. He'd been so certain she was his *céile* mate. But that could not be, not when Sinann . . .

Now he understood the nagging sense of urgency. Every Druzai of Coruain knew Merrick would wed a powerful sorceress before his thirtieth year. He knew the mate he chose was going to be the key element in the struggle for Druzai survival. He'd had a great deal of advice on the subject from his father and the elders, for there could be no more serious a crisis than what faced them now.

Merrick had chosen well, and he would not renege. He needed to hurry with his task here and get back to Sinann, make her his mate, and combat Eilinora's assault on Coruain.

Merrick swore quietly when he thought of all the times he'd tapped into his powers and used magic—he'd used it numerous times in the Gypsy camp, again on the road to Carlisle, and finally, so often tonight, he could hardly keep track.

He shoved his fingers through his hair in frustration. If an Odhar hunter had been in the vicinity of any of these events, he could very well have found the bright, yellow residual sparks of his magic, and traced him here. And Jenny would be in grave danger.

Merrick looked toward the bed where she slept. Was she the Keating he'd been told to seek? She must be. But she carried no blood stone. Merrick had seen all her possessions . . .

All but one. He had not seen the locket she sought in Carlisle.

Matthew was gone when Jenny awoke. She washed and dressed, and was ready for the day by the time he returned to their room.

"Let's eat and go, then," he said.

"You're in a fine hurry this morning."

He did not reply, nor did he look at her. He merely unwrapped the parcel he'd brought and offered her its contents, a boiled egg and a piece of brown bread. He had not shaved, so his jaw was dark with the night's growth of whiskers, and his mood seemed just as black. Something had changed. "Aren't you going to have any?"

"I ate at the tea shop." He picked up his satchel and Jenny's bag and placed them near the door. A hole opened up in the pit of Jenny's stomach with his distant, cold attitude toward her.

"A-are we leaving?"

"Aye. I've found us a better place. Safer. We'll go as soon as you eat, then start looking for your Miss Lambton."

"What's happened, Matthew? Why are we running away?"

"We are no' running, Jenny. Merely moving on to our search for your locket."

Sensing his hurry to get going without any more talk, Jenny ate quickly, pulled on her cloak, and headed for the door. They went downstairs and saw no sign of Mrs. Welby, so they left the house and walked through the city center, past all its market stalls, to the Queen's Hotel. There were signs of last night's crowd—a broken window covered with wooden boards, shattered glass underfoot, and litter on the street. Jenny supposedthe hotel would be a better barrier to a mob if another one formed while they remained in Carlisle, but she nearly had to run to keep up with Matthew's pace.

"Matthew, are you angry about something?"

He gave a shake of his head, but said nothing, adding to Jenny's uneasiness. After all their intimacies, he had closed himself off from her. It was not like him.

"What about Moghire?" she asked.

"Already in the hotel's stable."

They entered the building, and Jenny was astonished with the opulence of the entry room. Two chandeliers lit the large expanse, and there was a fireplace at each end. She had never seen so much highly polished wood, or fine, rich, furniture. It seemed a place fit for royalty, and it occurred to Jenny that Matthew seemed quite at ease here.

It emphasized the differences between them.

A neatly dressed clerk in spectacles stood behind a tall desk, watching them over his glasses as Matthew led her to the grand staircase. Walking across the lush carpets toward the steps, Jenny felt self-conscious. Her clothing was anything but grand, and she wore no glittering jewelry on her hands or at her throat like the other women who turned to watch as they walked by. At least Matthew would have told the clerk they were man and wife.

Yet he did not touch her as they climbed to the second floor. He was behaving anything but husbandly.

Nor did he act like a lover.

They walked down a long, narrow hall lit by regularly spaced wall sconces. Halfway down the hall, he took a key from his coat and unlocked a door. He pushed it open, and when Jenny stepped into the room, he dropped her bag inside but did not follow. "This is your room." He turned slightly. "Mine is across the hall."

Despite everything . . . their intimacies and his denial of any prior attachments . . .

Jenny had known it would happen. She'd prepared herself for his leaving, yet tears burned the backs of her eyes, and the curious silver threads burst from her chest to smash one of the nearby wall sconces.

Matthew could not have seen the threads, for he

gave the broken sconce only a cursory glance, then returned his dark gaze to Jenny's. She pressed her lips tightly together to keep them from trembling. She would not cry.

She raised her chin, refusing to let him see how deeply his desertion hurt her. "You needn't stay, Matthew."

She took a deep breath and forced her voice to remain steady. "Wh-whatever responsibility you felt for me . . . I'm . . . well, I'm here safely, and I—"

"I'm going to help you find your locket."

She blinked away the moisture welling in her eyes and schooled her features into a neutral mask. "No. You should not delay going to Scotland," she said with a forced flippancy. "You've done your gentlemanly duty and seen me to Carlisle, and besides, you must have . . ."

Two well-dressed couples came into the hall, talking sociably together. As they approached, Jenny feared she might shatter into a hundred pieces for everyone to see.

But Matthew eased into the room and closed the door behind him. "I'm not leaving until you have your locket."

Jenny turned away to the window and swallowed the lump in her throat. She looked out at the street, where pedestrians hurried to and from their destinations, but she hardly noticed them.

"I do not need you anymore, Matthew," she said brightly. It never did any good to show any pain, but just made her more vulnerable.

And she'd been such a pathetic fool, so open to heartache. She turned and picked up her bag, and without looking at him, started for the door. But Matthew blocked her way.

"Excuse me," she said quietly.

"Where . . . What are you doing, lass?" His voice took on a tone of concern, but Jenny knew nothing had changed.

"I can't afford these lodgings. So if you'll let me by, I'll just go back to Mrs. Welby's house and see if she'll give me last night's room."

Ainchis! Merrick cursed quietly, under his breath. He wanted to take Jenny into his arms and dispel the bleak look in her soft, gray eyes. He wanted her to understand he was nothing like her uncle, or Mr. Ellis, but he feared he was. He had no choice but to abandon Jenny. Frustration and fury welled up inside him, fierce and brutal, unlike any he'd ever known.

He grabbed her shoulders, his fingers tightening over her delicate bones through the thick fabric of her cloak. He spoke harshly. "Doona be ridiculous."

Turning her to face him, he gathered her into his arms and felt her take a long, quivering breath. He scorned the fates that had put him in Jenny's path, that had made her care for him, even though she should not.

"You saved my life, Jenny," he said in a softer tone. "Let me help you now."

She dropped the bag and pushed away from

him. With a resolute expression, she left the room. Merrick followed her down to the main lobby, where she approached the clerk at the desk. "Can you tell me if there is a rum distillery in the city?"

"Aye, madam. There is one up away north in Caldewgate, past the Lanes."

"The Lanes?" Merrick asked.

The man frowned, his spectacles slipping down his nose. "Up near Fisher Street. But mind you take care wherever you go. There's been some trouble with the Irish and Scots weavers."

"Some trouble," Merrick muttered under his breath. "Aye."

"Thank you very much," said Jenny, lifting her skirt and going out to the street. She started in the direction the clerk had pointed out, proceeding as though she were alone. Her dismissal of him chafed. Badly.

For the first time in his life, Merrick could not analyze himself out of a predicament, nor would his warrior's skills serve him. There was no one to fight, and no way to change the oracle's prediction.

He'd come to the Tuath lands several times in the past on his father's orders, using his analytical skills to help various tribes avert disaster. Matthew knew his missions had been part of his training to become high chieftain, and he'd gained great respect for the Tuath people. He had enjoyed his forays here, but he'd always been glad to return home to Coruain.

His duties also included his father's work of diplomacy, of keeping the magical isles united and protected when challenges arose. It was unusual for a faction of Druzai to cause unrest, and that was not merely because of the Mac Lochlainn's vast powers. Kieran had believed in working out differences and solving problems diplomatically before any crisis could emerge.

This was a wholly different situation than any the Druzai had ever faced since Eilinora's treason a millennium ago.

She had created violent unrest among the clans, taking delight in causing mistrust and misunderstandings, fomenting prejudices and causing wars. She'd encouraged the Druids, protégés of the Druzai, to use their powers to contribute to the disaster.

The details of the witch's rise to power and her defeat had been lost with time. But since those ancient days when she'd been captured and imprisoned, the Druzai had had little interest in her.

Until now, when she was free from her prison.

Merrick felt a sharp pang of grief at the loss of his father. No one had foreseen Eilinora's assault on Coruain House. The witch had disabled her father's stone guardians who were in place to warn of impending trouble, and caught Kieran alone and unprotected. The entity that had helped Eilinora seemed to wield even more power than the witch herself possessed. Merrick wondered if Ana had identified it, or gleaned the extent of its powers. Mayhap that was why she'd called to him so desperately from the *ceirtlín.*

Mayhap she sensed the connection growing between him and Jenny and had tried to warn him to keep his distance. If only he'd known . . .

He stayed beside her as she made her trek northward, watching her proceed as though the distance he'd put between them meant naught to her. She was a courageous woman, so focused and determined to make her own way, far from Bresland School, away from him.

His desertion would not destroy her.

Jenny regretted declining Matthew's offer to hire a coach for the trip to the distillery when they walked past terrible slums with crowded, broken-down buildings and suffocating ash pits, where the smells of degraded humanity ran thick. Small children in much worse shape than the Gypsies ran free in the streets. They were poorly clothed and pale-skinned, and had to play among the debris that had fallen from the ancient buildings.

A group of ragtag youths approached them as they headed north. "Ye've got a shilling, ain't you," said the leader, a well-developed boy in his late teens. He was the largest, with sallow skin and big hands and feet. His companions looked like big bullies, too.

"Stand aside and let the lady pass," said Matthew in a civil tone, then he bent slightly and spoke quietly to her, but she could not hear him.

It was clearly not the time to ask him to repeat his words in her good ear.

"Lady? She your doxie, mate?"

"Doona be stupid, lad." He took Jenny's arm and started to move them around the boys, but their challengers did not stand still. They scattered to surround them, and Matthew was outnumbered, eight to one. No one from the vicinity came to give assistance, and even the occasional wagon driver spurred his horse to go quickly past the obvious trouble.

"Let us pass lads, and there could be a few shillings for each of you when we return."

Jenny tensed, certain the young men would attack. She did not doubt that Matthew could hold his own against one, or even four, of these fellows. She'd seen the warrior in him deal with the highwaymen who'd attacked her. But surely he could not win against eight. It was terrifying to think what this vicious gang could do to him . . . to them . . .

Jenny looked up and down the street, but no rescue was coming. She forced the tingle in her chest to snake out and reach for a broken-down wagon, to use it somehow to distract everyone. But the fibers wavered out of control and sent a sudden shower of bricks skittering down the chimneys of the surrounding buildings. A billowing cloud of black smoke descended upon them, choking them as well as hiding them. Matthew released her arm and moved in front of her, pushing her behind him as he spoke to the young men through the black miasma.

Their assailants coughed and rubbed their eyes, but they did not back down, in spite of the thick, suffocating cloud swirling around them.

"'Tis a foolish path you're takin'," Matthew said. Moving so quickly that Jenny hardly saw his hands, he picked up two of the young men at once and tossed them aside. He then delivered blows to two more, who doubled over and ran. The other four followed them, apparently unwilling to test their skills against the big Scot in the midst of a black maelstrom of smoke.

"Let's go, Jenny. Move quickly, before they change their minds." Jenny lifted her skirts and ran. Matthew stayed beside her, holding her arm to steady her as they hastened up the street, away from the smoke that choked the district, and on toward the castle. Once they were in safer territory, Jenny put some distance between them, even as she thanked him for helping her out of danger.

He glanced around. "No' a carriage in sight," he said. "Jenny, lass . . . if another dangerous situation arises, you must promise to do as I say, and quickly."

She gave a halfhearted nod. As long as he insisted on staying with her, she could do worse than trust his judgment. "I will. But you'll have to try to remember to speak into my left ear. I cannot hear from my right."

He stopped abruptly, and Jenny turned to see what had happened. As far as she could tell, there was nothing, though a muscle in his jaw flexed tightly.

"There may have been other times when you thought I was ignoring you, and I apologize," she said formally. "I don't always hear everything."

He started to reach toward her deaf ear, but pulled his hand back abruptly, muttering his favorite Gaelic curse.

Jenny felt as though he'd slapped her. He'd already made it clear that he no longer wanted any intimacy between them. Turning quickly away, she took a deep breath and resumed walking.

"Jenny, wait." He caught up to her and matched her pace, walking at her left side. "Was it always this way? Being half deaf?"

She swallowed the burning sensation in the back of her throat. "It happened at school."

"How? How does a child lose her hearing?"

"When a headmaster . . ." She shook her head. "It does not matter, Matthew. It happened a long time ago and I've adjusted. I should have mentioned it earlier, but I hardly think of it anymore."

She stole a glance up at Matthew's face, but he walked on with his brows furrowed low over his eyes, as though her partial deafness was the worst of their worries and their encounter with the destitute youths in the Lanes had been only a slight inconvenience. Jenny could not help but wonder what had changed since the night before, turning his mood so black.

It could be only one thing.

"Did you . . . Has your memory . . . Have you remembered?" she asked, dreading his reply.

He hesitated, his bearing stiff and forbidding.

He kept his eyes on the street ahead as he answered. "I . . . Our predicament is the same as it was yesterday."

But it wasn't. He'd split them up, taking two hotel rooms. Jenny could not bring herself to ask him about that, not after all they'd shared this past week. If nothing had changed, Matthew would have told the hotel clerk the same story they'd used with the Moffats and Mrs. Welby—that they were a married couple.

Her heartache threatened to choke her. Her breath stuck fast in her chest, and she did not think she could bear another minute beside him, knowing that it was over between them. She glanced around, searching for a place to run, but none of the nearby streets was welcoming, and the Lanes were back the way they'd come.

"Come away now, lass."

She felt him behind her, and he spoke so gently, Jenny could almost believe he'd come back to her.

Almost.

Finding her pendant meant little. She had to get away from him now, before her heart broke.

She turned to flee, hurrying down the street as fast as she could walk. Tears blurred her vision, but she managed to follow a southward path, turning into a street alongside a huge cathedral.

"Jenny!"

She could not bear to face him now, but when he caught her and took hold of her arm, she had no choice.

"We'll find your locket."

"I don't care, Matthew. Harriet can have it."

"I doona understand—"

"Then you're a bigger fool than I!" She tried to yank her arm away, but he would not let her go.

"Jenny, we are so close."

"To the thing that will make it possible for me to survive without you, Matthew. Are you so anxious to help me get it so that you can be free of me?"

"Jenny—"

"You are free already. Go. We have no promises between us. I don't n-need you."

She hated the way her voice quivered, and knew that anger would serve her far better than this pathetic, naïve misery. It would have been so much better if she'd refused his help after leaving the Gypsies. They would not be having this discussion now, and she might have arrived in Carlisle with her heart intact.

His eyes clouded with some emotion Jenny could not identify. She turned away from him, intending to go back to the hotel and collect her bag. She felt colder and emptier than she'd ever felt before.

He stopped her, speaking quietly, dangerously. "Do you no' think I could give you enough gold to keep you for a year or more, lass?"

Jenny took a shaky breath.

"I want you to have your locket back . . . The one thing of value you've ever managed to keep."

She supposed he thought he was being kind, but he could not possibly know how foolishly important she'd allowed him to become. "'Tis not your worry, Matthew. I can manage on my—"

"Come now, Jenny," he said softly. "We're nearly there. Allow me to help you."

Resigned, she let him lead her to the top of Abbey Street, where they took a turn to go outside the city walls. They walked past the workhouse and came upon a dark brick, one-story building with a tall smokestack at the back. Carved into the stonework over the door was the name "Davenport Distilleries." Jenny took a deep breath and went inside, aware that the moment she found Harriet and retrieved her locket, Matthew would feel free to take his leave.

There was no formal foyer inside the building, but the distillery itself rose up just inside the door. It was a large, high-ceilinged room with huge metal vats and a number of men doing some kind of work around them. A tall wooden staircase scaled one wall, its broad second-floor landing leading to two closed doors with frosted windows. One had the word "Manager" on it. The other read, "Accounts." Matthew started up the stairs, and Jenny followed to the landing at the top. She waited beside Matthew as he knocked on the manager's door.

A man in shirt sleeves with a thick mustache opened the door and demanded, "What is it?"

"I'm looking for one of your workers."

"Who's asking?" the fellow demanded.

"Matthew Keating. I'm looking for a man called Lambton. He's . . . er, due to receive a reward."

Jenny let the blatant lie pass, quickly understanding why he'd used such a ruse.

"A reward? For what?"

"That's for me to tell Lambton."

The manager turned and spoke to someone inside. "Jenkins, have we got a Lambton in our employ?"

"No. No Lambton," was the brusque reply from within. "Never did have one, either."

Jenny pushed forward. "Are you certain?" she asked, unsure whether to feel glum or elated. "His sister said he was a rum—that he made rum in Carlisle. Would there be any other—"

"Davenport's the only rum distiller in town. And we don't know of any Lambton." Dismissing them, he started to close the door, but Jenny stopped him.

"I was told specifically that he was a rum dubber. He *must* be employed here."

The man with the mustache looked horrified at first, then his face broke into a grin. "Rum dubber, you say? Then he's a housebreaker, miss. He's got nothing to do with any legitimate business, unless it's to steal from them."

Chapter 10

"**T**hank you, sir," Matthew said, and guided Jenny down the stairs, hurrying when they heard a sudden loud crack and the splintering of wood on the steps.

"It's coming apart, Jenny. Hurry!" Moving quickly, he scooped her up and lifted her, carrying her down the stairs faster than she could have run by herself.

Jenny was surprised the entire staircase did not collapse, but only a few balusters cracked and fell away from the stairs. She and Matthew made it all the way down to the main floor while the men in the office came out to see what had caused the disturbance.

"Are you all right?" called the man they'd just spoken to.

"Aye," Matthew called up to him as he set Jenny down on her feet. "But you'd better have someone reinforce that staircase before you try to come down."

They left the building, but Matthew turned to look at where they'd just been. His brow furrowed in puzzlement, as well it might. There was no earthly reason for those balusters to crack and split away from the staircase, yet Jenny knew she was responsible, since the morning had been one of the worst of her life. She had not seen the silver fibers this time, but she'd felt the tingling in her chest and seen the flicker of sparks on the ground.

Matthew gave a quick shake of his head, as though dismissing the distillery's structural problems, and faced Jenny, taking hold of both her upper arms. "Did I understand the man? Lambton is a thief?"

She shrugged and extricated herself from his grasp. "Harriet said her brother was a rum dubber. I thought she meant he made rum. I didn't realize it was a slang term." She started back down toward the workhouse, gazing absently past Matthew at the huge expanse of the city beyond them.

"There must be ten thousand people in Carlisle. I was a fool to think I could ever find Harriet." She swallowed her dejection and kept walking as Matthew fell into step behind her.

She tried to think how long it had been since she had left Bresland. With or without her locket, she was expected at Darbury merely a fortnight after receiving her confirmation letter. A few days had passed between the date she'd received the letter and her final confrontation with Reverend Usher. She'd lost track of time since she'd met Matthew, but there could not be many more days before she had to report to Darbury.

As they walked past the workhouse, Jenny felt a rising sense of panic. She might lose her governess position if she did not arrive on the specified date. She needed to concern herself with survival, and not some wild chase through Carlisle in search of a burglar's sister.

She had to face the fact that her locket was long gone, and that Matthew no longer had any reason to remain in Carlisle.

He might not remember everything yet, but in all their days together, she'd never seen him brood the way he did now. Some memory had driven a wedge between them.

And Jenny had plenty of experience to know when she was not wanted.

"How do we find a rum dubber?" he asked.

"In a village the size of Kirtwarren, it would be simple. But it cannot be done in a city this size. The search is over, Matthew."

He frowned darkly. "You intend to give up?"

Jenny covered her quivering mouth with one hand, her heart feeling as though it could explode. She had not felt such wretchedness at Mr. Ellis's abandonment, yet she'd known Matthew only a few days. An intense few days.

"Your locket . . . 'Tis all you have of your family." He touched his wrist where he wore his coppery torque, and Jenny was fairly certain that he remembered something of it now. But he said nothing to her. He did not want to tell her what he'd remembered, effectively closing her out of his thoughts and plans. She picked up her pace, nearly running in her haste to be alone with her misery.

"Jenny," he said, quickly catching up. "There must be some way to search for a thief—"

"It's done, Matthew. Finished. Time for me to go to Darbury, and for you—"

"One more try, Jenny. If I can find Lambton, I'm sure I can find your locket. Where would we look for a thief—"

"If he knew where to find Mr. Lambton," she said with frustration, "a magistrate would have put him in the House of Corrections."

"Magistrate? Where do you find such a person?"

Why could he not leave her alone in her misery? "There must be a magistrate somewhere in the city, but I don't see how—"

"Mayhap Lambton has come to this magistrate's attention."

She turned and looked up at him, tamping down the despair that threatened to well up and spill over. "Matthew, there is no p-point—"

"I know Lambton's name. I can ask questions. If he's a thief, do you no' think 'tis likely he's known by the authorities?"

The sorrow in Jenny's eyes cut Merrick deeply. Had he not needed the locket himself, he still would have done everything in his power to retrieve it for her. Yet he knew its recovery would not be sufficient to wipe the anguish from her eyes. He knew that her life had consisted of one loss after the next, yet he could do naught to change that.

He had to leave her, too.

"Matthew." Her throat moved as she swallowed thickly. "I've resigned myself—"

He took her hand and continued on their way. "We'll find it, Jenny. 'Tis my fault you were taken off the Lambton woman's trail. I want to make it up to you."

Her pretty brows rose. "Make it up to me?" she whispered, her chin quivering in distress.

Mo oirg. They'd gone much farther together than his performing a simple favor for her. He'd taken her innocence and declared that she belonged to him. Now he was doing all he could to keep her at arm's length. He could hardly tell her that he was a Druzai sorcerer—a warrior from her antiquity—who'd come to find her locket and take the magical stone within, yet he owed her some kind of explanation.

Matthew pulled her to a stop and moved to face her, taking hold of both her arms. "Jenny, I realized you were right about my memories . . . I doona know what my responsibilities are . . ."

But he did, and they did not include her, at least not beyond making sure that her future held a situation far better than the one that awaited her at Darbury. He knew better than to act directly, having learned on his previous visits to Tuath that subtlety worked best.

Not even the most astute seer could predict every detail about the future, which made overt interference dangerous. Merrick had personally seen that gentle guidance and the occasional magical spell was all that was needed to save the Tuath from themselves.

He'd used subtlety in helping King Arthwyr to establish peace and prosperity within his kingdom. More than six centuries later, he had put himself in a position to *suggest* that King John's barons might force the king to a binding agreement, and then he used a touch of magic to lead the king to Runnymede. And he'd helped prevent a massive, bloody Irish uprising by giving his contemporary Brian Boru the power to unite the Irish Celts, if only temporarily.

None of those tasks had been terribly complicated. Finding the *brìgha*-stone was proving to be a much more important and challenging feat.

Forcing himself to leave Jenny was going to be nearly impossible. She was his, yet he could not claim her as his own. With all his powers and talents, he could not change what the Druzai oracle had prophesied nearly thirty years before.

Once he found Jenny's locket and took the *brìgha*-stone from it, he could risk enough magic to restore her hearing and provide her with security and independence before he took his leave. With luck, contentment and happiness would follow.

What a bastard he'd been all morning, irritable and frustrated now that he remembered his quest and knew the reality of his circumstances. He'd been certain Jenny was his *céile* mate, that they would bond for life, completing each other in the Druzai custom. He did not understand how he could have been so mistaken about his connection to her. Even now, he wanted to be inside her, wanted to take her hard and as fiercely as he'd done the night before.

He sensed the stiffness of her body as they walked together, felt the distance she drove between them.

Merrick muttered a few unsavory curses, in both Druzai and English. 'Twas difficult to comprehend how his physical bond with a Tuath woman could have been so intense. He could think of no Druzai lore or learning on the subject, for Druzai and Tuath had remained separate for more than a millennium, but for his own few, short encounters.

He thought of Sinann and wondered if their mating could ever reach the heights he'd shared with Jenny. He discovered he was not eager to find out.

When they had come within a few paces of the hotel, Merrick stopped Jenny. "I've already paid for your room here, lass. Do me the favor of waiting in your room while I go to the magistrate and ask about Lambton."

She made no reply, but pressed her lips tightly together and headed up the staircase ahead of him. He followed her to her door and unlocked it for her, then stood and watched as she went inside. "I'll come back with news as soon as I—"

Keeping her eyes ahead, she nodded.

"Jenny . . ." He wanted to feel her in his arms, to taste her mouth and lie alongside her, comforting her. But he could offer her naught. Such intimacy would not be fair to either of them. She'd been wise to try to hold him at arm's length after seeing Ana in the *ceirtlín*, but for reasons she would never guess.

Jenny pushed back the curtain of the bedroom window and watched Matthew walk away from the hotel. When he was out of sight, she took a seat on a straight-backed chair across from the bed and tried to clear her mind of all that had happened in the past week. She could spend no more time bemoaning the risk she'd taken with Matthew. She had to report to the master of Darbury on the fifteenth, and as far as she could reckon, it must already be the thirteenth. She needed to leave Carlisle no later than the morrow if she wanted to arrive on time to take the post at Darbury.

Her locket was not recoverable. No matter how Matthew tried to retrieve it, she knew the odds were against his success.

A lump formed in her throat, and the backs of her eyes burned. She felt moisture on her cheeks, but wiped them dry, upset that she'd become such a pitiful gump. She had not wept since Norah's death, refusing to allow herself to become so vulnerable again.

Because it hurt so badly.

She pressed one hand to the center of her chest and took a deep breath as the four walls of the bedroom threatened to close in on her. Sniffling away her tears, she turned her attention to the cursed force within her that had cracked the balusters at the distillery. Jenny had been so upset when she'd learned about Harriet's brother, there was no question that she was responsible for the damage.

But it was controllable. She knew that from the incident at the riverbank after she'd set off alone from the Gypsy camp. She'd seen it again when she and Matthew had been confronted by the ruffians in the Lanes . . . well, nearly controllable that time. She'd intended to knock over the ruined wagon and provide a distraction, but she'd caused the bricks to start crumbling from the chimneys instead.

Concentrating her efforts to produce the familiar hot prickling in her chest, she managed to project the strange, silvery threads toward the bed. She set her jaw and narrowed her eyes, forcing her brain to guide the luminous fibers. Her chest burned and her breathing became tight, but she managed to control the path of the fibers and make them slip under the quilt.

Her mind compelled the threads to pull the quilt back. It was a struggle to maintain control, drawing the strands to the edge of the blanket with her thoughts. She focused her concentration and narrowed her awareness, using the threads like fingers to pull the blanket down, but suddenly she lost her tenuous control over the fibers. They whipped up to the ceiling and bounced down to the desk near the window, slamming into the drawer and pulling it out violently. Tiny yellow sparks flew all over the room, coming to rest on the floor around her.

Jenny broke off in a sweat and sat down hard in the chair, feeling some satisfaction that she was beginning to understand how to control the force within her. Now she needed to discover the means to prevent it from causing accidents like the one at Davenport's Distillery, or the one that had just occurred.

It did not seem to be a matter of tamping down her emotions completely, though that would certainly be a welcome talent when she and Matthew parted. She decided she should be able to recognize the early sensations—the burning and tingling in her chest—and the sense of energy flowing from a point just above her heart. Once she did that, she might be able to stop the silvery threads from rising of their own volition to cause damage to whatever they happened to encounter.

But no matter how much control she gained over the threads, she could not change the inevitable.

The Isle of Coruain, 981

With a suddenness that startled Ana, her breaths flowed from her lungs much more easily. The Odhar's attacks against the protective swathe still continued, but Eilinora's *personal* assault was gone. While the witch's absence was a relief, 'twas also a worry.

"She's gone," Ana said, pushing up from her pallet. Though her legs were not yet fully healed and her limbs felt weak and depleted, at least she could breathe. Her heart could pump normally again.

"Eilinora?"

Ana nodded to the elders who remained beside her at Coruain House. "I can no longer sense her presence."

"Then where has she . . ." Cianán gave a worried glance toward Liam. *"Ainchis ua oirg,* has she gone to find Merrick and Brogan?"

"Aye," said Ana with a worried shudder.

"Your cousins are no fools, *mo curadh,"* said Liam. "The Mac Lochlainn know how to keep themselves concealed."

"But our use of magic comes so naturally," said Cianán. "If they slip up just once—"

"We can only hope that they do no' slip up," Liam retorted.

Cianán began to pace while Ana and the other elders returned their full attention to the protection of Coruain. She dearly hoped her beloved cousins managed to escape the Odhar's notice, or

Coruain would suffer a disaster unlike anything it had ever known. Merrick and Brogan were to have used assumed names so the Odhar would not inadvertently stumble upon Mac Lochlainns in Tuath, and they were to use no magic to draw an Odhar hunter to them.

But so many things could happen. If an Odhar seer had located the *brìgha*-stones, Eilinora's path might very well cross those of Merrick and Brogan, for they would find themselves searching in the same territories. Or the witch might be able to recognize them through some other means, in some way they had not anticipated.

While Ana used the greater part of her powers to shield Coruain, she had not sufficient energy to try to see Brogan and Merrick. Even if she did, she could do naught to help them. Her cousins were entirely alone in their quest for the blood stones.

Carlisle, March 1826

The hotel clerk gave Merrick directions to the house of the magistrate, a prominent man named Albert Denison. He walked a few blocks through streets that were vastly different from the Lanes, to Denison's house. After being admitted by a servant, he was led ceremoniously into a richly appointed study.

A well-dressed woman was coming out of the room at the same time, with the man of the house right behind her. Touching the small of her back,

Denison gave her a kiss on the side of her neck. She gave a playful gasp, then a laugh, and went her way, leaving Merrick feeling as though he'd been coldcocked. The small gesture of playful affection between husband and wife was something he might have enjoyed with Jenny . . . but Sinann was a dignified member of the elder class who would have certain expectations of a noble husband.

He blew out a deep breath and faced Denison, a smiling gentleman with a thick dark beard, wearing a gray suit of clothes, similar to those Merrick wore. Merrick introduced himself, finally using the name he and Brogan had agreed on before they'd left Coruain. He shook hands with the magistrate and took the seat he indicated. "What brings you to Carlisle, Mr. Locke?"

"I'm looking for a man—a known thief."

"Aren't we all, then?" Denison replied. "Er, looking for them, I mean."

Merrick gave a nod. "He has a sister by the name of Harriet Lambton. Beyond that, I know nothing of him."

"What is your complaint?"

"'Tis actually the man's sister who stole something of value from my . . ." How should he refer to Jenny? He slid his hands down his trews and told the same lie he'd used to take their rooms at the hotel. ". . . my sister."

"And you think you might be able to get it back?"

"I'd hoped that by finding some trace of Lambton, we might locate the sister."

"Lambton. You believe that's the brother's name as well?"

"As far as we know, the woman is unmarried, so I assume so."

Denison opened a drawer of his desk and took out a blank sheaf of paper, on which he wrote one line. He dried the ink, then folded the paper. "Take this to the town hall and ask for Adam Phelps. He's a clerk in the law office—quite an efficient man—who might be able to help you. As for myself, I have no particular recollection of any Lambton."

Merrick thanked the magistrate and took his leave, again catching sight of Mrs. Denison in the foyer with two pretty young children. All three were putting on coats to go out. 'Twas no wonder Denison's mood was one of smiling contentment with such a loving wife and comely children. Merrick would surely feel the same if only . . .

He closed off that line of thought and took another short walk, which brought him to the building where the town's business was transacted. Asking for Phelps at the door, he handed the official the paper given him by Mr. Denison, and was ushered down a wide hall. A number of people loitered in the corridor, some sitting on chairs, waiting for appointments, others looking at newspapers or gazing absently out the windows.

At the back of the building was a stark office with Phelps's name painted on the door. Merrick went inside, introduced himself, and restated his purpose. In a starkly businesslike manner, Phelps left the office for a few minutes, and soon returned with a stack of papers.

The clerk took a seat behind his desk, leaned forward in his chair, and started leafing through the pages. "We keep files, although they are not always complete. I make no promises here, Mr. Locke."

'Twould be so easy for Merrick to use magic to search the city for Lambton, or even to sift through the clerk's stack of papers. But he remained patient, and waited for Phelps to complete his search. He needed to focus his full attention on finding Lambton and his sister, and be scrupulous not to use any magic in doing so. He could not believe how careless he'd been before regaining his memory, using the magic that had come so naturally to him.

He was fortunate, so far, that Eilinora's hunters had not located any magical sparks and confronted him. Surely, by now, the witch had discovered that one of the *brìgha*-stones was hidden somewhere near or in Carlisle, in this time period. And as she searched for it, she would be keeping watch for signs of any Druzai about. She would not want any interference.

Merrick's use of magic had put Jenny at risk. He did not want to think what Eilinora might do to her while she wielded his father's scepter. The chieftain's staff was the most powerful talisman in all of Coruain. Used by Eilinora or by the entity that had freed her, it could only have devastating results. Merrick felt a renewed urgency to find Lambton and get the blood stone from his sister.

As Phelps paged through the stack of reports, the man picked out one particular sheaf and then another, setting them aside while he finished going through each and every page in the stack. He finally took the two papers he'd chosen and turned them on the desk to face Merrick.

"There are two named Lambton. The first is Jack, aged twenty-six, a stocky little fellow by his description, and a known burglar."

Merrick looked at the notes of the cases Jack Lambton had been accused of. Then he made a mental note of the location of the last house where he'd been known to stay. "You've tried to arrest him, obviously."

"Oh aye. Had a number of complaints, but he seems a slippery one." He pointed to an entry at the bottom of the page. "Here's his wife. Says she doesn't know where he is, either."

"Do you believe her?"

Phelps shrugged. "Who knows? He might stop in every now and then. Long enough to get another bairn on her. She's got four or five already."

Merrick turned his attention to the other Lambton. Frank. The description was of a taller man with white-blond hair, a year older than Jack.

"This one is an arsonist, too?" he asked.

"Who knows? He's a bad actor all the way 'round."
Phelps pointed to several other entries on the page.
"Had some education by the looks of this report, but
turned to murder, vandalism, inciting riots—"

"Like the one near here last night?"

The clerk raised an eyebrow. "You heard about
that?"

"My . . . er, sister and I got caught in it."

"Big, strapping Scotsman like you wouldn't
have been hurt. But best to keep your sister off the
streets after dark. I suspect the fools will not be
stupid enough to come out again tonight, not with
the militia at the ready."

Merrick studied the report on Frank Lambton.
"No one's seen him since this last accusation of
murder?"

"No, or the constables would have brought him
in. Could be he's left town."

Which would be disastrous for Merrick. Time
was running out.

"I'll send the constables 'round to the places
where he's known to hang about. Maybe—"

"We'd like to find his sister, just to ask her about
the item she stole from us. Mayhap we'll be able to
recover it. Where are these houses?"

"Down in the Lanes. Trust me, you don't want
to go there. Let me look into it." Merrick followed
Phelps to the door. "Where can I find you if we
uncover any information?"

"The Queen's Hotel, but I would ask that you
delay your inquiries. I'd like to surprise Lambton
myself, if you catch my meaning."

Phelps nodded. The two men shook hands once again, and Merrick went out toward the front of the building, encountering two tall men dressed in black. They were the same two constables who'd come 'round the Gypsy camp, looking for Jenny. The older man was with them, too, his features harsh and angular. Usher.

Merrick picked up a discarded newspaper and took a seat on one of the chairs.

"We'll not get far here, posing as constables of the law," said one of the men as they approached.

Usher ignored his cohort and kept walking, his stride purposeful, his expression arrogant. His greatcoat flapped behind him as he walked, and his suit was rumpled, clearly not having been changed in days. By the bits of straw on his waistcoat, Matthew figured he must have found some rather poor lodgings over the last few days. Still, he wore a stiffly starched collar, his black stock was neatly tied, and his watch chain and fob were securely fastened at his waist.

"Doubtful we'll find her here, anyway," said the second man as they walked past Merrick. He stood up and followed them.

"The farmer and his wife said the little whore had been on her way to Carlisle," said Usher. "Obviously up to no good."

"You know, all this is getting beyond my talents, Usher," said one of the men. "I'll take my money now, if you please."

"I don't like it, either. Even Mr. Ellis said she was not likely to steal—"

The headmaster made a harsh sound and tossed a few coins at the men, letting the money scatter all over the floor. Then he proceeded down the hall, his stride as regal as a high chieftain's, and turned into an office not far from the one Merrick had just vacated.

Chapter 11

J enny paced the short length of her small hotel room and decided to leave for Darbury now. No doubt she could learn the estate's direction from the hotel clerk or someone else in town, and it was early enough to walk the few miles. It seemed the best course of action, to leave now, before Matthew returned and told her he could not find Harriet, and that it was time for them to separate.

Or worse, that he planned to take her to Darbury himself. She did not think she could bear it, not after all they'd been through together, after the intimacies they'd shared.

She knew by the change in his attitude that he remembered something. It could be that parts of his memory were still missing, but Jenny was certain he knew something about his past. And he did not want to tell her what it was.

She could guess.

Pressing a hand against the center of her chest to ease the ache, Jenny opened her travel bag and took out her Bible, searching through the pages

until the letter from Darbury fell out. She un-
folded the missive, checking the date she was to
report for her new post. She'd been correct, and
only needed to verify today's date and the location of the estate. Her understanding was that it
lay north of Carlisle, but only a few miles away. It
should be an easy walk.

She repacked her bag and closed it securely,
then looked in the drawer of the writing table for
a pen and ink, for she could not go without at least
leaving a note for Matthew. Sinking down into
the chair, she realized she did not know what to
write. She considered telling him to come to Darbury for her if he found he had no binding ties in
Scotland.

Yet in all her years at Bresland, she'd never asked
anyone for anything. She'd borne the cold, uncaring environment and all her punishments, aware
that there was no one to help her. She would not
beg Matthew to remember her once he returned
to his life.

She took a deep, quivering breath. She was not
a beggar, nor was she a coward. Much worse had
happened to her than living through a difficult
farewell.

She tossed the pen on the desk and pulled on
her cloak. Her small room here was too similar to
the one she would likely be given at Darbury. In
spite of Matthew's wishes, she left it and walked
down to the street where they'd been caught up
in the previous night's disturbance. There were
shops as well as open stalls, and she wandered

through them, avoiding the tobacconist's shop. She could not avoid thinking through all that had happened in the past few days and concluding that Matthew had recovered enough of his memory to know where he belonged. It seemed he was not in any great hurry to return there, else he would not be so determined to retrieve her pendant.

Jenny didn't know why he bothered.

By late afternoon, a cold drizzle started to fall, enough to deter her walk to Darbury. She would just have to spend some of her money on a hackney coach to take her there later, after she made her farewell to Matthew in person.

She shrank into the warmth of her cloak and hood, and hurried back to the hotel. Loath to spend any more time in the cold and lonely room, she remained in the lobby, where servants had built up the fires in the grates.

Merrick bristled with anger as Usher disappeared behind the door of the office. There had to be some reason the headmaster was so intent upon finding Jenny and taking her back to Bresland, even hiring his own "constables" to do so. Bardo's suggestion that Jenny knew something damaging about the man rang true, although whatever it was, Jenny seemed not to be aware of it. Mayhap Usher believed she'd heard something that he'd rather keep private.

Mayhap he was unaware of the damage he'd done to Jenny's hearing.

Merrick did not like to think of the cold, bleak

existence Jenny had known at Bresland, and swore viciously at the thought of the blow Usher must have given her to destroy her hearing. 'Twas all Merrick could do not to drag the man from the office where he'd gone, and show him a thing or two about discipline.

The two hired constables left the building, and Merrick kept an eye on them as they mounted their horses and rode away. Without the two cohorts, 'twould be so easy to isolate Usher and deal with him in the same manner he'd handled wee Jenny for so many years. But a mere thrashing would be too lenient. The man deserved a much more far-reaching punishment. Merrick intended to give it due consideration.

He kept an eye on the office where Usher had his business and came to his feet when the door opened and the headmaster came out. Merrick could not resist confronting the man. He stepped into Usher's path, his chest burning to wreak havoc on the man, there and then. He controlled the urge to use magic on him.

"Stand aside," Usher said.

Merrick did not move. He looked into the man's eyes and tried to gauge whether 'twas pure evil that drove him, or some kind of madness. He quickly saw that it was utter malice that dwelled in Usher's heart, and decided to let the headmaster stew over the possibility that his secrets—whatever they were—were about to be exposed.

"Your reckoning will soon be upon you, man," Merrick said.

The headmaster's pale cheeks went bright red, and Merrick knew he'd hit upon a nerve. He wasted no further time with the man, but walked away, taking his leave of the town building and Usher, who stood fast.

Reassured by the knowledge that Jenny remained safely inside the hotel, Merrick gave no further thought to his plans for Usher. For now, he hoped the headmaster spent several uneasy hours wondering what was known about him.

He turned his attention to the search for Harriet Lambton, considering the addresses in Phelps's reports. Whether they were actually valid had yet to be seen. Merrick intended to check for himself, but he could not do it dressed as he was, as a target for the kind of ruffians they'd clashed with earlier in the Lanes. He walked toward the shops in the center of town and encountered a rag-and-bone man. Pawing through his cart, he looked for a jumper and trews that he could wear, clothes that would not set him apart from every other man in the Lanes.

"I'll need shoes," he said to the rag collector after he found some old clothes that looked as though they would fit him.

"Nae so easy to find, mate," said the dealer, who gaped at Matthew's big feet. "C'mon—I'll take ye 'round to a shop where ye can buy shoes at the second hand."

'Twas not easy to locate a pair of shoes that did not pinch Merrick's feet, but he eventually found some that were workable. He paid the shopkeeper to wrap his good suit and keep it for him until he returned, and dressed in the old clothes. But for their rough texture and drab colors, the brown trews and loose gray jumper were more like his Coruain clothes than the fine suit he'd been wearing all this time.

Setting off for the Lanes on foot, Merrick realized he might locate Harriet Lambton right away. And if he found the locket and the stone within, he should return immediately to the Astar Columns and back through time to Coruain.

Yet the thought of leaving Jenny alone and waiting for him at the hotel was disquieting. He owed her some explanation of his actions, even if he had to lie about having a wife in Scotland. At least that was a tale she could believe. 'Twas one she already believed.

Merrick went up Fisher Street and turned into Rosemary Lane. He saw a number of unsavory characters sitting on broken-down chairs in dried-up gardens, with naught to do but watch the foot traffic. But there were no gangs of youths looking for trouble. Stopping in the midst of the debris on the street, he tossed a coin to one of the men and asked if he knew where to find Blue Bell Lane.

After receiving directions, he hiked deeper into the poor district, where houses and shops were so crowded together, 'twas difficult to breathe. He passed an old church whose walls were crumbling, though two stone statues of ancient statesmen in robes remained intact. A small black sìthean leaped from nowhere onto the shoulder

of one of the statues, making Merrick suspect
the stone statesmen were actually dragheens.
He wondered how they'd managed to escape the
blight that had penetrated the neighborhood, and
why they'd stayed.

"Begone, sìthean!" he said in a hushed tone.

One of the dragheens blinked its eyes and
gazed directly at Merrick as the sìthean squealed
and jumped down, running away into a ruined
building nearby.

Merrick looked up at the dragheen, glad to find
allies here. He'd known some of the stone guardians had remained in Tuath after the Druzai
exodus to Coruain, but thought it fortuitous to
find these two who might actually be able to help
him.

"Guardian?"

"Aye," said a crackling voice. "But who are you
to ask? *To know?*"

The second dragheen merely tipped his head
slightly and waited for Merrick's reply.

"I am Merrick Mac Lochlainn, son of Kieran of
Coruain."

"'Tis himself," said the first dragheen to the
other.

"Aye, Doughal."

"What do you mean?" Merrick asked, carefully
looking 'round for anyone who might be lurking
nearby to witness his exchange with the two stone
creatures. Dragheens of various forms were not
unusual on Coruain, but here within Tuath lands,
they kept entirely to themselves, maintaining a

secret presence. They moved slowly, if at all, as was their wont, speaking to no one but each other, and not with words.

"We know of the Mac Lochlainn," said one, his voice rough with disuse.

"We know of Merrick and Brogan and the search for the stones," said the other.

Merrick frowned, deep in thought. "How could you know this?"

The first dragheen made a low sound. "'Twas foretold."

"By whom?" he queried, surprised that the stone creatures already knew of him.

"'Tis not known."

"An ancient oracle foretold it," said Doughal, contradicting the other.

"A Druzai oracle?" Merrick asked.

"Mayhap, m'lord. Or a powerful seer. 'Twas long ago, well before e'en yer time."

"We are at yer service, m'lord."

"Do you know where the blood stone is hidden?" Merrick asked.

"Alas, m'lord," said one dragheen.

"Torin and I know naught."

"And the words of the oracle . . . or seer? Do you know what was said?"

A harsh sound came from both creatures in unison, and Merrick knew they would say no more about any prophecy they had heard. 'Twas the way of the dragheen. They were benign creatures who lived according to their own rules, whispering suggestions to the minds of the unwary, and alerting their allies of impending dangers. There had always been dragheen contingents guarding Coruain House, but Eilinora had managed to destroy every last one of those who guarded Kieran before they could give warning to the chieftain. Merrick believed the witch had intended to flaunt her exceptional mastery over them.

"I am looking for a woman called Harriet Lambton. Do you know of her?"

Torin answered, his voice the harsh sound of gravel trickling across stone. "Nay, m'lord."

"Mayhap you've heard of a man with the same name? Jack or Frank Lambton?"

"Aye. These we know."

"No' brothers, m'lord," said Torin.

"Cousins, mayhap," Doughal remarked.

"Or no relation at all."

"Please," Merrick interjected, his patience depleted by the dragheens' slow banter. "What do you know of these Lambtons?"

The dragheens turned still and silent as two young girls wearing dark shawls walked past, looking warily at Merrick. He gave a nod and bent down to tie the lace of his worn and uncomfortable work shoe. When the girls had passed, Doughal gave him a general idea of where to find each of the Lambton men. While there was no guarantee that either man was connected to Harriet Lambton, they were the only clues Merrick had to follow.

He took his leave and followed the dragheen's directions to an adjacent crowded lane of shabby houses where the smell of privies and cesspits was nearly overpowering. Many of the houses were deserted, and there were narrow, dark alleyways at intervals where rats and other vermin scurried, unchecked.

He knocked on the first door specified by the dragheens. A filthy, poorly clad child pulled it open, but he was pushed aside by a work-worn woman who closed the door but for a crack. Through that small space, she spoke curtly to Merrick. "Aye," she stated harshly. "What's yer business?"

"Looking for Jack Lambton. I've got something for him."

"There's nae tha' any Scotsman would have that he'd want, eh?" said the woman.

"What about his sister? Is she here?"

The woman's expression went blank. "Sister? Jack's got nae sister."

Merrick tipped his hat and backed away. "Then I am verra sorry to have bothered you, ma'am."

As he picked his way through the littered alley to the next location, a fellow with curly dark hair ran past, bumping into him. Merrick felt his pocket and realized the lad had taken the coins he'd stashed there.

Merrick thought of postponing his search for Lambton to go after the thief, but the lad clearly had greater need of the money than Merrick. There was much more back at the hotel, and a few more coins in his other pocket, too.

Besides, he needed to find Lambton. The *brìgha*-stone might be very near, signifying an end to his quest.

Retracing his steps, Merrick found the place where the dragheens had told him to look for Frank, but it was a ruin of a building that looked uninhabitable. Merrick found no one inside, and doubted the place had been more than a deserted hovel for a very long time.

Sure he could find someone else to ask about Lambton's whereabouts, Merrick left the spot and moved on, sighting a seedy tavern on the far side of a row of run-down wooden buildings. As it started to rain, he walked over to the place and went inside, where a number of rough-looking men stood at the bar, drinking. Merrick joined them.

He ordered a mug of ale and turned to the drinkers next to him. None of them fit Lambton's description. "Would any of you know of a man called Lambton? Frank Lambton?"

The men pointedly ignored him and continued talking among themselves. 'Twould be so easy to use a blathering charm to loosen their tongues, but if Eilinora or any of her minions were nearby, they might hear the magic in his voice, and see the sparks his magic would cause. He was not going to make that mistake again.

"I've got a profitable proposition for Lambton, if anyone knows him . . ."

"Nae Lambton hereabouts," said one of them.

"Is that so?"

Each man leveled a threatening glare in Merrick's direction, as though 'twould take but one more word to incite them to pounce on him. But Merrick towered over every last one of them, exuding the confidence of a man who had no fear.

And he was becoming just frustrated enough not to mind cracking a few heads together. Being robbed so easily did not bode well, nor did missing Lambton at every turn.

"I found Jack's wife," Merrick said. "But Jack is no' the Lambton I seek. I'm guessing someone will know where Frank might be."

He lifted his ale and turned to size up the rest of the tavern. The interior was dank and dark, lit by an inadequate chandelier hanging from the center of the ceiling. There were scarred wooden tables and benches in the room, and a few chairs scattered haphazardly. Not a single sconce or candle brightened the place, nor was there a fire burning in the hearth. A number of grimy paintings in heavy frames hung on the walls, and one or two women plied their unsavory trade in the darkened corners.

Merrick put down his mug. "'Tis a pity you'll no' partake of the reward for finding Lambton."

He went outside and started to walk away when a woman in a thin woolen cloak stopped him under the leaky eaves of a nearby hovel. "I heard ye inside. Looking fer Frank."

"You know him?"

"Aye. Everyone knows Frank. But he's nae one t' make himself known t' strangers."

"Where can I find him?"

She was a pretty lass, though poverty and hard living was taking its toll. A colorful bruise on one cheekbone illustrated the rough living she made, and the whites of her eyes were tainted a bloody red. She held out her grimy hand, palm up. "What's it worth t' ye?"

"Tell me how to find him and I will be verra generous."

She took back her hand. "He likes t' lasses. New blood is wha' he wants."

Merrick noted that her hair was light-colored, and he figured her skin would be fair, too, if only it met with water and soap on occasion.

"No' you, then?"

"Nay." She touched her injured cheek. "He's nae interested in me nae more."

"You're suggesting I lure him to the tavern with a woman unknown to him?"

She shrugged and held her hand out once again. "I jus' know what I know. What ye do wit' it be yer own business."

Merrick looked down the lane for signs of an available woman, even though there was unlikely to be any "new blood" about. He looked back at the girl.

"Bring her 'round to the Old Scratch," she said, "and Frank will hear about it. Like a bee t' honey he'll be."

*   *   *

Matthew finally came into the hotel lobby, so tall and handsome it made Jenny's heart skip just to see him walking toward her as though there were nothing on his mind but her. But she knew differently, and had only waited long enough to tell him she was leaving for Darbury.

"Jenny, lass. Come with me," he said, shifting the parcels he carried so that he had a free hand to take her elbow and escort her upstairs. "We're going to find your friend Harriet tonight."

"No, Matthew, I've already—"

"We're verra close, Jenny, lass. Tonight, we'll have your locket."

She let him escort her into her room, dismayed that it took but a word and his slightest touch to draw her into the quest she no longer cared about. She memorized each of his features, down to the dimple that appeared in his cheek when he spoke. She inhaled deeply of his scent and let the timbre of his voice roll through her.

"There are two men called Lambton who are known thieves."

"Which one do we want?"

"Unfortunately, 'tis Frank. The other one has no sister, but a wife and children. He would likely be much easier to locate."

He started to unwrap the smaller of the two packages, and Jenny did not have the heart to tell him her locket had lost its importance. He was so determined to do this one thing for her, and she could not bring herself to separate from him just yet.

"How do you plan to . . ." She saw a bright blue dress rolled tightly in the wrapper, and looked up at Matthew with questioning eyes.

"I know 'tis not your usual fashion."

She smoothed down the skirt of the somber black gown she wore. Lacking in style and color, it was just like every other speck of clothes she'd worn since her arrival at Bresland, with the exception of the colorful Gypsy skirt and blouse Rupa had given her. Lifting the garish blue dress from the bed, she saw that it had no sleeves to speak of, and the neckline dipped so low it was absolutely indecent. He could not possibly mean for her to wear it.

She sat down in the chair across from the bed.

"Jenny, listen to me."

"Surely this is not for me?"

"I spent some time in the Lanes, searching for Frank Lambton."

Jenny wrinkled her nose with distaste at the memory of the district where they'd been accosted on their way to the distillery.

Matthew took a seat on the bed, his demeanor different from what it had been earlier. The search pleased him and seemed to draw them close again, but Jenny knew better than to trust it.

"Frank Lambton runs in the opposition direction when anyone asks about him, and he's got friends who shield him. But I found that he frequents a public house up in a place they call Feathers Court. I'm hoping to lure him out."

"Lure him . . . ?" Jenny's eyes wandered to the dress, and she realized what he was asking. "You want . . . I'm . . . bait?"

"Believe me, I tried all afternoon to find him, but he managed to elude me at every turn. And his sister is just as bad. Worse. No one has ever even heard of her."

Jenny swallowed and nearly refused.

But she could not, not when her locket might actually be within reach. Besides, the little charade he proposed would delay her departure for only another hour or two.

"What do you want me to do?"

Merrick stood abruptly and went to the window, dragging one hand across his face. Now that he'd spoken it aloud, the idea of setting Jenny up to draw Lambton out rankled. He'd left the Old Scratch and found a concealed place where he could watch for the bastard to join his cronies at the tavern. But the rum dubber never wandered into Feathers Court.

Merrick knew he had no choice. He'd gone back to the secondhand shop and changed clothes, then picked up the only vaguely suitable dress that was to be had, and bought it for Jenny. When he'd seen her in the lobby, something inside him had shifted.

"Mayhap 'tis no' such a good idea after all, lass." There was no guarantee they would find Harriet even if her brother *did* turn up.

He started to put away the wretched little gown, but Jenny stilled his hands, her expression one of resignation. "'Tis the only way to find Harriet and retrieve my pendant?"

He nodded. "I canna think of any other way." Not without magic. His visions of Ana indicated that the situation on Coruain was dire, and he'd wasted too much time already.

"Then we have no choice, do we?"

Merrick's chest swelled with deep respect and admiration for this courageous lass who possessed no magic to protect her. As frightened as she was, she did not let her fear prevent her from going along with his dangerous plan.

"From what I gathered this afternoon, Lambton will go for any new female who comes 'round."

"You think he'll show himself for m-me?" she asked, as though she could not believe a man would cross the burning fires of Hades for her.

Mo oirg, he would cross the fires of Hades and battle all the Odhar for her.

He closed his eyes and tamped down the rising tide of emotions he had no right to feel. "Aye, lass," he said. She was not Druzai, and he had his duty to his people.

"If you dress in that"—he gestured to the revealing gown—"and go to the Old Scratch, Lambton will turn up."

Jenny paled.

"Ach, Jenny. I know 'tis a poor plan," he said, deciding he would not put her at risk, no matter what the cost. He had to find some other way. "Forget that I—"

"No, Matthew. I can do it."

He jabbed his fingers through his hair and muttered a curse. He wanted to take her into his arms and tell her they need not go through with his plan, but he could not. He had no choice but to get the blood stone, and he had to return to Coruain. Alone. The plan to use Jenny to lure Lambton and find his sister through him was the best one—the only one.

"What do I . . . H-how am I to . . ."

She was so perfect, she would need to do naught to attract the man. "You'll go inside the tavern and walk up to the bar. Order a drink. Smile and appear to be . . ."

Turning away, he rubbed his hand across the lower half of his face in frustration. *Ainchis ua oirg*, he did not think he could watch Jenny offer herself as bait for a low character like Lambton. His mouth went dry at the thought of her walking into that filthy tavern, to be eyed by the dense ruffians and drunkards at the bar.

"Jenny. *Moileen*." Ach, but he should not call her that. She was not his Druzai mate. She could be naught to him.

And yet he had to use her to get the blood stone, else Ana and countless others would die.

"I should appear to be what, Matthew?" Her pretty throat moved as she swallowed thickly, and he could barely suppress the urge to press his lips to the pulse that fluttered there.

"Appear to be a comely lass waiting for her lover," he said, his voice sounding harsh to his own ears. "I'll be nearby, wearing these." He opened the second package and showed her the rough trews and jumper he'd worn all afternoon. "No one will touch you, Jenny. I swear it."

He was loath to leave her alone, but he needed to regain some objectivity. He carried the old clothes to his own room across the hall, but 'twas a cold and empty place without Jenny.

Bringing Sinann's face to mind, he tried to imagine her, instead of Jenny, waiting for him in that simple Tuath room, ready to execute his dangerous plan. But he could not.

Sinann was the sorceress most likely to help him deal with the current crisis when he returned to Coruain. Months ago, his father and the elders had urged him to take the beautiful sorceress as his mate. But he had not done so, partly because of Ana's quietly voiced reservations, citing Sinann's apparent disinterest in Druzai affairs.

Merrick had not objected to her propensity for playing riddle games and working complex puzzles with the other noble idlers of Coruain. Merrick had enjoyed the occasional *crìoch-fàile* puzzle and was quite good at them. But there were far more important occupations for the Druzai high chieftain and his mate.

Now he wondered how Sinann could be at the heart of their struggle for survival.

How he could ever call her *céile* mate.

Merrick dressed in the old clothes, then removed the thin band that held his hair at his nape. He left his room, reminding himself of the impor-

tance of his success with Lambton. He could not
let all that he had come to feel for Jenny distract
him from his purpose. She let him into her room
after his quick knock.

The sight of her in the candlelight took his
breath away. The bright, shiny blue cloth of the
dress left her shoulders and the slopes of her
breasts bare. Drawn in tight at her waist, it hugged
her hips and legs. His cock sprang to life at the
memory of all that the gown concealed, and all
the pleasures they'd shared, arousing him to the
point of pain.

"Are you all right?" she asked, trying ineffectu-
ally to cover her chest with her hands. "I know I'm
not very—"

"No, lass. You are . . . stunning."

She blushed pink and turned her back to him.

"You needn't give false compliments, Matthew.
I know my shortcomings."

"I'm no' ly—"

"The buttons run down the back of the bodice.
I couldn't reach all of them."

The fine skin of her back was exposed in the
narrow vee created by the opening in the gown.
Merrick's hands itched to touch her. He wanted to
take her to the bed and make love to her there, to
tell her that all would be well. Though he knew
better, he could not help himself from pressing his
lips to the slight hollow at the side of her neck.

Chapter 12

She sighed deeply when he slipped his hands under the edges of the gown and pushed the bodice down to her waist, pulling her back against his hard arousal, and he knew she was not as indifferent to him as she tried to let on. Her breasts were barely concealed under her thin white shift, and her nipples pebbled against it. Merrick struggled for breath, for the control he needed to keep himself from cupping their fullness, from laying her on the bed and showing her how irresistible she was.

Using all the restraint he could muster, he drew the sleeves back up her arms, sliding them over her shoulders.

"We canna," he said, the truth of his words hitting him forcefully. He quickly fastened the buttons down her back and put some distance between them. "I need to help you find the locket and then . . ."

"You'll return to your wife in Scotland."

"Jenny . . ."

Abruptly, she gathered up her cloak and threw

it over her shoulders. Keeping her head down, she spoke soberly. "We should go, don't you think?"

No, he did not want to leave. But prudence won out, and they left the hotel by a side entrance to avoid being noticed in their shabby attire by the hotel staff. Merrick hired a coach to take them close to the Lanes, and from there, they walked. He wanted to take her hand, to turn 'round and get her back to the quiet warmth and safety of the hotel. But he could not delude himself. This was the only way to find Lambton.

Jenny did not cower as they walked, nor did she bear the same beaten-down appearance as the other women he'd seen in the city. But she looked entirely too vulnerable. Merrick had no doubt he could protect her from Lambton or any other ruffian who approached her.

But he vowed to use magic to keep her safe if it became necessary, and damn the consequences. He would deal with Eilinora or any other Odhar if they showed themselves.

"You'll need to go in alone," Merrick said. "We canna give the impression of being together."

"Where will you be?"

"Close behind you, but I'll act as though I doona know you."

They walked past the dragheens near the church, and Merrick gave them an imperceptible shake of his head. He sensed that Jenny's nerves were raw enough without having these stone creatures speaking to her. They continued on, heading into Feathers Court.

"Look." He pointed to the row of empty buildings, not far from their destination. "'Tis possible we'll become separated, and if we do, I want you to turn into this passageway. Go 'round to the back and hide inside the building." He did not mention the rats.

"Where will you be, Matthew?"

"I'll be following Frank Lambton."

She shivered perceptibly and pulled her cloak tight. "I've never been inside a public house, Matthew. I'm not sure exactly what I should—"

He put his hands on her shoulders. "When you go to the bar, just ask for a mug of ale." 'Twould be better for her to ask the men at the bar to buy for her, but he could not let her face that. He'd given her some coins, so he knew she had sufficient money, but not so much as to attract the wrong kind of attention. "Take the drink to a table in the center of the room. Doona go into any dark corners."

She nodded. "Then what?"

"You wait. Take your shawl down from your head so your hair is uncovered." And let the whoresons at the bar peruse her bare shoulders and soft fullness of her breasts. "*Mo oirg,*" he muttered under his breath, wishing for the thousandth time there was some other way to draw Lambton out.

Jenny gave a quick nod and turned to walk down to the tavern alone.

"Jenny," he called quietly after her, "you may no' see me, but I'll be nearby. Doona be afraid in there."

* * *

With a mug of ale in her hand, Jenny turned around and searched for a likely spot to perch. The only light in the place came from a few sputtering candles in a dusty, old iron chandelier that hung from the center of the ceiling. Her feet stuck to the floor, and as she walked to the table, she was tempted to ask for a cloth to wipe it down first. Hell would freeze over before she actually drank from the mug given her by the barkeep.

Silence had descended on the place when she'd come in, and the men at the bar did not resume their talk, even after Jenny took her seat. She avoided looking at them, preferring to glance around the room. But when she saw the reason Matthew had warned her to stay away from the dark corners, she blushed hotly. And nearly panicked.

What if one of those ruffians dragged her into a corner and forced her to her knees to—

The door creaked open and Matthew came in. Relief flooded through Jenny, even though he did not come near her. He stayed at the bar and started talking to the patrons, without mentioning Frank Lambton. The men did not answer him, but kept their attention on Jenny.

Their watery gazes made her skin crawl.

She remembered Matthew's instructions, to take off her cloak and appear as though she were waiting for a lover. Lowering the hood of her cloak, she found she could not make herself remove it, not while wearing the revealing gown underneath. Instead, she opened the fastening at the neck and pulled the edges apart to some degree, but not off her shoulders.

One of the men at the bar left his place and approached her. "Eh, dolly lass—ye be lookin' fer a man t' take away yer worries?"

Jenny forced herself to keep her expression neutral, or even a bit aloof as she looked at the filthy drunkard with his foul breath and missing teeth. Sending a silent prayer of pity for the man's poor wife, she thanked heaven that she'd at least received an education at Bresland and would never have need to rely upon such a man for her livelihood.

"Not the likes of you," she said, and turned away in disgust.

"Why, ye little—"

"Watch it, Kip," said another man. "This toffee-nosed bitch be fresh meat. Ye know the Gaffer'll want first crack at 'er."

Kip growled and stepped away, leaving Jenny to wonder who the Gaffer was. The second man sat down across from her. His face was greasy, and he'd tied what was left of his thin hair into a queue at the back of his neck. He still had most of his teeth, but they were jagged and brown.

"Werst t' from?" he asked. "We've nae seen ye afore."

"My business, sir."

"Oh, so high-and-mighty," barked the man, lifting his chin and holding his nose in a parody of Jenny's superior attitude. The rest of the men in the tavern laughed and slapped one another's backs, adding their own mockery to his.

Jenny cast a quick glance toward Matthew and saw his dark expression. He was going to come to her defense if she didn't do something, and then they might never find Frank Lambton. She stood abruptly. "Maybe not so high-and-mighty, but certainly too good for the likes of you!"

She hoped she'd managed to do enough to attract Harriet's brother to the tavern, but was too nervous to sit still. "And who is the Gaffer, anyway?"

"I am," came the answer from the entryway.

He was a large man with hair the color of sun-bleached straw, same as Harriet. And as he came into the tavern, all the other patrons moved aside to give him the choicest place at the center of the bar. But he did not move. He stood still and let his small, pale eyes wander over Jenny's body.

A fine stubble of reddish-blond hair covered his chin and cheeks, and an angry red gash graced the bridge of his nose. His mouth was a thin, sneering line of implacability. Jenny had no doubt he was Harriet's brother.

Now that she'd drawn him out, she wondered what Matthew was going to do with him. They hadn't discussed what the plan would be, once they found him.

"I've heard of you," Jenny said, though her knees were knocking together under her skirts. She did not want to look at Matthew, afraid he might do something rash, but needing him to do . . . something.

"Oh, aye? From who?"

"Harriet. Your sister. She told me to look you up if I ever came to town." Her mouth went completely dry, and she had no idea how to continue the conversation or what she hoped to accomplish with it.

"So now ye've found me." He spread his arms wide, as though to display his wares. Jenny saw that his hands were the size of hams, and she stepped back.

"I-I don't suppose your sister is in town . . ."

He smacked his lips once. "Let's nae talk about that mordy cow."

Jenny backed up as he closed in on her, ignoring the loud guffaws at the gross slight of his sister.

"I got me a reet cushty room nearby wit' a bed. Jus' a short walk down the ginnel."

Grabbing Jenny's arm, he pulled her close and lowered his head as if he intended to kiss her.

But he jumped away suddenly, and not of his own volition. Matthew had grabbed him and yanked him away from her.

Lambton reacted immediately, whirling on Matthew and swinging one of his meaty fists at him. Matthew ducked, and Lambton lost his balance with the momentum of his blow, giving Matthew an opening to shove the man into the bar. Lambton landed on two of the men standing there, who took exception to the inadvertent assault and shoved him back.

"Jenny, get out of here!"

Lambton and the two men at the bar exchanged shoves and punches, but they quickly turned to the outsider who had instigated the trouble. Matthew moved to shield Jenny as the three men closed in on him. "Go, Jenny!"

"I'm not leaving you!" She held on to the back of his jumper as he avoided the first blow and mounted an attack of his own. Jenny did not have time to wonder if this was what he'd intended all along when he grabbed Lambton again and used him as a propellant against the other two attackers. The three men fell into one of the tables, which cracked and splintered, and crashed down in a thousand pieces. Jenny scooted away as the women in the corners shrieked and scattered, their male patrons adjusting their trews as they came out of the darkness to join in the fray.

Jenny shuddered at the sight of them and headed for cover, but one of the men at the bar grabbed her and spun her around. She felt a familiar prickling near her heart, and the silvery threads of her power appeared. She tried to control them, but they seemed to fly from her chest to the ceiling, pulling the ancient chandelier from its anchor, smashing it into a table beneath.

The chandelier and table collapsed to the floor, distracting her assailant just enough for her to get away from him and get clear of what was quickly becoming a full-fledged brawl. The prudent thing would be for her to get out of there, but with punches being thrown in every direction, she did not want to leave Matthew. She was reluctant to try unleashing the powerful threads again, afraid that whatever disaster they caused might hurt Matthew.

Every man in the tavern became engaged in the fight, and most of them seemed intent on destroying Matthew. Jenny moved away from the few who were brawling independently, and circled around to where Matthew was using his size and strength against Lambton and his cohorts. He punched and ducked blows, shoving and using his attackers' own lumbering size against them. But Jenny did not think he could win without help against so many.

She picked up the remains of a broken chair and swung it at the back of one man's legs. She hit him so hard, he went down with a crash. No one seemed to notice the one less attacker, so she did the same thing to another of Matthew's assailants. This time, one of the other men took note of her actions and made a grab for her.

She screamed.

The ugly, beady-eyed Tuath managed to jerk Jenny's cloak from her shoulders as she scrambled away, leaving her much too exposed in the damned dress Merrick had bought her. Though she managed to get away into the shadows, it did not ease his worry about her.

She might be indomitable, but she was not invulnerable. Any one of these Tuath brutes could break her in two, and now a few small fires had sprung up where the chandelier's candles had scattered. "Jenny," he muttered, furious with her. He should have known she wouldn't leave when he told her to go. Now he had to get both of them out of the building that was rapidly filling with smoke.

He moved fast, using nonmagical talents common to all Druzai warriors, to hammer at Lambton and the others. He was anxious to finish them off and get out of the tavern, and away to the hidden place where he could watch for Lambton to leave the Old Scratch. Fielding punches as well as dirty attacks, he caught sight of Jenny as she ran behind the bar and grabbed two bottles of whiskey. "No! *Mo oirg, bhur eiridinn cròlot aimsith!*" he shouted, more terrified than he'd ever been in his life. "Get out, Jenny!"

But she returned to the fray and crashed a bottle over the head of one man, then did the same to another. In spite of his frustration with her, Matthew had to suppress a grin at her audacity.

He caught her eye and shouted over the clamor. "Go 'round to the door, lass! Do it!"

"Only with you!" she shouted back.

Merrick found himself muttering yet another low curse and shot her a look that would brook no defiance. She turned and wavered only a second, then made her way across the floor that was now wet with whiskey and covered with splinters of glass and wood. She made it to the door just as Merrick leveled the man closest to him.

Lambton came at him again, but Merrick did not want to disable him completely. He wanted the man capable of walking out of the tavern and leading him to his sister. If only the scoundrel hadn't made a grab for Jenny so soon, they might have learned more about the sister's location without all this useless violence.

He had to admit that Jenny's efforts during the brawl had helped to thin out the crowd against him, though a few still refused to give up. 'Twas utter chaos inside, with the fire growing and the smoke thickening.

Merrick fought his way to a corner of the tavern and put his back against the wall. Then he sidled toward the door, following in Jenny's tracks. He considered conjuring a quick blinding spell to get away without being seen, but knew 'twould be too risky. Instead, he yanked a heavily framed painting from the wall and smashed it over the heads of Lambton and two others. While they struggled to extricate themselves from the splintering wood and torn canvas, Merrick reached Jenny, grabbed her arm, and pushed her out the door.

"Come on!"

She ran alongside him, turning to look back toward the tavern.

"No time to gape, lass!" Merrick pulled her into the alleyway where he'd told her to hide if things became dodgy inside the tavern. Turning sideways, they edged their way through the narrow passageway as the men came pouring out of the tavern after them.

"In here!" Merrick whispered when they reached the end. They turned 'round a stone corner and pushed through the rickety door of a vacant building. "Wait here for me while I follow him."

Some small thing skittered away in the dark, and Jenny grabbed his arm. "No! Don't leave me here alone!" She'd lost her cloak and was shivering with cold and possibly fear. Merrick was torn. He knew he could not just abandon her and leave her there.

"Come on, then—out here!" Using another route altogether, they left the building. Merrick grabbed her arm, leading her quickly through the maze of buildings and back alleyways as he pulled off his woolen jumper.

He pressed it into her hands. "Put this on, but keep moving," he whispered urgently. "And if we become separated, make your way back to the dra— to the two statues we passed near the old church."

"Where are we going, Matthew?"

"I have an idea, but you'll have to trust me, *moileen*. And do as I say this time!"

The fire had drawn onlookers from their hovels, and they were creating crowds in which Merrick and Jenny could lose themselves. At the same time, they interfered with Merrick being able to catch sight of Lambton to follow him.

The mob started to turn ugly as it had done the night before. There were shouts and screams as the people decided to run toward the town center where they'd gathered the night before. Merrick caught sight of Lambton in the crowd. "There he is!"

Swallowed up in his jumper, Jenny held his hand tightly and hurried to keep up with him. They raced down the crowded lane, pushing their way past everyone who impeded their path, but the man was getting too far ahead.

"Matthew! Go on without me!" Jenny cried, almost breathless.

He slowed and pulled her against him with one arm 'round her shoulders. "Nay, lass. We'll never get to him through this horde. Now that I know who he is, I'll be able to catch him on the morrow."

"I can find my way back to the hotel . . . Go on—"

"No' tonight, Jenny."

There was no point in allowing themselves to become bogged down in the mob. Merrick wasn't going to catch Lambton this way, even without her. Better to come back later, or in the morning, after the crowd had dispersed.

He could use *himself* as bait next time. After thrashing the man as soundly as he'd done, Merrick was sure Lambton would feel he had a score to settle. All Merrick would need to do was show up in the vicinity of the Old Scratch and boast of his conquest. Lambton would hear of it and come to him like a spark to flint.

Most importantly, Jenny could stay in the safety of her room at the Queen's Hotel while Merrick went searching for Lambton and the sister.

The constables routed the crowd, and they heard gunfire coming from the direction of the Lanes. Jenny jumped and screamed at the sudden, startling noise that was so much louder than the Gypsy boys' gunpowder. Merrick hurried her away from the crowd, circling 'round to the back of the hotel to the servants' entrance. A surprised maid opened the door to them, and Merrick drew Jenny inside.

He did not stop to make explanations, but drew Jenny along a dim passageway to a narrow wooden staircase. They climbed it and reached a service area, then found the door to the lobby. Going through it, they headed for the staircase and quickly made it to Jenny's room.

She was still shaking when Merrick closed the door behind them.

He pulled her into his arms and held her. "Hush, *moileen*. You're safe now."

He skated his hands down her back, rubbing her body and warming her. "Ah, *moileen*, would that we were born of the same place and time," he whispered into her right ear, aware that she could not hear him.

He knew he should leave her now that their time together was coming to an end, for he would surely locate the locket on the morrow. This would be their last night together.

When her shivering subsided, he helped her remove his oversized jumper, then unfastened the buttons of her dress for her. A moment later, she was standing in her shift and Matthew was turning down the blankets of her bed. "Climb in, Jenny."

She moved to the far side of the bed, allowing space for him to join her, something he should not do, for the temptation to possess her was too strong. There was no magic on earth that could keep him from wanting her. "Jenny . . ."

There were things he needed to tell her. About Usher. He intended to deal with the headmaster before he left, but could do naught before he was ready to leave for Coruain. In the event that there was some further delay in his finding the locket, Jenny might need to protect herself. She needed to know Usher was nearby.

Casting his better judgment aside, Merrick pulled off his shoes, his shirt and trews, and climbed in with her. He lay on his side and faced her in the dark room. "I saw your headmaster earlier today."

"Reverend Usher? Where?"

Her trembling returned, so he drew her into his arms to soothe her and warm her.

"He was at the town hall this afternoon with the same two constables from the Gypsy camp."

She made a small sound of despair.

"Doona worry about him, *moileen*." He brushed his lips across her forehead. "I will take care of him for you—"

"What can you possibly d-do, Matthew?"

He could not explain how he intended to destroy Usher, so he changed the subject. "Why is he so bent on finding you, Jenny? You know that

Bardo was right. Since you took none of his possessions, you must be a threat to his good name."

He could hear her swallow above the noise of the crowd outside. "I don't have any idea how I could be. No one ever took the least notice that the headmaster beat his students. Even Mr. Ellis thought Reverend Usher's disciplinary actions were justified."

Bristling at the thought of a physician who did not see fit to come to the children's defense against a bullying tyrant, Merrick slid one hand all the way down her back, and thought again of the scar Usher had given her. "Mayhap 'tis something you saw. Did he ever scar another child as he did you?"

"I don't know about scars . . . He liked to single out the smaller girls, the ones with light hair. Me, in particular. Even Norah mentioned it."

"Norah?"

"My friend who died. She once saw the headmaster thrashing me and threatened to tell the old doctor who sometimes tended us."

"I doona understand. If Usher beat all the children . . . You mean to say your beatings were worse . . . ?"

Her shaking became worse and he drew her even closer. "Jenny, lass?"

"He liked to . . . to strike m-my . . . my naked backside."

"Ainchis," he said under his breath.

"With his bare hand."

The man was not only a monster, he was a deviant. "Did he do this to anyone else?"

"He told me never to speak of it . . . to anyone."

Matthew made a rude sign. "He'd have said the same to any others. Could this be the reason the headmaster hunts you? To prevent you from telling anyone else?"

"He would have to hunt all the other girls who were at school then. Many of them suspected . . ."

"But they've gone from Bresland?" he asked as a theory formed in his mind.

"I'm the only one who stayed. I could not find a position anywhere, no matter where I advertised."

"So you remained at Bresland as a teacher. Did you have no other options?"

"Marriage seemed a possibility for a time, but my only suitor believed all that Reverend Usher told him about me and decided . . ." She pulled back, and Matthew could see her puzzled expression. "Do you think he intentionally kept me at school?"

"I canna say for certain, Jenny." But he suspected it was so.

"I never received any responses to my advertisements. None at all, not until the post that came when Usher was ill and could not leave his bed." She looked over at him. "Oh, Matthew, you are right! He did not want me to leave!"

"Now we must try to understand why. What do you know that is so dangerous to Reverend Usher?"

Jenny tried to remember every altercation she'd ever had with the headmaster, from the time she'd asked for additional bread on her first day at school, to the words she'd exchanged with him the night Norah had died. But there had been so many.

"We tried to make ourselves invisible to him," she said. "All but Norah. She defied him to his face, and reaped harsh—"

"Punishments as harsh as your own?"

"Different. He . . ." She sat straight up in the bed.

"What is it, *moileen*," Matthew asked, pushing up to sit beside her.

"I remember . . ." She felt her heart pounding in her chest as a dark recollection came back to her. She went cold all over, and even the close proximity of Matthew's warm body did not take away the chill.

"You said he punished her . . . He left her outside in the cold?"

She swallowed a lump in her throat and nodded. "For interrupting him while he was beating me."

"One of those naked beatings?" His voice was a low growl.

"Norah said she was going to tell old Dr. Crandall about it. She even started walking to Kirtwarren . . . But the headmaster prevented her leaving and locked her in the privy all day. It was bitter cold, and when he finally let her out, she was chilled all the way through."

"But she was no' daunted by it?"

"No. Nothing frightened Norah, not like me."

Matthew pulled her into his arms and eased her back down to the bed. "You're the bravest lass I've ever known," he said.

"Hardly." Not when she intended to run away from all manner of wonderful possibilities merely to avoid being hurt by Matthew's own departure. She had not changed, not in the least. "I was a frightened mouse."

She'd hidden herself in a dark cupboard to avoid Usher's wrath . . . "When Norah got out of the privy, I heard her say that it did not matter what the headmaster did to her, she would see that everyone in Kirtwarren knew of his perversity."

"That's a lass."

"She was so chilled, they put her to bed in a sickroom away from the dormitory." It was not far from the tiny, dark place where Jenny had hidden herself.

"The headmaster and two teachers stayed with Norah," Jenny continued, "and when the hour grew late, he sent away the teachers. He ordered them to go and sleep so they would be ready for classes in the morning."

She felt tears streaming down her temples, and wiped them away more easily than she could the terrible memory of what had transpired that night. "The headmaster stayed with Norah, but after only a few minutes, he came out of the room."

"What then, *moileen*?"

"I could see him through the crack between the cupboard doors. He was brushing his hands together a-and . . . muttering to himself, but I couldn't really hear him . . . my ear. His footsteps echoed—they made an eerie, hollow sound as he walked down the hall."

"And then?"

"When I was sure he was gone, I sneaked out of the cupboard and went in to see Norah."

Matthew held her, but Jenny felt little comfort as she remembered the rest. "There was only a thin stream of moonlight through the window, but I could see her . . . facing away from the door. Her hair was disheveled, and she lay perfectly still. I went around to the opposite side of the bed and spoke to her, but she did not answer."

"What did you do?"

Jenny gulped back a sob. "I tidied the room. I was afraid Reverend Usher would punish her for the tousled bedclothes."

"Ach, Jenny."

"The teachers had been talking to her when they came out of the room . . . as though nothing was amiss. Yet only a few minutes later, she was dead."

"What did you do?"

"I was frightened, afraid the headmaster would find me there, and I would be in trouble, too. It didn't occur to me, then, that he'd killed her."

"Did he see you?"

"He caught me as I c-came out of the room, just as I feared he would." She felt her throat thicken. "I'd forgotten that. He marched me down to the chapel and made me stand on a chair before the altar through the rest of the night. It wasn't until morning that the other girls told me about Norah. There she was truly gone."

"You were obviously too distressed to take it all in," said Matthew, gently rubbing one hand across her back. "But now we know why he wanted to keep you at Bresland, and under his control."

"He thought I would go to the authorities?"

"How would he know you didna remember exactly what had happened?" he remarked. "The magistrate I met today was a reasonable man. I doona believe he would ignore your accusations."

"But if the headmaster told the constables I stole something . . ."

"I saw Usher pay them for their services, so I doubt they were true constables." His caresses slowed. "Lies are difficult to keep up. The headmaster must surely be desperate to maintain his."

Jenny felt drained. "He doesn't frighten me anymore. Now that I remember . . ."

"Aye. The truth is a powerful ally."

"No doubt you're right, Matthew," she said quietly. "But outside of Reverend Usher's sins, the only real truth for me is that I must be at Darbury tomorrow, or I will lose my position."

He did not speak for a moment. "Aye, *moileen.* 'Tis a truth that canna be avoided."

Jenny fell into a fitful sleep beside him. Merrick held her while the noise of the mob outside died down, and vowed that no one would ever hurt her again. He'd considered what to do about Usher and decided 'twould be simple enough to plant the questions that would bring Usher up before a magistrate and make him answer for little Norah's murder and his vicious treatment of the Bresland lasses. Merrick needed only a few more details from Jenny, and then he would work his subtle magic.

After he retrieved the locket and had the *brìgha-stone* in hand, 'twould take only a quick spell or two to see that Usher never hurt another child. A few more magical words would place Jenny in a comfortable home of her own, mayhap a cottage on the eastern coast where she could face Coruain whenever she looked out her windows.

Yet she would not see him. And when Merrick returned home to his own place in time, Jenny would not even have been born.

The thought of going away made his stomach burn. Sinann would never come to mean half as much to him as Jenny had, within only a few short days. She was everything to him, just as a true *céile* mate would be. *Ainchis ua oirg*, she *was* his *céile* mate. He loved her. There had to be a way to take her back to Coruain with him.

He had known of no Tuath who'd ever traveled to his magical isle. Yet he felt certain the spells that would protect him as he passed through the Astar Columns would protect Jenny, too. Merrick could no longer doubt that they had shared the magic of *sòlas*. He'd felt the merging of their *bràths*. He had to take her home.

The elders would have difficulty accepting a Tuath as the high chieftain's *céile* mate, and there was every likelihood that Sinann would be just as cruel as Usher, only in a different way. Merrick's spirits sank when he realized 'twould not be fair to take Jenny to his home isle, to a place where she did not belong. She would be far from everything that was familiar to her, thrown into a culture that might very well be hostile. Merrick knew that his brother believed the Tuath were inferior beings. No doubt his opinion was shared by others, by Druzai who could make Jenny's life a misery.

Mayhap 'twould be possible for Merrick to stay with her here. He did not want to subject her to the derision of highborn Druzai like Brogan and Sinann.

Other Druzai lords had remained in Tuath centuries before, when Eilinora had first been captured. But none of those men had prepared their entire lives to take on the responsibilities of high chieftain. None of them possessed the Mac Lochlainn power.

Merrick felt his chest squeeze with frustration and set about trying to analyze a solution to his dilemma. No one else on Coruain had been trained to rule. Brogan was often rash and hotheaded, and had vehemently spurned any designs on inheriting their father's scepter. Ana was already a powerful seer, well on her way to becoming a Druzai oracle. She would not rule. The elders and the Druzai people firmly held to the Mac Lochlainn line, so 'twas up to Merrick.

His blood ran cold when he faced the reality of his responsibilities. He could not shun them, no matter how much he wanted to, not after taking his investiture vows. He could not make a life here with Jenny.

The worst kind of emptiness weakened his *bràth* and threatened to drown him in anguish. His breath died in his chest, and his heart slowed to a deathly, irregular patter.

He tried to convince himself that Jenny would fare well on Coruain, but he could not. She did not know their customs, and though he could easily give her the Druzai language, he could not give her magic. She would be considered less than the least powerful Druzai, and be ridiculed by the likes of smug noblewomen like Sinann. Jenny would wither among his people.

Feeling discouraged, he eased out of the bed quietly, so as not to wake her. After dressing in the dark, he leaned over and brushed a light kiss on her forehead, aware of what he had to do. "I promise you, *moileen*," he whispered almost inaudibly, "I will make things right for you before I go."

'Twas not yet dawn, but Merrick's mood was as black as midnight. He went on foot to the Lanes where men still loitered, drinking from bottles and cursing their lot. Merrick made his way to the Old Scratch, which still remained standing. It seemed the fire had not taken sufficient hold to burn down the building. He heard noises from within.

Instead of going inside, he went to the broken-down garden wall across from the tavern, and sat on it, garnering a few curious looks from the men who wandered past. "You see Lambton," he said to one small group of lurkers, "tell him I'm looking to finish him off."

He waited awhile longer, saying much the same thing to a few others, then got up and took a circuitous route, back through an alleyway to the broken-down building next to the Old Scratch. He picked his way to a deserted shell of a room near the street and took up his post behind a grimy, broken window to watch the comings and goings of everyone who happened by.

There were no gaslights in this district, but in the early morning light, he recognized a number of the passersby, men who'd been drinking in the tavern when Lambton had come for Jenny. For Merrick, 'twas a matter of patience now, of waiting for the right man to arrive. After putting out the word that he was waiting, he did not think Lambton would resist the taunt.

An hour passed, and the streets came to life. People came out of their dwellings, and a few horse carts rambled down the lane. Finally, the man Merrick sought appeared. He went into the Old Scratch, but came out only a few minutes later with one of his cronies. Stopping outside with his hands on his hips, he turned his head to look up and down the street. He spoke to the man beside him, but Lambton was too far away for Merrick to hear what he said. When he did not find his quarry, he yawned and shoved his fingers through his hair. It looked as though he was off to find himself a bed.

Merrick quickly left his hiding place to follow Lambton. At the end of the alleyway, he stopped, waiting in the shadows for the burly blond to choose a direction. As soon as the man moved, Merrick went after him, staying far behind, anxious to catch him at home where his sister might also be.

Lambton took a serpentine route, going deep into an area where Merrick had not been before. There were enough people out on the street to prevent Merrick from being obvious, and he followed Lambton to a dingy, crumbling brick house, two stories tall. Most of the windows were cracked or broken out, and those were covered with rotting wood to keep out the cold.

Merrick waited until Lambton went inside, then caught up and slipped into the building behind him. All was quiet in the house. He listened for sounds of movement, then climbed the creaky stairs when he heard footsteps on the second floor. In the upstairs hall were two doors of raw, blistered wood, and they were both closed. Merrick stood outside the first door, listening, but there was no sound from within. He listened at the second door and heard movement. Quietly, he tried the door and found it unlocked.

Wary of such good luck, Merrick pushed it open, but remained outside, waiting. The flickering light of a candle gave some illumination to the room, and Lambton suddenly appeared just inside, and lunged for Merrick. 'Twas easy to sidestep the attack and grab Lambton by the collar and the waist of his trews. Merrick tossed him headfirst into the wall.

As the man shook his head to clear it, Merrick spoke. "I'm no' here to brawl with you, Lambton. I'm looking for your sister, Harriet."

Lambton rose to his feet, seemingly pacified by Merrick's statement, but he made a sudden dive and rammed Merrick in the midsection. Holding on to Lambton, Merrick quickly dropped down to the floor. Lying on his back, he raised his legs and connected with the man's belly, tossing him over his head. Then he rose to his feet.

"Where is she?"

A downstairs door opened, and someone shouted for them to pipe down. The two combatants ignored the demand.

"How would I know where she is?" Lambton crawled to his feet. "The bitch is a bleedin' pain in everybody's—"

"She came to you, did she no'?" Merrick took a quick glance into Lambton's room. "Did she find a position at a school? Or a private residence?" he asked, considering that Harriet had been a teacher, at least at Bresland. "Or is her thieving profitable enough to—"

Lambton threw a punch.

"Look," Merrick said, avoiding the punch as he grabbed Lambton's hand and twisted his arm 'round to the back of his body. "I'll pay you to take me to her. But mind, I'll no' give you a shilling if you try something foolish."

"'Ow much?"

"More than you'll see in any given week," Merrick said. "But naught until I see the woman herself and speak to her." He yanked up on Lambton's arm, just to punctuate his demand.

"Aye! Aye, damn ye. I'll take ye."

"Tell me where, first."

"She's not teachin' nae more," said Lambton. "Works in th' kitchen in some rich toff's house."

Merrick knocked Lambton to the floor, face-down, and kept hold of his wrists. "Where? What street?"

"Holm Street," Lambton bleated like a wounded sheep. "Why d'ye want 'er?"

"She stole something of importance at Bres-land. And I want it back." Merrick regretted that he could not use magic to bind the man's wrists behind him, and shackle his ankles, too. "What house in Holm Street?"

"'Ow do I know ye'll pay me to squeal on 'er?"

"You don't. But you might keep hold of your life if you tell me now, Lambton." He put more pressure on the man's trapped wrists.

"The Beattie house! Damn ye, ease up!"

The irate voice from the first floor returned. "Gawddamn ye up there! Shut yer traps and let us sleep!"

Merrick pulled Lambton up to his feet and grabbed his sherte. Before the man could react, he spun him 'round and coldcocked him. Knocked unconscious, Lambton slid down the wall to the floor, just outside his door. Merrick went inside

Lambton's room and took a more thorough look 'round this time, just in case the man had lied about his sister. When he did not find her hiding inside, he took the stairs by twos and hurried out of the building.

Now that it was past dawn, the city had come fully to life. Merrick took off at a run toward the church where the dragheens stood, with the hope that they would know the geography of the city.

"M'lord," said Doughal.

"Where is Holm Street?"

"Away south, m'lord," said Torin.

"And the Beattie house? Have you heard of it?"

Doughal looked at the other dragheen, and Merrick felt some unsaid communication between them. "We doona know. 'Tis likely new in the city."

"New? You mean less than five hundred years?"

"Well, aye," Doughal replied, as though the answer should be obvious.

"Never mind. I'll find it," Merrick said, and started on his way through the Lanes and back toward the center of the city.

"M'lord . . ." called Doughal. "Your lady . . ."

Merrick stopped. "Aye?"

Torin stretched his neck, making the rasping sound of gravel crunching underfoot. "She is no' . . . You didna want her to notice us."

"Is she no' Druzai?" Doughal asked.

"She is Tuath."

Both dragheens furrowed their brows and made the cold, hard, rasping sounds of stone rubbing against stone. "M'lord, if I may—"

"No, you may no', dragheen," Merrick said, jabbing his fingers through his hair. "I need no advice regarding my lady, and you would do well to remember she is *céile* mate of the Druzai high chieftain. Give her assistance if she crosses your path. But try no' to frighten her!"

Merrick did not wait for a response, but headed south, toward the center of the city, searching for Holm Street as he considered the dragheens' attitude toward Jenny. It confirmed what he already knew about his own people.

The more powerful Druzai might take care of their lesser folk who possessed minimal magic, but Merrick knew that if he took Jenny to Coruain, his peers would not look favorably upon her, a powerless Tuath who was not only in their midst, but was his own beloved *céile* mate.

They would know her as the woman who had broken the oracle's prophecy.

Chapter 13

The Isle of Coruain, 981

Ana was able to sit up and take nourishment, but she was physically too weak to leave the pallet in the great room of Coruain House. She feared that when it came time to battle Eilinora and her mentor, she would be of no use to her people. Merrick and Brogan had to find the *brìgha*-stones and bring them home. *Soon.* She did not know how much longer she and the Druzai elders could keep the Odhar from breaking through and invading the isles. Her sense of their attack had shifted.

"Something has changed," she said to the few elders who had remained at Coruain House through the long ordeal, persevering alongside her in the effort to keep the enemy from breaching their defenses.

"Aye, Ana," said Cianán. "I, too, sense something much darker than the witch."

Darker? Ana knew he was beyond darkness, a deep and vile malevolence that sucked away all life and light. She *knew* he thrived on death and destruction for their own sake.

"I worry for the high chieftain and his brother," said Cianán. "They are so vulnerable away in Tuath."

"There could be only one reason for Eilinora to leave the assault on Coruain to the Odhar," said Aenéas.

"Aye," Liam remarked. "To pursue those who would locate the *brìgha*-stones and return them to Coruain. She must have found where they were hidden."

"More likely, she found the Mac Lochlainns," said Cianán.

"And the other . . . he is so strong," Ana whispered, almost to herself.

"Aye. He must have immense power to have found Eilinora and the Odhar—"

"Who is he and why do we know naught of him?" Liam asked.

"How could he have broken the numinous bonds that held Eilinora for a thousand years?" Aenéas remarked. "I doona understand how he even found her. Was she no' hidden deep in a *bòcan* forest?"

Cianán turned to Ana. "Have you seen him, *mo curadh*?"

"He probes my mind," Ana said. "His intrusions are much more— They are darker and more cunning than Eilinora's."

"*Ainchis ua oirg,*" Cianán muttered, coming to Ana's side. "What has he seen?"

"Naught from me. Have you no' felt him poking through your own thoughts and memories?"

The elders looked at each other blankly.

"I've *seen* him prodding, probing you," said Ana. "'Tis well that you know naught of my cousins' quest."

"I have felt naught," said Aenéas, shocked at Ana's words. Clearly, neither elder had felt the intrusion. Cianán swore again, and Aenéas whirled away and stalked to the window, turning his full attention to their defenses.

Ana turned to Cianán and Liam. "He thinks I do no' sense him, but his invasion is like burning tentacles, probing, seeking. I fear that if Eilinora manages to find the blood stones before my cousins do, and she offers them to him—"

"Eilinora is his servant, then?"

Ana furrowed her brow. "Aye. She owes him for her freedom. She has become his handmaiden."

Her statement was met with silence as the elders considered it. Cianán paced while Aenéas stood perfectly still, looking out the windows to the cliffs beyond the crashing sea. Liam sat down hard near the fire, completely deflated.

Ana sensed their feelings of defeat and knew she had to bolster their spirits lest their own pessimism defeat them. "My cousins will bring home the stones and we will make our stand here, on the cliffs of Coruain, against the Odhar warriors and Eilinora . . . against *Pakal*." She looked up as the name came to her. "He calls himself Pakal."

Eilinora's malevolent lord allowed her to

glimpse him . . . a tall, muscular man with bronze skin. Symmetrical designs were painted on him from his neck to his shoulders and down his arms. Even his face had an intricate pattern painted on it, and thick rings of gold pierced his nose and ears. Black was his hair, cut dead straight across his brows and the back of his neck. He was like no one Ana had ever seen before.

She looked up at Cianán. "He is of the earth, but there is another world, a Tuath land. . .'Tis far from here, to the west. He and the other Lords of Death—"

"Lords of Death?"

Ana nodded, her head aching after her brief mental skirmish with Pakal. "He and others . . . this is what they call themselves. And their Tuath people are slaves to their brutal whims."

"Just as Eilinora would have enslaved the Druids and the other Tuath of her time."

"And destroyed the Druzai."

"I sense no vulnerabilities in him," Ana said dismally. "He is supremely confident of his abilities."

"Does he no' think there are any Druzai with equal power?"

"No. He does no' believe it."

"But there is one," said Aenéas. "A female who has the power to vanquish him."

"None have come forward to assist us with the shielding swathe," Cianán retorted angrily. "If there is any Druzai with power who has no'—"

"Where is your daughter, Aenéas?" asked Liam. "While we all struggle to maintain our defense against the Odhar assault, Sinann is strangely absent. Does she throw her *lòchran* light toward our protective fields?"

"Aenéas, Sinann's assistance would no' be amiss," Cianán added. "Look at Ana. She is weakening. 'Twould benefit us all to have your daughter's power in force against Pakal's assaults."

"I will ask her to come," said Aenéas.

"No," said Ana, unwilling to suffer the distraction of Sinann's presence. For the past few years, the woman had behaved as though she were already Merrick's *céile* mate, the woman chosen to prevent the monstrous disaster predicted by the oracle at Merrick's birth. "'Twill suffice for her to stay where she is and cast her energy to the shielding swathe. Any Druzai woman capable of thwarting a disaster of these proportions should have sufficient skill and power to prevent the Odhar from entering Coruain, no matter where she sits."

Ana had no energy to waste on thoughts of Sinann or any other Druzai woman who had designs on her cousin.

Carlisle, March 1826

Matthew was gone when Jenny awoke. She had felt the warmth and comfort of his body through most of her troubled night, but he'd left her during the morning's earliest hours. Perhaps his admission that the truth could not be avoided had spurred him to go.

She glanced to the desk, but saw no note there. His clothes and shoes were gone, yet she doubted he would leave her without a word. He'd likely gone in search of Lambton.

She crawled from the warm bed and dressed in her old Bresland gown. The blue dress Matthew had bought her lay discarded across the back of the chair. She picked it up and let the thin fabric slip through her fingers to drop to the floor. This time, it truly was time to prepare herself to leave.

With her emotions in turmoil, she felt the familiar prickling of silver fibers that suddenly burst out to create some havoc in the room. Jenny halted them, controlling their movements, drawing them back inside.

Her satisfaction at such newfound control was overshadowed by the acute loneliness she felt in Matthew's absence.

She packed her bag. Wrapping her shawl around her shoulders, she went down to the lobby. The locket was not what she wanted, but she was unsure whether she possessed the courage to stay and fight for her deepest desire. Matthew denied the full return of his memory, but Jenny sensed that he knew something of his past.

Yet she had to believe he would never have lain with her again if he were married or pledged to another woman. Perhaps he *had* stolen the gold, and he did not want to put her at risk.

"Madam," said the hotel clerk, "would you care for coffee?"

"No, thank you," she replied. She rubbed her forehead as though she could eliminate the ache, along with all her yearnings for a future with him. But she knew better.

"Do you know of a place called Darbury?" she asked the clerk.

"Aye, of course," replied the clerk. "Lord Keswick's estate."

"Where is it?"

"'Tis about eight or ten miles northeast. A very long walk, madam, if that's what you're thinking."

"Is there a coach that goes that way?" she asked, mindful of her limited funds.

"Oh aye, madam. There is one that leaves from Rickergate in about an hour."

Dismayed at the promptness of its departure, Jenny realized she could leave now and allow the rest of her life to be dictated by a cowardly decision. Or she could stay and show some backbone.

She set her bag down near one of the sofas and paced restlessly. Perhaps it was just as well to go to Darbury now. Matthew knew where to find her if he wanted to do so, and leaving now would preserve her pride.

She chewed her lip and tried to think of something besides the hollow feelings growing in her heart. She was no coward. She went to the front window of the lobby and crossed her arms over her chest. She was going to wait for Matthew. She loved him, and would face his difficulties with him.

Gazing absently out the window, she nearly choked when she saw Reverend Usher coming out of the chemist's shop across the street. Matthew had told her he'd seen the headmaster, so she should not have been so surprised.

But now that she remembered everything about Norah's death, she thought about confronting him with what she knew. Undecided, she watched as he opened his parcel, removed his purchase, and placed it in his trouser pocket.

And when he pushed aside his coat, Jenny saw her pendant on his waistcoat, dangling from a watch chain outside his pocket.

Merrick hastened through the Lanes, looking for a carriage for hire. Obviously, none frequented this neighborhood. Only the wagons carrying rags and waste drove through these poor streets.

Leaving the slums, he hailed the first carriage he saw. "Holm Street," he said to the driver as he started to get in.

"Ye have money, then?" asked the suspicious driver.

Merrick drew a shilling from his pocket and flipped it up to the man. If this fellow thought he looked disreputable, then 'twas unlikely he would make any headway in Holm Street. "Make that the Queen's Hotel, then."

A few minutes later, he arrived at the hotel and went up to Jenny's room. He knocked quietly, but there was no answer. 'Twas still early, so mayhap she was still asleep. They'd retired late, and Jenny's memory of her friend's death had been stressing. She'd spent a restless night in his arms, sleeping only short intervals before being awakened by some terrible dream.

He would let her sleep now, but before she left Carlisle for Darbury, he intended to give her some explanation about himself. Mayhap he could concoct some fiction that would assuage the hurt he knew she felt. 'Twas only equal to his own.

He wished there were some Druzai magic that could change how she felt. He would perform any spell that would take away the pain of their parting, but no magic could alter emotions. It could not bring back the dead, make one person love another, or make two people stop loving each other.

With a great sigh of regret, he went across the hall to his own room and washed off the grime of the Lanes and his altercation with Lambton, then changed into his better clothes. Dressed as a gentleman, he was more likely to be admitted to the Beattie house.

The hotel clerk hailed another carriage for Merrick and gave the driver his direction, and soon he was traveling to the south end of the city. The homes he passed were statelier than any he'd seen so far, but the black smoke that wafted up from each chimney darkened the neighborhood and obscured the sight of the crisp blue sky.

The coach made several turns, and finally came to a stop. The driver came 'round and asked where in Holm Street Merrick wanted to go.

"Do you know the Beattie house?"

"Nae, sir. But I'll find out fer ye."

The man trotted up to the first house on the street and skirted 'round to the back. He was gone only a few minutes before he returned. "Got it, sir. Friendly maids 'ereabouts, eh?" he remarked with a grin.

Merrick gave a nod and considered how the driver had gotten his information. 'Twas unlikely that Harriet Lambton would react favorably to a well-dressed man who came to her employer accusing her of thievery. Nor would the owner of the house appreciate a stranger coming to ask about one of the maids. 'Twas a puzzle.

When the coach came to a stop, Merrick asked the driver to step down.

"I've a job for you." He took several shillings from his pocket. "There is a kitchen maid inside the house, called Harriet Lambton, and I'd like to speak to her. Do you think you can get her to come out?"

"Oh well, I'm nae so sure—"

"I mean her no harm, and there'll be a sovereign for both of you if you can convince her to join me here."

Merrick took the driver's hand and turned it palm up, then he dropped a few shillings into it. "'Tis important."

"A sovereign more, ye say?"

"For each of you."

The man touched the brim of his hat and jogged away to the back of the house. Merrick sat back and waited, forcing himself to be patient, when all he wanted to do was accelerate the process with a quick spell. He could easily vanish and enter the house. 'Twould be no problem to locate Harriet and convince her to turn over the locket.

He thought about Jenny, and hoped she'd finally achieved some peace in her sleep. Certainly, it had been disturbing for her to remember what had happened to her friend, but it had to be worse to leave the memory lying dormant in the back of her mind. 'Twas how it had been for Merrick— he'd known he had an important task, and the niggling sensation of urgency had plagued him up until the return of his memory.

The headmaster's downfall was going to feel particularly rewarding, unlike Merrick's departure for Coruain. Leaving England was imminent, and it should be all he thought about. But the image of Jenny's face would not leave his mind. He could not forget the lively spark in her gray eyes or her courage under adversity. She'd been magnificent in the Old Scratch the previous night, never daunted by the danger all 'round them.

Merrick turned his attention to the side drive, where the coach driver was hurrying back with a small blond woman beside him. He opened the carriage door when she arrived. "Please come in."

She crossed her arms in front of her. "I'd rather stay out here, if ye don't mind." Her hair was nearly white, like her brother's, although her build was small and nothing like Frank's. She was almost childlike. With speech a bit more refined than her brother's, her manner was one part curious, the other part hostile. "Why are ye looking for me?"

"You were a teacher at Bresland School?"

She narrowed her pale eyes. "You've come from that foul old man? The headmaster? Well, you can just tell that boggin perv that he's not to come near me again or I'll—"

"I'm no' here for the headmaster. I've come to get Jenny Keating's locket back."

The woman's eyes went blank. "Her what?"

"Her locket," said Merrick, puzzled by Harriet's reaction. "A bit of silver jewelry on a chain. A pendant. Miss Keating said she wore it hidden under her dress, hanging 'round her neck most of the time, or in a pocket of her dress."

"I never saw any locket, guv. Now, if you're done . . ." She held her hand out and tipped her head toward the driver. "He said you'd give me a sovereign just to talk."

"Aye. And I will. Just a few more questions." But what to ask? The girl seemed completely unaware of Jenny's locket, although she could be lying. Merrick could easily determine if that were so . . .

"What did you mean about the headmaster?" he asked.

"Pinched me, he did. And more than once."

"For what reason?" Merrick asked, unable to understand why Usher would do such a thing.

"You've not been around much, have you, toff?"

"I suppose not."

"The headmaster likes his girls fair and small," she said. "And I'm not game for his antics. Got out of there as soon as the penny dropped. And good riddance, too."

"Did he pinch Miss Keating as well?"

She gave a bitter laugh and shook her head. "I'm sure there was a time or two . . . But he likes us small, and she's gotten much too . . . Well, ye know."

He did *not* know, nor did he want to know. "The locket . . . You're sure you never saw it?"

Harriet shook her head. "If I did, I'd have hocked it so I wouldn't have to be here, bustin' my . . ."

Merrick decided to risk a bit of magic to determine if she was telling the truth. The amount he used would be small, leaving few traces, hardly enough for an Odhar hunter to find.

"Torrun mo dearbh forhais," he whispered under his breath while Harriet continued to speak. A dull, blue light framed her body, and had Merrick not been looking for it, he'd have missed it, for it remained 'round her for only a fraction of a second before disintegrating into gray dust. But now he knew for certain that she was telling the truth. Harriet really did not know anything about the locket. Her only reason for leaving Bresland was Reverend Usher's unwanted advances.

Merrick concealed his disappointment and thanked the young woman. "Here's your sovereign, Miss Lambton." He tossed another coin to the driver and climbed inside, wondering how long it would take Moghire to carry him to Bresland School to search for the locket. Now that he knew why Usher was so anxious to keep Jenny there, Merrick had a suspicion he knew where to find it.

The Isle of Coruain, 981

Ana gazed incredulously at Sinann, who entered Coruain House with an entourage of her closest friends, sycophants who admired her beauty and skills. Skills at what, Ana was not quite sure, for the daughter of Aenéas seemed to use her talent only for solving complex riddles and puzzles.

Sinann could not possibly become Merrick's *céile* mate, no matter how lovely she might be, with her glossy dark hair and fetching amber eyes.

"I am told you are in need of my assistance," she said.

Ana's stomach turned. "Your *lòchran* to help shield the isles, Sinann."

A sudden, sharp-edged wind blew through the great hall, and Sinann staggered against it. The distraction of her entrance had altered the elders' shields for a fraction of a second, and Pakal used the moment to ride a bolt of *lòchran* light and emerge inside the great hall. All at once, he was standing at Sinann's back.

As the tempest blew through the room, small items were lifted and tossed about. Pakal whipped one painted arm 'round Sinann's neck and bent to her ear, giving her a quiet, irresistible *tànaiste* command.

Unable to deny Pakal when he spoke thus, Sinann shot a powerful *lòchran* blast toward Ana, knocking her to the pallet and holding her down. Ana struggled for air, fighting to repel the sorcerer's probes.

"Tell me of stones, Druzai!" Sinann cried above the fierce winds, neither the voice nor the words her own.

The elders crouched and held on to the furniture to avoid being thrown about the room; at the same time, they combated Pakal's attack and forced a calming of the winds. They fortified the shields as Pakal dissipated like an exorcised spirit.

Sinann fell to the ground, and her father, nearly spent, crawled to her side.

Ana heard Liam and Cianán calling to her, but she could not make out their words. The voice of the Lord of Death drowned out anything the elders tried to say. Ana closed her mind to the black tentacles that somehow reached past her defenses and slithered through her brain, searching, demanding, hurting. Ana pushed back against him, and with the help of the elders, drove Pakal from her thoughts.

With a surge of power, she reversed their roles. Rising to sit up on the pallet, she threw her own questing sensors to the dark enemy, piercing through his own barriers.

When she saw her uncle's scepter in Pakal's hands, she pushed herself to the edge of the pallet and swung her healing legs over the side. "You willna defeat us, Pakal. The Druzai will no' be victims to the rogue powers of the Lords of Death."

Inside his thoughts, she saw a triangular-shaped stone tower with hundreds of steps leading to the peak at the top. 'Twas dark, but thousands of torches lit the ground below, held by a seething mass of handsome, bronze-skinned people, whose bloodthirsty, frenzied energy fed Pakal. A young woman with bound hands was dragged to the top of the tower. She screamed in terror when her bonds were cut with a silver dagger, and then she cried out in horror as they tied her, spread-eagle, to an X-shaped frame.

Pakal's power swelled and grew when a white-robed man, whose hair was cut in the same blunt style, stood before the girl, wielding the knife. Ana braced herself, unable to banish Pakal's vision of the killing, of the sight of the poor victim's heart being cut from her chest while it still pulsed with life.

It sickened her, but she would not be cowed. "You will never take the heart from the Druzai people," Ana whispered into the black *bràth* that served as his soul. "We are beyond anything you have ever known. *Begone!*"

Carlisle, March 1826

By the time Jenny got out to the street, Usher was gone. An outdoor vendor was setting up shop nearby, and she turned to him for help. "Did you see a man here just a moment ago?" she asked. "He was tall and well dressed, with white hair."

"Aye," the man replied, pointing away from the city center, down the street. "'E hired a carriage. Right there. That's 'im—not too far gone."

She saw the one carriage, heading north. "That's the direction of the Lanes, is it not?"

"Aye, but not only the Lanes, miss. The cathedral is up tha' way, and the castle, too."

"Thank you." The headmaster was not going to the cathedral, nor was he on his way to see the sights at the castle. His sole reason for coming to Carlisle was to find her. After she remembered the night of Norah's death, it was perfectly clear that he'd kept her at Bresland intentionally. There might have been some earlier responses to the advertisements she'd made, but Usher must have confiscated them before she'd seen them. And he'd made certain that Mr. Ellis would break off their courtship, telling the young doctor tales about her intractable personality.

She shuddered at the thought of the headmaster coming into her room during the night and stealing her mother's pendant, for that was the only way he could have gotten it. No doubt he'd intended to hold that over her to keep her from leaving.

As angry as she'd ever been in her life, Jenny saw no other coaches in the vicinity but did not allow that to deter her. She set off on foot, keeping Usher's carriage in her sights as she hurried to catch up. Fortunately, the coach did not move very fast as it traveled in the direction of the tavern where she and Matthew had encountered Lambton the previous night.

How futile that excursion had been. For all this time, she'd thought Harriet had stolen her locket, but it had been in the headmaster's possession. Jenny hadn't needed to run from Bresland to pursue Harriet after all. She could have confronted Usher that last morning in his office, and demanded that he return her locket to her.

Which was what she intended to do now, although that was the least of her concerns. She was mindful that Usher was a vicious murderer. Jenny didn't know how he'd killed Norah, and she didn't want to know. But she intended to see that he paid for it. The magistrate in Kirtwarren would have to believe her.

Usher's carriage stopped and let him out. He did not look back in her direction, but stepped out and turned into the nearby lane as though he had not a worry or a care in the world. Jenny was repulsed by the sight of him.

She picked up her pace to a near run. There were many places to hide in the Lanes, but not many decent houses, and she wondered what kind of business would bring Usher to this district. But no matter where he went, she was determined to find him.

She reached the headmaster's carriage and stopped to look in the direction he had gone on foot. He was within shouting distance, walking past the old church where Matthew had told her to go if they became separated. Jenny hurried to catch up. She was closing on him when he turned into an alleyway, exactly like the one where she and Matthew had hidden the night before.

Before going into the alleyway after him, she looked around her and saw no one. The only traffic in the narrow street were the few horse-drawn rag and rubbish carts. Yet Jenny felt as though she were being watched by a hundred pairs of eyes, peeking furtively out of the grimy, cracked windows. Perhaps this was not such a good idea, to confront the headmaster here, away from any decent society. There was no one here to protect her . . . no one even to care if something untoward happened to her. Thinking better of it, she took a few steps back, then turned to leave.

But Reverend Usher blocked her path. She realized he'd doubled back intentionally to trap her.

"You'll not be leaving the Lanes, you wicked girl," he said, his voice low and dangerous.

"How dare you call me wicked. If there is any evil at Bresland School it is—"

"Defiant, obstinate, insolent female!" He took a step toward her, and though Jenny stepped back, she could not resist responding to the horrible man.

"I pity the poor girls who must stay at Bresland," she said in a challenging tone. "Although I doubt *you* will be headmaster much longer."

He continued to move toward Jenny, but she felt just as insolent as he'd called her. She was finished with cowering in fear of what might happen, and determined to do what was right.

"You are a murderer, Clement Usher."

He slipped his hands into his pockets, pushing the edges of his coat away. Jenny could see her mother's locket, dangling as though it were a common watch fob.

"And a thief, too."

He detached the locket and chain from his waistcoat and held it swinging from his fingers in front of her. "I thought perhaps I might use your precious trinket to hold you at Bresland. But your coming to Carlisle has worked much to my advantage."

Jenny continued to retreat.

"Mr. Ellis had grown quite fond of you. Even though I convinced him that he would not want you for his wife, he would have asked questions had you disappeared."

"Mr. Ellis?" Jenny asked weakly.

"Aye. Poor sot was so taken by your pretty little heart-shaped face . . ."

Jenny cringed at the headmaster's mocking tone and the malevolent expression in his eyes.

"Ellis did not want to hear about your faults. But I could not allow you to marry him. As I understand it, husbands and wives talk . . ."

"M-my faults?" Jenny asked, stunned by Usher's admission. She never expected him to confess that he'd ruined her chances for marriage with Mr. Ellis.

"I cannot let you tell anyone about Norah Martin's mishap—"

All at once, a man came out of a nearby doorway. Moving fast, he ran into Reverend Usher and shoved him hard, grabbing her locket from his hand. Usher fell to the ground.

Jenny took the opportunity to get away from Usher, who clearly intended to do her some damage and leave her in a rat-infested alleyway where no one would bother to wonder about her. Following in the thief's tracks, she ran toward the church, hoping there would be someplace to hide from the headmaster if he managed to come after her.

She arrived at the site of the two statues in front of the church, and saw a small black creature perched atop the shoulder of one of the tall stone statesmen. Jenny had never seen such an animal, but she became distracted by a horse-drawn rubbish cart, coming down the lane much too fast, careening out of control. Taking advantage of Jenny's distraction, the strange black creature jumped into her path, tripping her so that she went sprawling into the street.

It was a little, scaly beast with huge, pointed ears and bulging eyes, and it pulled Jenny's hair with glee, refusing to let her get up.

"Jenny!" came a shout from afar. She looked up to see Matthew, and guessed that the hotel clerk had told him in what direction she'd gone.

He was mounted on Moghire, coming up in the road behind the speeding horse cart. The driver shouted at the horses and tried to slow them, but they galloped on wildly. He jumped free of the runaway cart just as it tilted and overturned, smashing into the run-down dwellings that lined the lane. Jenny watched in horror as the horses raced toward her. All at once, Moghire made a spectacular leap over the detritus in the road, but it was too late.

She shut her eyes tightly, and prayed.

* * *

Matthew jumped from Moghire's back and ran to the site where the horses had run Jenny down. He fell to his knees beside her and leaned close, afraid to touch her broken body. *"Moileen!"*

Her injuries were grave. She was gashed and bleeding from her head, chest, and arms, and she was barely breathing. Yet in spite of her dire condition, she opened her eyes and looked up at him.

"Matthew," she whispered, her voice hardly an audible rasp. "A thief . . . my locket."

"I doona care about it, *moileen*. Just . . ."

She was going to die. And some fool rum dubber was getting away with the *brìgha*-stone.

Merrick had no choice but to chase the man down and get the locket from him. Gently, he brushed away a tiny trickle of blood from Jenny's nose. She had difficulty swallowing, but she managed to whisper a few short words. "I love you, Matthew . . ."

"Ach, lass . . ." Merrick rubbed tears from his cheeks and knew he could not let her die. He could try healing her, but he did not know if he had sufficient skill for it. He was no master healer like Rónán. There was only one other solution, but it would surely draw the Odhar to him. He could displace and prevent the accident from occurring. Displacement required a significant use of power, and there would be residual sparks trailing from here to the heavens. If Eilinora's minions were anywhere near, they would not miss it. But Merrick would do no less for this woman. He did not care if Eilinora herself arrived here and destroyed him on the spot.

He had to save Jenny.

'Twas necessary to act quickly, for he could move only a few minutes forward or back, and he needed as much time as possible before the accident to prevent the damned sìthean from pushing Jenny into the road.

Still leaning over her, he exerted the power and muttered the words that would take him back. *"Fèath cian mo aimsir daonnan a rec astar."*

And with those words he was suddenly back on Moghire, but this time, he knew what was about to happen. Jenny was hurrying toward the dragheens near the church and Usher was not far behind her.

Merrick had just enough time to ride into a narrow alley and move ahead of the runaway horse cart, coming out in front of the galloping vehicle. He dismounted just as a sìthean jumped from its perch on Torin's shoulder with the intention of tripping Jenny.

Matthew got to her first and kicked the beast away.

"Matthew!" Jenny cried as Merrick caught her in his arms. "Usher had my locket!"

Merrick pulled Jenny far from the road and the lurching wagon. He held her tightly, relishing the healthy, whole feel of her body against his. He cupped her face in his hands and kissed her. "Jenny, *moileen . . .*"

"A pickpocket took it, and now he's getting away!"

Merrick took a deep, shuddering breath. "Aye. Wait here!"

The thief was fast. Merrick could stop him with just one magical word, but he was reluctant to push his luck. He'd already used magic to assure himself that Harriet Lambton had not lied to him, and then he'd displaced. So far, Eilinora had not found him. He could not risk any more magic until he had the stone in hand.

The rum dubber turned a corner and tried to slip into a narrow doorway, but Merrick grabbed him and swung him 'round. But just as he took the locket from him, a piercing, inhuman screech paralyzed him, and he realized he'd been found. His entire body burned, from the soles of his feet to the top of his head, the fiery sensation making him feel nauseated, weak, and powerless. A bright flash blinded him momentarily, and an odd, acrid smell irritated his nose. When his vision cleared, he saw that he was standing in a barren landscape of gray and white.

A blast of luminous *lòchran*, more powerful than any Merrick had ever seen before, surged toward him. He ducked, but the *lòchran* caught his shoulder, knocking him to his knees, dislodging the locket from his hand. Merrick reached for it, but another blast came toward him, and he had to move quickly to avoid being seriously injured or killed.

"You will regret being born, Eilinora!" he muttered.

"Not Eilinora," said a male voice. "Pakal dei Mestarre."

The new adversary wasted no time, but used his power to yank Merrick off his feet and throw him in the air, rocketing him into the trunk of a tree, knocking the breath out of him.

Merrick's vision cleared, and he saw the imposing figure of a man, dressed in a black loincloth, his upper body and face covered with ink designs of red and black. A ring of gold dangled from his nose, and his black hair was cut straight across his forehead. Gold bands encircled both his ankles. He was no *jinni* nor a *seunn*, but Merrick realized he must be the creature who'd freed Eilinora.

He crouched and moved toward Pakal, gathering all his powers to mount his own assault.

The driver of the wagon jumped off before it smashed to bits, and Jenny watched him chase after his runaway team. In a morning full of disasters, the wagon accident might be the least of it.

"Danger," said a rough, deep voice that seemed to come from nowhere. Jenny turned around and saw no one and nothing but the two stone statues near the church.

"Is someone there?" she asked, thinking she'd heard the word with both her ears.

"He comes. Beware."

Reverend Usher came around a corner, wielding a knife. Jenny's instinct was to run, but when she sensed the heat of those powerful strands emanating from her chest, she stood and faced him. Usher seemed not to notice the silvery threads streaming from her breastbone, and Jenny gathered them in one hand and threw them at the headmaster, stopping him in his tracks as yellow sparks fell all around her.

He doubled over, apparently in pain.

"She is Druzai, Torin!" said the deep, gravelly voice in an expression of surprise. And though Jenny did not understand the words Druzai or Torin, she was certain she'd heard them with both ears, the same way she'd heard the voice in the woods, days ago.

"Are ye, lass?" said another rasping voice. "Druzai?"

Jenny did not turn to see who had spoken, so amazed was she by her control over Usher. "I am English, same as you!" she said breathlessly.

"Ah, but we are no' English. Nor could ye be, lass, no' with the *lòchran* lights comin' from yer breast."

They'd seen her threads! Jenny whirled around to determine who had spoken. One of the stone statues moved slightly, putting Jenny momentarily off balance.

"Aye, lass. We be dragheens."

The threads disintegrated, and Usher recovered enough to come at her again. "Evil one!" he shouted. "You will not—"

Jenny quickly gathered her strength and pierced him again, using better control than she'd been able to do until now. She knocked the knife from Usher's hand. "You will hang, Reverend Usher," she said quietly, "for Norah Martin's death."

The headmaster went pale. Jenny tried to bind his wrists behind him with the threads, but something pushed her off her feet. The breath whooshed from her lungs as a terrible sound pierced both her ears. She felt hot, as if someone had tossed her into a fire, and she could not save herself.

Everything suddenly went silent, and she found herself lying facedown in a strange forest of dark trees and gray grass. Thick black beetles crawled in and out of a nest not far from her eyes, and the smell of camphor assailed her.

She pushed herself up and away from the ugly insects and looked around her. It was a horrible place without any color at all. Even the sky was a dark gray. Huge, black birds that hunched over like vultures sat silently in the branches of the dark, shadowy trees, waiting, their white eyes watching while their sharp beaks twitched. There were massive, black, mosslike growths hanging from the trees like curtains, preventing Jenny from being able to see much more of the bleak landscape. It seemed to be a swampy area, although it was only mud, not water beneath her feet.

A loud crash sounded near her, and she jumped to her feet, poised to run. The sound came from a fearsome painted man who'd dropped from the air to land heavily on the ground in front of her.

Jenny blinked her eyes. First, talking statues . . . now, what? She could only think she was dreaming, that Reverend Usher had been a mere illusion in a dream.

"Jenny lass, run!"

She turned toward the sound of Matthew's voice. It sounded real, if distant, but she could not see him through the black moss.

"Get as far away as possible, Jenny!"

Another loud crack rent the air, and Jenny recoiled from the sound.

"Do not move, human!" said the painted man, now on his feet, and Jenny was suddenly very worried that this was not a dream. She started to back away, but tripped awkwardly as the painted man disintegrated before her eyes.

She swallowed. "Matthew?"

"Hush, lass. Doona call attention to yourself."

"I-is this r-real?"

"Aye . . . Hush now."

Jenny saw her locket lying in the mud, dented and cracked. She took hold of the chain and slipped it around her neck just as Matthew crept stealthily across the muck and came into view. Jenny started to run toward him, but screamed when the painted man appeared behind Matthew. The stranger lunged and knocked Matthew down, then slid one muscular, painted arm around his throat and pulled up, hard enough to break his neck. "Where is the stone, Druzai?" he demanded.

Matthew made a quick move and threw the other man off him. An ax suddenly appeared in the painted one's hand, and he swung it at Matthew, who seemed to melt on the spot, his body turning into a stream of . . . *of water*!

Jenny felt her heart stop as he took his familiar form again, several feet away. When he reappeared, his suit of clothes was gone. Instead, he wore loose, dark blue breeches and soft leather knee boots. His shirt had disappeared, leaving him bare-chested, looking like a primitive warrior of old, with his copper bracer at his wrist. He wasted no time, but pointed two fingers at the painted man. A thick beam of luminescence shot from his chest toward the enemy, and threw him down, yet Matthew had not even touched him.

Jenny could barely catch her breath at the sight of Matthew's unearthly power, and she realized the thick, shimmering light he'd sent toward the painted man was a mass of luminous fibers, the same fibers she'd used to stop Reverend Usher.

Jenny's thoughts were a jumble of confusion. The painted man had called Matthew Druzai— the same word used by . . . Oh dear heavens . . . *Had the stone man actually spoken to her?*

The painted man extended both hands in front of him, palms up, and a long, ornate rod of gold came to rest in them. It appeared to be a scepter of sorts, and he took it in one hand and pointed the plain end at Matthew, aiming it as though it were some kind of weapon.

It was no firearm, but just as lethal when a dark gray haze emanated from it, enveloping Matthew, choking him . . . killing him!

Jenny grabbed her locket and screamed, "Stop!"

The locket burned her hand, and she let it go. She ran toward Matthew, who dropped unconscious to the ground as the painted man snapped his wrist in Jenny's direction. Something hit her hard in the face, incapacitating her, keeping her from reaching Matthew's side.

Catching the locket in her hand once again, she willed the fibers of her own power to emerge and disable the enemy, just as she had done with Reverend Usher. Instead, a bright red beam of light appeared, and tiny, lethal needles shot out at the painted man, wounding him and knocking him senseless.

Jenny went to Matthew then, and crouched beside him. "Matthew, we haven't much time!" She looked back at the painted man, who was starting to move again. "We must get away!"

Matthew came around and looked up at her, puzzled and frowning. "I doona know how you got here lass, but—"

"Come on—we've got to get away! He'll soon be after us!"

Chapter 14

Merrick saw that she wore the locket 'round her neck. 'Twas an unprepossessing trinket of silver with a band of etchings, worn almost smooth 'round the middle. A poor ornament, 'twas dented and cracked, and Jenny deserved much better.

"Hide the locket, *moileen*!" he whispered as he took her hand and started pulling her through the *bòcan* woods. Pakal did not know that was where the stone was hidden, and he'd never believe Merrick would give possession of it to a Tuath lass.

She slipped it inside her bodice. "Matthew, what is this pl—"

"'Tis a dead forest, *moileen*, and no' a fit place for you. We need to get far away from Pakal and then I'll be able to shield us."

"The painted man? Who is he? How did we—"

"Ach, lass. No time to explain. There will soon be others. Run!"

They needed to get far away from Eilinora's mentor so that when he summoned the witch and her followers, they would not be able to follow

Jenny and him from the *bòcan* woods. If only Jenny had not come, Merrick would have faced the strange sorcerer alone. He had no doubt he could wield the blood stone and defeat the painted man himself, but Jenny was a distraction as well as a liability. He would not risk her safety here and now. He had to get them to Coruain, to the very place where he had decided she could not go. 'Twould be the only reasonably safe place for her.

Jenny pulled her skirts out of the way and ran through the trees alongside him until they reached a gray meadow covered with foul-smelling plants with spiky white leaves. "What do we do now?" she asked, just as the villains Merrick had hoped to avoid took shape before them. At least twenty Odhar rose up from the spikes, materializing from a dark haze that rose out of the ground. But there was no Eilinora.

The Odhar were mostly male, and they looked like any other Druzai, but for the malevolent gleam in their eyes and their boastful, warlike stance. They were fully confident of destroying him.

Merrick felt Jenny's fear, and he pulled her close, while wondering if he alone could overcome all these sorcerers together, even with the *brigha*-stone. He doubted it. For now, he had to elude Pakal and these foul warriors, get back to Coruain, and unite all the Druzai's strength behind him. With luck, Brogan would already have found the other stone and returned home.

The Odhar formed a long, eerie line merely fifty yards ahead, advancing toward them in silence.

Merrick did not doubt that Pakal was somewhere nearby, and Eilinora would soon appear.

"Hold on to me, lass, no matter what happens."

"Matthew?" Jenny whispered.

"There is much to tell you, Jenny."

He risked a glance behind him, and saw more of the Odhar advancing toward them as Pakal appeared among them, walking at a leisurely pace. As well he might.

Jenny turned her head slightly to look at him. "You're n-not from Scotland, are you?"

"Nay, lass, and I am no' Matthew Keating, either."

She was pale and worried, yet her expression was one of resolute strength.

"I love you, lass. Always remember that."

Merrick squeezed her hand tightly as the plants on the ground began to shudder and wave as if tossed by a powerful wind. The ground softened, and he and Jenny started to sink into it.

Merrick whipped 'round and faced Pakal, throwing a bolt of *lòchran* that pulled tangling ropes of black moss from the trees and wrapped 'round Pakal and his line of Odhar. 'Twas nothing like the powerful, luminous strands that had held Eilinora for so long, but enough to give him the opportunity to harden the ground, to pull Jenny into his arms and leap.

Jenny felt as though she were flying when Matthew carried her through the air, although the sensation was not nearly as frightening as facing the painted man and his followers. Matthew made a movement with his hand, and she saw a cluster of silvery threads shoot through his fingers to the air below them, causing filmy gray walls to appear around them. He set them down on the murky floor.

"*Moileen*, there is no' much time," he said. He cupped her face and bent to take her mouth in a kiss that melted her bones. When his tongue mated with hers and he dropped his hands to her hips to pull her tight against him, Jenny could not think about where they were, or where they'd been.

He suddenly broke away. "*Mo oirg*, I've needed to taste you . . ."

"Matthew, what—"

"Pakal is enemy to my people, the Druzai."

"Druzai? Then the stone creatures actually . . ." She felt as though the strange, shadowy floor was collapsing beneath her feet.

He cupped her shoulders in his hands. "I am Merrick Mac Lochlainn, high chieftain of the Druzai people. I came from Coruain to England for the stone that's hidden within your locket."

She pressed her hand against her bodice and felt the locket inside. "A stone? There's no. . ."

"Aye, lass. I doona know how it came into your possession, but 'tis a magical talisman."

"And when you have it, you will return to your people?" She swallowed tightly. The locket pressed heavily upon her chest, against her heart. Now that he had what he needed . . .

"We canna get to Coruain from here, but they will soon find us."

"We?"

"Aye, lass. You doona think I'll be leaving you now?"

Emotion welled in Jenny's breast, and she slid her hands up his chest and around his neck. Meeting his lips with her own, she poured all the passion she felt for him into their kiss.

"Ach, Jenny, what you do to me."

She felt fortified by his dark gaze and by his touch, but it was clear they could not remain where they were. He'd said there was not much time. "What can we do, Matt . . . Merrick . . ." It seemed so strange to know his true name, to call him by any name but Matthew.

"We must get back to Tuath . . . to England. How did you get here, Jenny?"

"I don't know." She frowned, considering all that had happened before Merrick had arrived in the Lanes and gone after the pickpocket. "Reverend Usher had come for me . . . He was going to kill me to keep anyone from learning about Norah. But suddenly I found myself in that black forest, and the painted man—Pakal—told me to be still."

Merrick let out a deep breath. "We are shielded for the moment, but I sense Pakal's probing. We must get back."

"What should I do?"

"Just hold on."

Since there wasn't time to ask him about the luminous fibers she'd seen him use, she closed her eyes tightly and felt the same burning sensation that had accompanied her to this place. When she opened her eyes, she discovered she was back in the Lanes of Carlisle, right beside the stone men who'd spoken to her. Moghire stood quiescent with his reins looped inside one of the stone hands.

Someone snatched her arm and pulled her 'round. Jenny flinched away from Reverend Usher, who looked down at the knife in his hand. He suddenly lunged at Jenny, but Merrick intervened, grabbing the man's wrist and holding tightly until the knife fell. Then he took the headmaster by the throat and squeezed while Usher struggled and gasped for air, his gnarled fingers pulling desperately at Merrick's hands.

Merrick suddenly released him, and Usher collapsed to the ground. "A quick death is too good for you, old man. You will soon suffer the consequences of your sins."

Merrick spoke a few quiet words, and Jenny saw a tiny trail of bright sparks encircle the headmaster. They fascinated her, but Merrick drew her away and lifted her onto Moghire's back. He pulled a brown waistcoat from his pack and put it on, then mounted behind her. He spoke again in Gaelic—no, Druzai—to the horse, and the animal took off at a gallop. Without another word, they passed the astonished residents of the Lanes who'd come to see the accident with the horse cart, and the disturbance with the old man near the church.

Merrick hardly noticed them. "I canna risk any more magic to get us to the coast, Jenny. Moghire will have to get us there."

"Why the coast?" she asked, her elation at staying with Merrick overshadowed by her bewilderment over all that had happened, and what he meant to do next.

"'Tis our only entry to the portal that will take us to Coruain."

"Is there a ship? Or . . ."

"No, *moileen*. We must swim."

Jenny's blood ran cold. She turned to face him fully as they rode through the streets toward Caldewgate. "I cannot swim, Merrick."

"Doona worry, lass. I'll get you to the Astar Columns."

"What about Pakal?" who was her more immediate concern. She would worry about Astar Columns—whatever they were—when they got there.

"He can trace us only through my magic—"

"You mean those tiny, dancing sparks you threw around Reverend Usher?"

He looked dumbfounded at her words. "You saw them? The sparks?"

"Of course."

"*Mo oirg*, Jenny. What else do you see?"

"Threads. Silvery—"

"*Ainchis, moileen*. You are a *hunter*!"

The Isle of Coruain, 981

There was an ominous lull in Pakal's attack. Ana sensed the power of only a few Odhar assaulting the protective shield. 'Twas more worrisome than a full bombardment, for it meant that Eilinora and Pakal were utterly confident of their success. She dreaded the moment when she would learn that her cousins had been discovered and the *brigha*-stones lost to their enemies.

Yet that could not possibly be. She knew that Merrick would return to defeat the Odhar with the sorceress who was destined to become his *céile* mate.

The prophecy could not be wrong. Merrick and Brogan *had* to succeed.

She sat up and swung her legs over the side of her pallet. Cianán lay sleeping on a nearby sofa, while Liam watched the heavy clouds that moved sluggishly across the gray-green sky. It had been a week since they'd seen the sun, a week since Ana's cousins had gone on their quest.

The bruises on her legs remained, but they would heal on their own, or Rónán would heal them when there was time. Gingerly, she took to her feet, but was reluctant to take a step. She closed her eyes and held still, relishing the moment of relative peace.

The sound of quiet voices brought her to attention, and she looked to the door of the great hall just as Brogan walked through, wearing Tuath clothes, and hanging on to the hand of a beautiful stranger with long, disheveled auburn hair.

So surprised was Ana, she could not speak. But Brogan came to her and swept her into his arms.

"Ach, wee Ana, you've no' had an easy time of it, have you?"

"Brogan!" She found herself weeping with relief and joy. "I was so worried."

"And taxed to the limit, by the look of you." He set her down and extended his hand to the young woman who remained near the door. "We've got the blood stone, Ana."

The lovely stranger opened her hand, and Ana saw the red stone, glowing brightly. She did not understand.

"She is Sarah, my *céile* mate," said Brogan.

"You found her in . . . in . . ."

"In England, aye. She had the stone. After all my searching—"

"You are welcome here, Sarah *céile* Mac Lochlainn," said Ana, taking Sarah's hand and greeting her in the Druzai fashion.

Carlisle, March 1826

Jenny and Merrick crossed the bridge and rode past the workhouse. "Merrick," she said, and the sound of his true name from her lips was pleasing to his ears. "I don't understand you. I have never hunted."

'Twas not easy to converse as Moghire carried them swiftly to the western edge of town, but he was anxious to learn more about her. She had seen the sparks created when he'd used his magic on Usher—yet she had not gone through the usual process of hunters. His brother was one of that breed, and Merrick knew that Brogan did some shifting of reality in order to hunt. Brogan said hunting made him vulnerable because he could not see the physical world except in vague shadows.

Yet Jenny had done naught but look. It raised many questions in Merrick's mind.

"Moileen, who were your parents?"

"Charlotte and Simon Keating, of Windermere."

"What more do you know of them? Were they Druzai?"

"Of course not," she replied, turning to give him a puzzled look. "They were not . . . magicians."

Merrick let the word slide. Druzai were not *magicians,* and Jenny would soon find that out.

Her mother had possessed the *brìgha*-stone. And Jenny was a hunter without knowing it. Was it possible that her ancestors had been some of the Druzai who'd remained in Tuath, and had somehow *forgotten* their heritage over the ages? Merrick could not imagine how, but it seemed the only explanation.

He pulled her back against him and spoke into her healthy ear. *"Sibh ar mèinn, moileen."* First and foremost, he could take her to Coruain. She might not be a fully developed sorceress, but she was Druzai, and she was a hunter. As soon as they reached the water's edge and dismounted, he would ask her to become his wife, his mate for life. 'Twas only right that she make her own decision before he took her to the Astar Columns and away from everything that was familiar to her.

"What will those sparks do to Reverend Usher?" she asked.

"The sparks themselves will do naught. They're merely traces of the spell I conjured. But the spell will compel the headmaster to visit the magistrate at Kirtwarren."

"Why?"

"Even now, Usher feels driven to confess his ill deeds, all of them, no matter how small." Though Merrick would have preferred to mete out a harsh and humiliating punishment of his own, he still believed that subtlety was best. He had to be satisfied with knowing Bresland's headmaster would receive a grim Tuath penalty.

He felt Jenny's hands tighten over his own. "He'll hang."

Merrick shrugged, unconcerned. He had come close to killing the man with his own hands. "That may be so."

They rode in silence until long after they'd left the city. Merrick slowed at one point to take his bearings and to see if he could get a whiff of the sea. Once he decided on their course, he turned Moghire to face Carlisle. "Jenny, look back. Do you see any sparks?"

"Only a few. But they're far back."

"None close to us, though?"

She shook her head, but Merrick did not rest easy. The Odhar had to know they were headed for the sea, and even though he and Jenny were well ahead of them, he did not want to leave a clear trail to follow.

He quickly turned them to a northwesterly path and gave Moghire his head. Galloping across flat fields, Merrick was mindful of the urgency to get through the Astar Columns, back to the relative safety of Coruain. He could not count on help from Jenny. Though he was certain she was Druzai, he doubted she had ever learned to wield her *lòchran*. She knew no charms or spells. 'Twas even possible she did not possess any Druzai power beyond her ability to see magic.

It did not matter. He loved her and hoped she would welcome his request that she leave Tuath and become his wife in Coruain.

Jenny was terrified. It was only because of Merrick's strong arms around her and his solid body behind her that she managed to keep from dissolving into a puddle of nerves. The swift ride on the back of the white gelding was frightening enough, but there were so many questions. In spite of their rapid flight across the countryside, she had to ask. "Who is Pakal?"

"We will speak of him later, *moileen*."

It was impossible to talk while riding at breakneck speed, but curiosity bedeviled her. "What about my locket?"

"The stone inside is a powerful talisman," he replied loudly, in order to be heard above the wind. "'Tis our only weapon against Pakal."

He pulled her tight against him. "As soon as we reach the sea, I will tell you more."

He kicked his heels into Moghire's sides, and the steed hurtled forward at an even greater speed than before. The galloping hooves rattled her teeth, and the cold wind blew through her hair, but Merrick's body warmed her and kept her secure.

She felt the locket under her bodice, resting between her breasts. It had glowed in her hand, creating a painful heat, but when she'd directed its light at Pakal, she'd seen fiery red needles shooting out like projectiles. They'd done some damage to him, but not enough to disable him completely.

She wished she'd had a chance to use the dark red stone on him once again before Merrick had whisked her away from that ashen place. If she had, perhaps they would not need to be galloping so desperately now.

"Pakal reminds me of a picture I once saw," she said, although her voice did not compete well with the jostling of their gallop, and the wind at their faces. "He looks like a native of the Americas."

"Americas?" He sounded as though he'd never heard of the Western continents.

Jenny nodded, and decided to explain later.

Finally, the beach came into sight and Merrick brought Moghire to a slow trot. They looked for signs of pursuers, and saw none, but Jenny did not believe they would be safe for long.

Neither did Merrick. "I doona know the extent of Pakal's powers, Jenny. He might well have another way of finding us. He located Eilinora, after all."

"Who is Eilinora? Is she the red-haired lady we saw in the Gypsy's globe?"

"Ach, *moileen*," he said. "There is so much you doona know. The red-haired lass is my cousin, Ana. She is home in Coruain, but desperate for the return of the blood stones."

She touched the locket under her dress.

"Aye, you carry one of the stones of power. Eilinora is a powerful sorceress, an enemy of the Druzai. Pakal freed her from her prison, a *bòcan* forest like the one—"

"That horrible, gray, murky place?"

"Aye. She escaped and somehow found a way to Coruain. She killed my father and stole his scepter . . ."

"Oh, Merrick, I am so terribly sorry for your loss," she said, reaching up to caress his cheek.

He covered her hand with his own. "Pakal is unknown to us . . . who he is . . . whence he came . . . But he and Eilinora stole the Druzai chieftain's scepter from my father's dead hands. 'Tis a powerful talisman used for the good of our people."

"But Eilinora?"

"In her possession, 'tis a powerful weapon."

"And my locket holds a special stone that fires red needles wherever it's aimed."

"Red needles?"

She nodded. "When I touched it . . . when I held it up near Pakal, it shot some kind of bright, fiery projectiles. Maybe they were not needles. Didn't you see them?"

"No, Jenny. Only you. And hunters like you."

* * *

They rode to the edge of the water and dismounted, and Merrick lifted Jenny down. Standing on the dry sand, he took her hands in his. "We havena much time, but I must ask you now, before . . ."

He kissed her knuckles and looked at the woman he'd chosen for his *céile* mate. She was no noble sorceress like Ana, or even Sinann, but an untrained fledgling whose skills were unknown. Yet she was the one whose soul spoke to his. He would have no other.

"Jenny lass, I love you. My world is verra different from yours, but I want you to join me in Coruain as my *céile* mate, my consort. My wife."

His heart clenched uneasily when she did not reply immediately. "I've given you little reason to trust me, *moileen*. Nor has anyone else in your—"

She stopped him with her fingers against his lips, and spoke quietly, unsteadily. "Yes, Merrick, I'll come with you, wherever we must go."

His heart rebounded. "I willna leave you, *moileen*. You must trust that I'll always care for you as I do now." He drew her into his arms and held her tightly, aware that he asked much of her.

She leaned slightly back and looked up at him with an expression of wonder in her eyes. "I . . . I believe you."

He kissed her softly. "That's my brave Jenny. I will prove myself worthy of you."

He felt her tremulous sigh. Hoping to reassure her, he kept her hand in his and turned to

Moghire. He spoke in his own familiar language, and the horse whinnied and shook his head, then turned and cantered away south.

"Where is he going, Merrick?"

"I sent him back to the Gypsies. They will care for him and give him the respect he deserves."

Jenny did not watch Moghire depart, but turned and faced the sea, eyeing the water nervously.

"We must enter the sea, *moileen*, but the spell I cast will take us safely to the Astar Columns."

"Are they in Coruain?"

"Jenny, I must take you back through time. Nearly a thousand years in your past. 'Tis through the Astar Columns that we must pass in order to return to my time and place."

She said naught.

"Doona go so pale, lass. I will take care of you."

"No, I . . . Do you feel it?"

"What is it, lass?"

"The air is shimmering. They're coming."

He saw them then, Eilinora's minions, coming toward them on foot, their hazy features becoming clearer as they came closer. They sent bolts of *lòchran* at Merrick and Jenny, and he managed to shield them from the attack. Jenny clutched his arm, but his attention had to remain fully on their protection. One gap in their defenses could be fatal.

"'Tis Pakal!" she whispered.

Merrick saw him coming toward them across the beach. The strange sorcerer was an unknown entity—Merrick did not know the extent of his power. "Jenny. Hang on to me, no matter what." He had to do something unexpected, and do it quickly, else he would not be able to get them to the Astar Columns. He wasn't sure if Pakal had access to his own portal to Coruain, or if he'd even been part of the actual attack upon Kieran. But he did not want the painted sorcerer to follow them.

"Jenny!" he shouted when he felt her let go of his arm. She turned abruptly and faced Pakal. Merrick saw the chain of her locket caught up in her fingers and knew she had it—and the stone—hidden in her hand.

Holding Kieran's scepter, Pakal opened his arms as though he intended to embrace them, but Jenny raised her arm and opened her hand. A bright, red light that even Merrick could see swirled 'round them, creating a vicious wind that crippled the Odhar where they stood. Small, bloody gashes appeared on their bodies, and Merrick realized they were being hit by the needles Jenny had described. They fell, each one disintegrating into a dense, red powder.

Pakal crouched down to the ground, then laid himself flat in an attempt to avoid the fiery red eruption that came from the glowing stone in Jenny's hand.

Sweat broke out on her forehead, and she grimaced as though the effort of wielding the stone caused her pain.

"Can you keep it up, *moileen*?"

She gave him a brief nod, clearly unwilling to

break her concentration, but they could not defeat Pakal with just one stone.

Before the painted sorcerer had a chance to mount his own attack, Merrick conjured a filmy sea barrier to encase them like a silken cocoon, which would protect them in the water. Moving fast, he drew Jenny into the surf. "Command the stone to keep up the attack after we're gone."

"Merrick, I don't know how!"

"Put your mind to it, Jenny. *Make* it so." Trusting that she could do it instinctively, he pulled her into deeper water and dived down, quickly saying the words that would take them to the Astar Columns. He hoped the *brìgha*-stone would keep Pakal occupied for the few minutes it would take to get there and pass through the portal, for he did not want to risk a battle so far beneath the sea.

Jenny quivered in his arms, and he lifted her chin with one finger and kissed her, pouring all that he felt for her into his kiss. She was everything to him, and he knew now that he would have abdicated his position as high chieftain if she had refused to leave Tuath. Life without her would be untenable.

Her arms slid 'round him, and when she opened to him, Merrick felt a shifting of his physical body to his *sòlas* being. They began to merge just as they reached the coldest depths of the Coruain Sea.

Merrick broke away, shaken by the strength of their connection. With no more than a kiss, they'd nearly come to *sòlas*. "Ach, lass. What you do to me," he said, his voice raspy and hollow.

The Astar Columns came into sight. Holding tightly to Jenny, he said the words that would take them through, and swam between the columns. *Lòchran* crackled from one column to the other, barely touching their bodies through the protective field Merrick maintained for them. 'Twas a much easier way to traverse time and space, than going unshielded by magic as Merrick and Brogan had had to do when leaving Coruain.

When the passage was complete, Merrick pushed off the seabed and propelled them to the surface. He felt Jenny panic and start to struggle inside their cocoon. He held her securely. "Almost there, *moileen*."

He summoned a *wealrach*, one of the mighty birds that hunted in the cliffs and waters of the bay. Jenny clenched her arms 'round his neck when the heavily scaled bird dropped down onto the surface of the water beside them, and extended its massive wings. "Doona fear, lass. 'Twill take us home."

He helped her grab hold of its wing, then scramble up onto its back. Merrick followed and took his place behind her, all at once circling her waist with his arms, and commanding the bird to carry them to Coruain House. Dispensing with the sea barrier, he spoke to the *wealrach*, then to Jenny. "He willna let you fall, *moileen*. Try to rest easy."

The *wealrach* took a flying leap from the water, and Jenny grabbed Merrick's arms. "'Tis my home, Jenny," he said, very glad to see the mountains and vales of the isle, but deadly worried when he saw flashes of *lòchran* light attempting to penetrate through the odd, gray-green skies. 'Twas clear that all was not well.

He kept an eye on the hostile lightning and trusted that the *wealrach*'s instincts would keep them safe.

He'd been aware of Jenny's burning need to ask questions all during their flight from Carlisle to the sea. But now she was deathly silent, holding him tight enough to bruise him. He nuzzled her ear.

"The *brìgha*-stones were hidden eons ago," he said, as much to distract her from her nervousness as to give her some answers. 'Twas quiet and peaceful in the air high above the water, with only the wisp of the *wealrach*'s gracefully billowing wings on either side of them.

Merrick closed his eyes and felt the breeze in his hair, and breathed deeply of Jenny's pure, feminine scent. He wished they were returning to a tranquil, peaceful isle. Instead, he feared his *céile* mate would have to meet her new life on Coruain through even more deadly trials than they'd already faced.

"My brother did not even believe in the stones until Ana saw them. When I came to your world in search of the stone you've worn 'round your neck all these years, I only knew to search for Keating, on the road to Carlisle."

The huge bird took them over the primary city of Coruain, then climbed high to circle over the cliffs where Coruain House was located. Jenny's fingers dug into his arms when the bird caught a vortex of wind and rode it downward in wide circles. Everything was going to be so new and foreign to Jenny. Merrick hoped she would have a chance to meet Ana—and hopefully, Brogan—before Pakal found them.

But he doubted it.

"Brogan was to search a place called Ravenfield, in England, in another era altogether." Merrick said to her. "I hope he found the stone he sought, for I doona think we can defeat Eilinora and Pakal with only the one stone you carry inside your locket. No' while they possess my father's scepter."

A burst of *lòchran* crashed through the shield over the isles, but Merrick saw that it was repelled by a dark-haired man standing on the cliffs. He saw the chieftain's dragheen guards lined up in formation behind the man, outside Coruain House. In his mind, Merrick heard the dragheen voices speaking of terrible troubles.

"Look, below, *moileen*. 'Tis Coruain House. And my brother, Brogan, standing on the cliff side."

The Isle of Coruain, 981

The huge bird descended, coming in a wide circle around the beautiful house before landing on the blessed ground. Though she'd been frightened nearly out of her wits, Jenny could not deny that the ride through the air had been wondrous. Merrick leaped off the bird and extended his hand to help her dismount. Her knees buckled, but Merrick supported her.

"Please tell me there are no more . . ." After all that had happened, she could withstand a mere flight through the air. She took a deep breath and straightened, though she kept hold of Merrick's hand. "I am all right."

"Aye. Verra much all right," he said warmly, taking her in his arms and touching his mouth to hers. Jenny leaned into him when he pulled her tightly against him, and allowed herself to forget—momentarily—about the coming challenge.

"You make a braw entrance, brother," said the handsome young man near the cliff's edge.

Merrick lifted his head and released Jenny, keeping her close. "Aye, Brogan, but only because Pakal is right behind us. We've seen no sign of Eilinora."

Brogan clasped Merrick's forearm as Merrick did the same, then the two men pulled each other into a brotherly embrace. Jenny was struck by the similarities in their appearance, both in features and in build. Brogan wore the same kind of loose trews Merrick now wore, only his were light gray. He wore a deep blue tunic, belted at his waist.

He made a simple but formal bow toward Jenny. "I am Brogan Mac Lochlainn."

"Brogan, this is Jenny *céile* Mac Lochlainn," said Merrick, ignoring the widening of Brogan's eyes as well as Jenny's questioning ones. She did not realize she had already taken his name. "We intend to wed as soon as Pakal and Eilinora are vanquished. Did you find your stone?"

At the mention of the *brìgha*-stone, Jenny took the chain from her neck and handed the locket to Merrick. She was not the one who should wield it.

"Aye, Merrick." He touched a leather pouch hanging from his belt. "But there is one less enemy to worry about. Eilinora is dead." Brogan turned and started for the house with Merrick and Jenny alongside him.

"You killed her?" Merrick asked.

Brogan nodded. "The witch's power was naught against the stone, but she relinquished Kieran's scepter to Pakal."

"Aye. We saw it."

"Then you saw Pakal."

"Aye. He canna be far behind," said Merrick.

They walked in silence for a few paces. "There will no' be much time to plan our defense."

Jenny's step faltered when the red-haired woman from the Gypsy's glass ball stepped out of the beautiful wood and glass building on the cliff. She wore loose silk trews of a green so rich, it reminded Jenny of the grass at home, and a long, cream-colored tunic over them. She walked carefully, as if every step pained her.

Jenny knew she must be Ana when Merrick embraced her and kissed her on each cheek.

Beside her was another young lady, also near Jenny's age, wearing a more conventional gown.

She looked to be as far out of her element as Jenny felt. She was very pretty, and when Brogan slid his arm around her, her hazel-green eyes lit up. There was an aura about them . . . Somehow, Jenny could see that their *sòlas* beings were joined.

"Allow me to present my own *céile* mate, Sarah," said Brogan, but before proper greetings could be made, the ground behind Jenny cracked.

The air turned cold, and a sudden downpour of sharp, icy pellets rained down on them. Fierce, circling winds tore at their clothes, and lightning crashed from sky to ground. Jenny held on to her blowing skirts and watched in horror when one of the cliffs on the far side of the dale broke away and collapsed into the sea below with a thunderous, deafening crash.

A filmy apparition formed out of the air and came toward them, with even more warriors right behind.

"Pakal!" Jenny whispered.

"Take care," cried Ana. "His *tànaiste* spell is—" The sorcerer whipped his arms up and out, extending the gold scepter toward Merrick and the others, speaking to them in such deep, quiet tones that Jenny could not hear.

Instantly, the two men dived at each other's throats while Sarah headed slowly toward the cliff, struggling as though she were being dragged there. Ana fell to her knees and grabbed at her neck, pulling away an invisible rope.

Bright sparks of magic surrounded them, nearly blinding Jenny. And she realized Pakal must have used some terrible magic to cause madness in the others. Reaching for her locket, she suddenly remembered she no longer had it. Desperate to get to it, she started for Merrick, but Pakal darted behind her and grabbed her arms.

Jenny felt his breath at her ear, but could not hear his words.

"*Stop it!*" she cried, struggling to get away as Merrick and his brother fought viciously, throwing punches, each one doing everything he could to destroy the other.

Her luminous threads shot out from her chest, and, without thinking, she projected them back, toward the evil entity that held her in place. She used her small ability to wrap them firmly around his neck. Then she somehow managed to tighten them.

Chapter 15

"**D**estroy him before he destroys you!" The words spoken by the painted sorcerer were more compelling than any Merrick had ever heard, and he could not seem to stop himself from attacking Brogan, from wishing him dead, yearning for a weapon to finish him off.

Ignoring the freezing rain, he threw his brother over his shoulder, brutally tossing him to the ground. But Brogan regained his feet and came at Merrick again with destruction in his eyes and a roar of pure hatred in his throat. Clearly, his brother felt the same fierce need for annihilation.

Brogan put his hands 'round Merrick's neck and squeezed even as he slid one leg behind Merrick's and tripped him. Merrick rolled away to the edge of the cliff as Brogan kicked. He grabbed Brogan's leg and pulled him down, delivering what was to be a killing blow, but Brogan dodged it. Brogan sidled closer to the edge of the precipice, grabbing Merrick and taking him with him. Merrick shoved Brogan onto his belly in the mud and hammered one knee into his back. Brogan pushed up on all fours and knocked Merrick away.

Hatred burned deep in Merrick's belly, and he wanted naught but to end the life of this—

Jenny's scream penetrated his madness.

Merrick caught sight of her at the opposite end of the cliff with Pakal standing behind her, holding her 'round her neck with one arm. With his other he was struggling against some kind of onslaught—

Mo oirg, the stone!

"Sarah!" Brogan shouted, suddenly catching sight of his own mate at the precipice of the cliff.

The two brothers pulled away from each other abruptly. Merrick yanked Jenny's chain from his neck and split open the cracked locket. Even though he could not dispel the virulent hatred he felt for Brogan, the sight of Jenny's struggle was enough to distract him from the need to kill his brother.

"Ainchis ua oirg!" Brogan muttered, leaping to his feet to run for Sarah. He grabbed her 'round her waist and pulled her from the cliff's precipitous edge. Holding on to her tightly, Brogan drew a blood stone from the pouch at his belt.

He shouted to Merrick, "We must help Jenny!"

But Merrick had already aimed the power of his stone at Pakal and the Odhar that stood behind him. Jenny was somehow managing to hold the sorcerer at bay, but she was clearly weakening. When the first burst of energy from the *brìgha*-stone hit Pakal, small, bloody gashes appeared on the faces and shoulders of the sorcerer and his invaders.

With a shocked expression on his ornately painted face, Pakal released Jenny, and she fell to the ground. Freed from whatever power Jenny had used on him, Pakal and the Odhar regrouped and unleashed their own formidable attack. Pakal used the scepter to deliver a crushing blow to Merrick, knocking the air from his lungs and leveling him to the sodden ground. The stone fell from his hand, rolling just out of his reach.

Brogan aimed the flashing spears of light from his stone at the Odhar, destroying them the same way Jenny had done on the beach. But the one stone alone could not vanquish Pakal. The painted sorcerer took a step backward at the onslaught, but it was not enough. Struggling for breath, Merrick rose to his knees and fought against the power of Pakal's assault. He saw Jenny reach for the blood stone that had rolled to her. She held it up and turned it to the painted man, adding the strength of its magic to that of the stone Brogan wielded.

Pakal dropped the scepter, but did not go down easily. The very air around them tore into black gashes, and when he shouted some foreign incantation, a heavy, screeching vacuum swirled 'round all of them and tried to swallow them into the empty voids in the air.

Jenny dug her fingers into the ground and held on. Fighting the suction Pakal created, Merrick crawled to her and helped her to sit up. Holding her tight and anchoring her to the ground, he sat behind her, straddling her body with his legs. He cupped her hand with his own and added his power to hers as she raised the *brìgha*-stone against Pakal once again, while Sarah and Brogan did the same.

The icy rain stopped suddenly. Ana limped forward and reached for Kieran's scepter. Standing between her two cousins, she raised the thick, gold rod and aimed it at Pakal. His painted body took on a whole new design of red gashes that rent his flesh.

The Druzai did not relent in their combined assault. Pakal jerked uncontrollably, and the dark voids disappeared, stopping their vacuous screeching. In silence, Pakal's black *bràth* fled his body, succumbing to the powerful *brìgha* assault, and dissipating into the air as his body fell to the ground and shattered into scraps and fragments of red and black.

A warm wind blew away the miasma of Pakal's attack, and the sky returned to its normal cerulean blue. What remained of the painted sorcerer blew over the cliff and into the sea, but not even the *wealrachs* would dive for that unsavory feast.

"'Tis over," said the dragheen commander, his voice heavier than usual and rough with emotion. "Welcome home, young lords."

Merrick turned toward the guardians who'd lined up in front of Coruain House and gave them a nod.

Merrick helped Jenny to her feet and took her hand in his. Brogan and Sarah came to flank them on one side, and Ana on the other. Jenny felt weak and spent, but she knew it was over. Pakal was truly destroyed.

"We must find the portal used by Pakal to find Eilinora."

"And us," Merrick added. "He found us in Tuath."

"He and Eilinora found us, too," said Brogan, slipping his arms around Sarah and brushing a kiss on her forehead.

"There are more of them . . . Lords of Death," said Ana. "I see them."

"Aye, then," said Merrick. "By all means, destroy the portal."

For a moment, Jenny was afraid they would decide they needed to go after the other death sorcerers like Pakal. Yet she knew she could face it with Merrick at her side.

"They derive their power from fear and hatred," said Ana. "Soon they will destroy each other. But we canna let them find us first."

"You are right, cousin. We must obliterate the passage between our worlds."

Sarah came forward and touched Ana's hand. "I think I can help you find it."

Jenny felt the stone in her hand, pulsing with life. "And I believe I can help you destroy it," she said.

Ana took Jenny's and Sarah's hands in hers, smiling as three men in loose robes and a sleek, dark-haired sorceress pushed through the stone guards and came to them.

"Lords Merrick and Brogan—"

"'Tis as it was foretold," said the dark-haired woman, who smiled broadly, keeping her eyes on Merrick.

Merrick took Jenny's hand in his and squeezed tightly.

"But no' as you thought, Sinann," one of the men said, taking her arm to draw her away. "Come with me, daughter, and leave the chieftain—"

"Oh, but it is, Father. 'Twas with our combined power that the threat was vanquished. While we stayed behind the dragheen line, we directed our *lòchran* into the battle and prevented the foretold disaster."

Jenny did not understand the subtleties here, but she was obviously missing something. Cupping Jenny's hand, Merrick lifted their two hands together and opened them, showing the woman the glowing blood stone that Jenny held.

Merrick said nothing, but the sight of the stone made Sinann blush deeply red. "But I . . ." A muscle in her jaw clenched tightly, and she whirled away from them, pushing past her father.

"The crisis is past, my lord," said the man with complete formality. "We will leave you to your—"

"A question, *mo curadh*," the white-haired man said to Jenny.

Feeling overwhelmed by the respect and the strange title bestowed upon her, Jenny replied, "Yes?"

"How did you repel Pakal's *tànaiste* command? 'Tis not long since we saw the power of it in Coruain House . . . when he used it on Lady Sinann."

"His *tànaiste* command?"

"Aye. Did he no' command you to destroy the high chieftain and his brother?"

Jenny bit her lip as she realized what Pakal must have whispered in her ear, and thanked heaven for the first time in her life for her partial deafness.

The Isle of Coruain, Lughnasa Day, 981

Far below the cliffs of Coruain, beside a stone grotto where the highest waterfall of the isle fell, Merrick stood beside Jenny and faced the most senior of the elders, Cianán Mag Uidhir. Hundreds of Druzai stood behind them to bear witness to the chieftain's vows to his lady, the sorceress from another world, whose bravery and tenacity had saved them from Pakal's dark conquest.

Merrick leaned down and spoke into her healed ear, "Doona be nervous lass. I love you with all that I am, with all that I will ever be." Then he took her hands in his as Cianán began the ceremony. "*Curdaith* Merrick Mac Lochlainn, is this the woman of your choosing, your true *céile* mate?"

"Aye. Jenny Keating is the other half of my *bràth*."

"And do you commit your life, your *bràth*, and your love to Jenny Keating for all the years you will live?"

"I do."

Merrick lifted Jenny's hand and kissed her fingers. He'd known when she'd struck the first blow to help him fight the highwaymen on the road to Carlisle, that there could be no other woman for him.

"Jenny Keating, is this the man of your choosing, your true *céile* mate?"

"Aye," she said, standing straight and queenly in her silken robes as she repeated the Druzai marriage vows. "Merrick Mac Lochlainn is the other half of my *bràth*."

"And do you commit your life, your *bràth*, and your love to Merrick Mac Lochlainn, high chieftain of all the Druzai, for all the years you will live?" Cianán asked.

She turned to gaze up at Merrick, clearly undaunted by the enormity of her vow. "I do," she said. "I love you with my body, my heart, and my soul."

The waterfall's brilliant rainbows were reflected in her eyes, and Merrick lowered his head and kissed his mate, knowing 'twas a perfect portent of the awesome future they would share.